Republic

Republic

Leon Paulin

ISBN 978-0-473-47768-4

Cover design and layout DIY Publishing Ltd

Dedication

For Sylvia, my long-suffering and affectionate wife,
and our two beautiful daughters Sophia and Suzie.

And to those people who take the time out of their lives
to read this book.

Acknowledgements

To my mother Sylvia, namesake of my wife, who was a prolific writer of letters, before the unromantic email age. She showed me very early the great power of thoughts, words and dreams. "Remember, thoughts are things," she was fond of saying.

I know she wouldn't have approved of my attempts to conjure what I see as some fundamental human truths. She would have got hung up on the images and the language, which to her would be simply "foul or uncouth" – words pretty much out of the vocabulary now replaced by political correctness. So I say to any would-be writers out there, don't put it off any longer; don't be put off by anyone. Write your truth.

Contents

Chapter One

Life without liberty is like a body without spirit

– Kahlil Gibran

CASTLEMERE, NEW Zealand, Pluto's Republic, March 2003.

"You're fired, Crust," said Robert Dalton, Manager of Castlemere Roading Corp. He stroked his silver grey moustache.

"Bullshit. I was only five minutes late." Nate scratched the wispy hair on his chin. *Prick.*

"It's a new era, Crust. It's all about efficiency, and you're surplus to requirements." He straightened his tie. "You can thank Dodger Blackwatch and his regime for that."

As Dalton continued explaining the reforms, Nate listened but said nothing.

"You can finish now," Dalton said. "Clean out your locker and I'll have your final pay made up Thursday."

"Just like that."

"Your attitude is bad. Sort out your priorities – work or surfing."

"I intend to." Nate held his middle finger aloft. He

wrenched open the office door and slammed it behind him, heading for his locker. He quickly emptied its contents into an old backpack. If he was lucky, Mike and Goose would still be at the pub.

They were. It was hot in the Oasis Hotel, and Nate felt his face redden with anger and heat as he made his way over. He thumped his fist on the chunky wooden table. "Guess what, guys? I've been fucking fired. The latest victim of Dodger Blackwatch and his three-year plans." He coughed as the wafts of marijuana, tobacco and booze reached him. "Surplus to requirements."

Goose tossed a handful of long blond hair over his bony shoulder and glared into Nate's light brown eyes. "I'm sorry mate but...what about the future – of the Republic, your children and your children's children?"

"I never think that far ahead," Nate said. "His priorities were thinking about the surf, and how he was going to finance his life, in that order."

Mike's body tensed as he turned to face them. "How can the Republic prosper?" he said. "Consumers at the mercy of competition and the free market, victims deemed to get what they deserve." He sighed in exasperation.

"You're like a lefty prima donna," said Goose. "The economy got so bad under the old protectionism and government intervention. There was no alternative."

The veins on Mike's neck stood out. "State assets funded by the taxpayer sold off to pitiless corporates in the private sector to pay back debt. Wealth goes into a few hands and the public are ripped off by what used to be government services."

"The fucking *bastards*," said Nate. He gazed out the window. It would be a great day for surf. The sun was warm on his forearms through the glass. It was just as well he didn't often think about politics, because every time he did, he felt angry, ripped off. Not necessarily weak, but fucking powerless.

"Didn't you hear?" said Goose. "Communism and the Berlin Wall have fallen." He laughed.

"I'm talking about democracy and decency," Mike said. "And we get massive cuts in education, health, affordable housing ... and suicides and epidemics of self-harm, eating disorders, depression and loneliness." His voice rose. "Because ... especially young people, they can't live up to the perfect role models the media pushes." He made a fist with his right hand.

Nate could identify. He wasn't telling him anything.

"It's up to the individual to sort this stuff, not the market," said Goose. "The plebs need to get entrepreneurial, sell themselves, gain unearned income like the big shakers and movers."

Mike's eyes were wild. "Well fuck you and your parasitic jungle mentality. What if you suffer from performance anxiety and social phobia because you struggle to live on casual work without unions? Many feel isolated." He cleared his throat. "There's a sense of loss of caring, meaning and community. Money is God."

"Get real," said Goose. "It's always been like that. Anyway, the best things in life are still free."

"I reckon he's got a point." The corners of Nate's mouth softened. "Well, as long as I can breathe, doss on the street, eat bananas and cornflakes and beg, I'll be fine." He grinned. "I get real stoked, thinking about a final solution – for bankers and politicians."

Mike supped his Guinness. His dark brown eyes peered out from under a fringe of black hair. "We don't need another holocaust. If you want to know where the power lies, just follow the money."

Goose said, "Fucking conspiracy theorists. No idea of high finance."

Nate had enough problems financing his own life without worrying about the Republic's debt. It didn't make much difference who the government borrowed from; it was the ordinary people who had to pay it back with their hard-earned taxes. And it seemed to him, even in his short life, that the plebs, the real financiers, had been abused throughout history. But lately he had a vague feeling that a strange ferment was happening; one he couldn't quite put into words.

The surfer trio got up to replenish their drinks and sauntered over to the bar. Balanced on barstools, they ogled a female biker in a micro-mini, lining up a shot on the pool table. Splayed legs left her vulnerable. A wedge of black knickers kick-started primal urges.

Goose said, "I'd like to pot her."

Nate's blood pressure shot up as one biker – a scraggy, bald, paunchy guy – grabbed her from behind with the arrogance of a feudal lord. She jerked to her feet and slapped his face, but he continued to kiss and maul her, and she couldn't escape his chafed, oil-stained fingers.

The bikers cheered, but Nate's blood pressure was rising and it was all he could do to stop himself jumping in. He needn't have worried. Sacrificing her manicured nails, the girl gouged the fat guy's arms with their *LOVE* and *HATE* tattoos. The fat guy winced as angry welts appeared on his skin. Another tattoo, of a homemade dagger, dripped blood.

Everybody gawked, while Nate's instincts screamed. He tapped the fat guy on the shoulder.

"What the fuck?" The fat guy spun around with a defensive right hook.

Nate blocked it with his right arm.

"Looking to be a hero, surfer boy?" He threw a left.

Nate blocked it and delivered a front kick to his balls.

The fat guy buckled, and stuttered in pain. "Ah! Waste 'em."

Nate kneed him in the head. *Boomf!* He fell backwards onto the floor and curled into a foetal position. Blood dribbled from his cut mouth.

A guy with long black hair, his skin covered in tats, pulled a hunting knife.

"Pud it away, Shane," the president said. He was a

giant with shaggy hair and beard. "Before someone gets hurt." He turned to Nate. "I'm impressed, dude."

Nate beamed. The president and the long-haired guy picked the fat guy up from the floor and sat him down to recover. The blond escaped to the ladies. Nate swaggered back to the bar and sat down alongside the others.

"You stupid bastard, Nate!" Goose kicked the brass rail around the bottom of the bar. "You could have gotten us all killed."

"Bloody domestics!" Mike said.

Jack, the barman, refilled their beers and muttered, "Crazy bloody kid."

"Somebody had to step in," said Nate. "She was being groped." If he'd had a sister, he hoped someone would have stepped in to help her in a similar situation.

Goose looked at his watch. "I told Greta I wouldn't be long."

"So?" Mike raised his eyebrows.

Goose tried to rescue some machismo. "I have to help the boss with the new parts database."

"Let them wait." Nate thumped his mug down, spilling beer on the bar. He was tired of his life being dictated by the fucking clock.

"I'll second that!" Jack, the barman, looked at Goose. "We all need time to chill out."

Goose rubbed the sleep out of his eyes and yawned. "Not in my contract. I get three …" he cleared his throat, "amended to four weeks holiday a year. Five days sick pay. Otherwise I work when and as required."

"Well, you signed the contract," Mike said, as if that explained it all. "Who held the gun to your head?"

Jack wiped the beer spills off the bar. "Talk about a pound of flesh."

Bikers glared at them, in case the language was directed at them. They seemed satisfied it wasn't, and continued their pool.

Mike leaned an elbow on the bar, glass in hand. "Joce's upset about the courses I'm taking at uni." He imitated her sarcastic tone: "They're not career orientated enough."

Where was this conversation going?

Jack slid Mike another beer with a wicked smile. "Maybe she's right. You don't want to end up pushing pints."

Goose's Adam's apple moved like the throat of a turkey gobbler. "You can't be too careful. You don't want to fall victim to the tyranny of the vagina."

Mike stared intensely into his beer mug, as if it were a crystal ball. "Don't refer to Jocelyn in that … biological way!"

Goose laughed. "Why defend their mercenary pink bits?"

Nate stifled a giggle.

Mike climbed on his soapbox. "The problem is guys have a mutant Y chromosome." He took a deep breath.

"We've lost market share because of our destructive need to rape and plunder to finance our egos and libidos."

"Speak for yourself." Goose's fist hit the bar hard. His eyes were wild.

Nate lit a cigarette and inhaled, in languid anticipation of Mike's speech.

The bar became Mike's lectern. "Eggs have outclassed sperm when it comes to reproduction."

"I'll believe it when I see it," heckled Goose.

"Me too," said Nate.

Mike went on, tongue in cheek. "Ovaries and vaginas are the ultimate producers and consumers, and have been co-opted by big business." He glugged his beer. "The vagina orgasms on money and power – it is the souped-up engine of the free market which desires everything and fills everything with desire."

Nate belched smoke over their heads. He didn't know about theories. They always seemed to be dropped by those wanting converts. And he wasn't going to be one of them. Although, in Mike's case, he was probably rehashing some weird book he'd read, going for their reaction.

Goose fanned the smoke out of his face. "Don't blow that shit in my face," he snarled. "Now who's talking about women as if they're nothing more than biology?"

Jack took down a fluted wineglass, polished it and eyed it with suspicion. "Yeah, but nowadays it's any port in a storm."

Mike gulped the dregs of his mug and slid it back to Jack to refill. "Right. The principle is the same. Any orifice that fuels desire is a surrogate vagina and holds power over the one who desires – it's the case of the soft overcoming the hard. What some call *conquering by yielding*."

"That's pretty weird." Nate had never heard that before.

"Go the Republic!" Goose shouted at the big-screen TV, keeping one ear on the discussion. A Plutonian Republic rugby player with a conviction for taking performance-enhanced drugs scored a try.

"Why don't they call it a do?" Mike said to nobody in particular.

Goose threw his hands up in excitement. "The Republic is winning, and all you can talk about is the philosophy of the fuck. What happened to your patriotism?"

"They tell me it's the last refuge of a scoundrel." Mike shook the hair out of his eyes.

Nate blew smoke. "I'll never get a hot chick." All this mumbo jumbo went over his head. He knew if he wanted one he was going to have to impress a girl in some way. He had to admit there was some truth in Mike's twisted theories. But they were best left unvoiced if you wanted to attract the opposite sex.

Goose flapped his cap to disperse the smoke. "You don't have to be a genius to know the short answer to that – get a job."

Nate was well aware of that. "Fuck you."

Mike ran his fingers over his bristled face and mounted his hobby horse. "Joe Penis ruled with full economic power while they needed brute strength and cannon fodder. But now, the sceptre has been passed to the vagina."

"Yeah, but they're only employing them 'cos they're cheaper than guys," Nate offered.

Goose took a deep slug of his beer and shook his head. "They've always ruled." He narrowed his eyes at Mike to make sure he got the point. "The original boobeosie, sitting on the means of reproduction, distribution and exchange. And every time they open or cross their legs, the dollar goes up or down."

Mike's eyes glowed dark. His breath was impatient. "Fascinating. The last man who expressed those views got tied naked to a tree with a rapist sign around his neck."

Goose grinned in defiance. "Well, someone has to say it. They're getting out of hand."

Mike's mouth dropped in disgust. "Now that *is* disrespectful." He lobbed a philosophical grenade, which exploded on cue. "Did you know men are mutated females?"

"You might be, sweetie," said Goose, his masculinity affronted, "but I'm sure I'm not." He wrenched the peak of his cap around, peered out from underneath, and beat out a rap pattern on the bar. "Once we were great apes ... hominids ... Neanderthals ... primates ... now hermaphrodites … with chipolata clits … spermatozoa ovaries … tits … and that's no shit."

"That the latest line peddled at uni?" Jack let out a deep laugh. "What happened to we are all fifty-thousand-year-old Africans?"

Nate lit a cigarette and drew back hard. "What's the point of having a friggin' cock if you've lost your main attraction?"

Mike broke in. "The new sexual politics has created new forms of old power relations, which make us governable as sexualized social units, transgender, gays, and lesbian rainbow families are equal to heterosexual ones but they all prostrate themselves before the primal vagina and the free market."

Nate was amazed at the workings of Mike's mind. He certainly couldn't be accused of being apathetic, or indifferent to the straight-jacketed thinking of many in the Republic. Goose could be fairly out there too.

Mike blew Nate's smoke back. He was back on topic. "The Republic uses the promise of freedom and tolerance to fulfil its anti-social, anti-democratic and violent agenda. It's also racist and neo-colonial."

"At last – a politician I would vote for!" Nate said. Even though he reckoned Mike was now making things up. "Still can't believe it." He raised his eyes to the ceiling and shook his head in frustration as he remembered his reality. "I've been made redundant, useless!"

"At least you know why," said Mike. "We had

similar governments before; it's why so many hate neoliberalism – capitalism with the gloves off. Basically it's naked greed and bugger your neighbour. It's time we celebrated more uselessness."

That certainly described Nate's life. He had no disposable income. He would have enough for a week or so, for the necessities, till his severance pay ran out. But the luxury of a girlfriend was out of the question in the immediate future. He was unskilled, poor, and at the mercy of market forces.

Goose swished his beer in his glass. "It's a boss's and a woman's prerogative to slap your hand." He took a gulp. "And I bet it wasn't the first time."

"No." Nate didn't see the significance. "But this time I got heaps of shit, about reforms, efficiency and profitability, individual employment contracts. The prick told me not to bother re-applying – I wasn't hungry or skilled enough to succeed."

Mike pushed his dark fringe out of his eyes. "Haven't you heard all human relations are money relations?"

"Be fair." Goose kicked the bar. "You didn't work for their benefit – the job fitted in with your surfing. You never put your heart into the profit-making equation."

Nate sat erect, squared his shoulders and pushed his chest out. "Fuck you! I worked m'guts out for those pricks."

Goose looked taken aback. Then his expression changed to smug satisfaction. "The world doesn't need another pair of hands."

"It needs a heart transplant," Mike quipped.

"Fuck the world." Nate placed his empty glass upside down on the bar – the universal symbol for *I want a fight*.

Goose winked at Mike and Jack. "You've got one hell of a bad attitude. If you changed that, I might be able to get you a job at work detailing cars."

"Thanks." Nate's mouth tightened. "But I want to be free to surf."

"Waste of time. You won't make the pro circuit in my lifetime – the competition's too good."

Mike rested a warm hand on Nate's shoulder. "Competition dragged the stone blocks up the pyramids and the workers into slavery."

"Why can't you accept the necessity of the three-year plans?" said Goose. He crossed his legs and tucked them under the stool. "We've been living beyond our means, a budget away from a banana republic." He appealed to their logic. "Can't you see? Basic economic survival is dependent on individual responsibility and international competitiveness." He let out an exasperated sigh. "Perhaps you guys prefer the gurglar?"

"You sound like a fucking politician," Nate said. Was there no end to this crap?

"More like the six o'clock news," Mike said.

The giant biker and his old lady approached the bar. Jack moved down to serve him. "Same again?"

The giant carried two empty jugs in each hand. His big-breasted girlfriend in clingy leather pants and black singlet followed with another two. "You're a fucken mind reader." The big guy held the jugs in the air. "Good stoush?"

"We don't encourage that behaviour here." Jack's voice quivered.

"We don't look for trouble." The giant placed his jugs on the bar. "But it finds us. Quaint place y'got."

"We like it, don't we guys?" Jack tried to include the others, desperate for back up.

Echoing silence.

"What brings you guys – and gals – to my quaint little alehouse?"

"Just cruising. Ain't that right, Queenie?" The big man snatched her two empty jugs and passed her the two full ones.

"Right, Wolfy. Cruisin'." She flaunted two full, firm breasts at the other guys. Her left breast wet-nursed a tattooed skull.

"Awesome tat," Nate said, with her tits in mind. "Don't go in for them myself. I don't like needles." It brought on a surreal vision of her boobs being popped, like over-inflated balloons.

"Did one of you dudes say you wanted a job?" The giant spoke in the direction of the surfers.

"Me." Nate pointed to himself. "But I've got something lined up ..." He faltered. "In tit ... tilt slab construction."

"The pay's peanuts and it's fucken dangerous." Wolf squeezed Queenie's tattooed breast. "If you wanna make some real bread, real easy, look me up." He flicked Nate a business card that read *Pariah Dog and Associates / Consultants in Leisure and Credit Control*. On the other side: *No Job too Tough*.

Queenie wriggled out of his grasp and sashayed back to her table with maximum arse and breast sway and minimum spillage. The surfers' eyes followed her back to her table.

Mike brought them back to the now. "Nate, how'd you like to tag along with me, Goose and the girls for drinks and dinner tonight?"

"No thanks." Nate lit a smoke. "I'd feel like a fucking gooseberry."

One day he'd have his own woman. They were hard to get, because they were less sexually obsessed and ready for sex than men, which put them in a position of power in the sex game. And there was a surplus of guys chasing them. It all came down to supply and demand. Anyway, he needed to save as much money as possible, not splurge on a meal that might look good but wouldn't satisfy his hunger.

Chapter Two

*The History of all hitherto existing society is the
history of class struggles."*

– Karl Marx

AT FOUR thirty on Saturday afternoon, Nate drove
home the long way, skirting the industrial area of
Claxton to avoid the booze bus and breathalyser. His
eyes scanned the rubber factories and tanneries that
poured noxious by products into Claxton stream, now
an open drain. Most industry had long since closed or
moved operations offshore for cheap labour.

Gearboxes, differentials, old tyres and rims, doors
and various car panels lay strewn in the mud banks,
visible when the tide was out. A few metres of brackish
liquid remained, stinking of formaldehyde, flowing
from this putrid stream to the estuary and eventually,
the open sea.

He stopped for a train at the railway crossing. The
Ting! Ting! Ting! of railway bells and the flash of lights
brought him back to the moment. The train came from
Castlemere Port with a kilometre of containers. The
lights flashed a warning in his head. He reflected on

what he'd learned from Mike.

Legislation decreed everything must run at a profit. This train and railway which cut his advance, had once belonged to the people of Pluto's Republic. An overseas consortium bought it and a good lump of the money, which used to provide a good rail service made use of the long suffering taxpayer and much of the profits went overseas. Most state-owned assets had been fully or partially sold off, including banks, shipping companies, the national airline and the country's main airport, plus various energy companies, along with many others transferred from public ownership to the private sector.

When the train had passed, he followed the serpentine road and hills that wound between the city of Castlemere and the port. Trade tariffs had been cut, so there was yard after yard of containers, from China and other low-wage economies, packed solid in stacks like property on a monopoly board. Huge forklifts offloaded trucks, and gangs of workers emptied the containers onto pallets, tagged for destinations in the Republic. Local manufacturers hadn't been able to compete against cheap imports, and had closed or moved offshore where workers could be paid a dollar a day. Yards boasted three-metre-high galvanized mesh topped by razor wire that would be the envy of high-security prisons.

He came to the bend by the mouth of the estuary, and saw the blue and red flashing lights of several police cars on the beach road. Traffic was bottlenecked at the Y intersection ahead. One branch of the road went via the beach, the other around the back of the village. He chose the latter, which led to the hills that overlooked the bay.

As he reached the top of the switchback, the sun slid down over the Alps. He shivered and began the descent to the fibro cement shack below. A smudged image moved through the misted kitchen window. He parked in the worn tracks alongside the house. The appetizing aroma of beef casserole met him at the front door.

Tiff was peeling potatoes as he pushed open the kitchen door. She wore a red and yellow floral print dress and plain white apron. A blue scarf was pulled tight over her straight honey blond hair. She was in her early twenties, the same generation as him and Daryl. She'd lived with them the past six months, since Nate's parents' death in a fatal car accident caused by his father Don's drunkenness.

"Heard anything about the cop cars down the beach?" He threw the question at Tiff's skinny back.

"I've been studying all afternoon." She turned to face him. "Ask Daryl."

"Daryl!" he yelled.

"Keep your hair on." Daryl sauntered through the hallway door into the kitchen and slouched in a chair at the colonial table.

"Did yah see the cop cars down the beach?" Nate slumped into the armchair by the door.

"Yeah. Some poor fucker got squashed under a

concrete slab. They got an ambulance, but too late."

"How'd you find out?"

"I talked to a hard hat on the site. Hey – that's the place you're working Monday." He didn't give Nate the opportunity to answer. "They were pushing a deadline – the ties weren't put on properly. The poor fucker was the meat in the sandwich. Hard hat reckoned they were taking short cuts. It was all about the folding stuff."

"Money?"

"No, flaky puff pastry. Of course money."

Daryl flicked on the TV. "Wonder what they'll say on here?"

Nate pulled out a cigarette from a full packet. "Any bikers downtown?"

"I saw the big fella and his gang, terrorizing the garden bar of the Mitre." Daryl's eyes brightened. "They're a brotherhood – like masons." He loosened his oil company tie. "They put you through rituals, like being pissed on."

Nate raised his eyebrows. "If they're a brotherhood, how come they've got gash with them?"

"Someone's got to do the menial stuff, not to mention the obvious, right Tiff?"

Tiff turned around and advanced on the table, stopping with her hands on her hips. She glared at Daryl. "They're all under the power of Satan and they're all on their way to hell unless they accept the Lord Jesus Christ, repent and turn their lives around."

"Can't see them doing that." Daryl flipped the pages

of the *Press*. "They're having far too much fun."

She went to turn away, but stopped. "And by the way, let's get something else straight. I cook because I am a servant of the Lord. She breathed deep. "When I serve you I serve Him, not because I am a woman, and not because I favour either of you!"

"Well I guess we know where we stand, eh, Nate? The best-fed flatmates in hell." He broke into uncontrollable laughter.

Nate smirked. "I know where I stand. I'm going up front to check out the surf before dark."

Tiff's and Daryl's voices echoed from the kitchen while Nate shuffled along to the front room.

"You're like the crackling of thorns under a pot," Tiff said.

"Speaking of pot," said Daryl, "how long till dinner? I'm starving."

"As long as it takes."

"One fisherman's basket," said the dark-haired waitress. She had a broad accent and the deep petalled lips of a Dublin Bay rose.

Mike hailed the waitress. "Over here – I'm the basket case."

The others responded with the pathetic chuckle he deserved.

Mike and Goose sat at opposite ends of the table, the two women facing each other at the sides. Mike ran a hand over his tight-fitting green cords and picked some lint off his cream safari-style jacket. Goose was wearing Levi's and a lavender polo shirt. Out of his car salesman's suit, he could be from any walk of life.

"Vegetarian salad?" the waitress asked.

"Thank you." Greta's breasts jiggled as she beckoned the waitress. Mike imagined her gravity-challenged breasts were supported by her most comfortable bra.

"Eat enough rabbit food and in your next life you'll come back as a grasshopper," he teased.

Greta didn't reply at once. Mike scrutinised her. Her long wavy red hair was held up with a jade comb; make-up covered the freckles on her face and retroussé nose. Large gold hoop earrings swung from her ears. Her perfume was musky.

"I'd settle for a super model's body," she said. "No tits, and legs up to my armpits."

The waiter opened the bottle and discreetly poured the wine.

"Hold that image." Mike sipped his wine and nodded acceptance. "They say the last thought on your mind influences your next incarnation." He looked out of the floor-to-ceiling windows of the restaurant, to the view of Sunvale beach. The waves were small, glassy and translucent. The moon was close to full phase and left a silver slick on the water. They were so close to the sea he could hear the gentle whoosh of waves on the hard sand. A couple walked hand in hand along the beach in a picture postcard portrait of ideal romantic love.

"Hey! You guys have got your food." Goose rattled his cutlery.

Greta frowned. "Steak takes longer."

Goose laughed. "I'm hungry, that's all."

Greta's eyes flashed in disgust. "You must have an internal parasite."

Goose gave her a steely glare. "External would be more to the point."

Jocelyn smiled at Mike. "I like my steak rare, like my men." One delicate hand caressed her blue pleated skirt and tailored jacket, and the other fingered her pearls as if they were rosary beads. "I like to see the pink hue of blood when I cut it with my knife."

Mike said nothing, breathing in the delicate zephyrs of her Chanel perfume.

"You carnivore," Goose replied. "We're supposed to be civilized. Think of the poor beast – once it was an innocent bobby calf, gambolling in a field."

"Don't even think such things. Many of Dad's clients are in the agrarian sector," Jocelyn snapped.

Mike smiled at Greta and Goose.

Ignoring Mike, Jocelyn continued, her tone condescending. "Mockery, or idle speculation, must not jeopardize people's livelihoods in the Republic."

A cell phone rang at the next table. "That reminds me." Jocelyn glared at Mike. "I've been receiving calls on my cell phone from Nate, for you." She breathed in sharply.

"What made you think you had the right to give him my number?"

Mike nonchalantly checked out the legs of the waitress serving at the next table. "I didn't think you'd mind – if it was urgent."

"When has surfing been a matter of urgency?" She raised her eyebrows. "Dad bought that phone so he could contact me twenty-four seven. I don't want the line monopolized by every beach bum no hoper."

"Nate's not a no hoper." Mike made desperate eye contact with Jocelyn, pleading for mitigation.

Goose came to the rescue. "By the way, guys," he said, beaming. "Did I tell you? I'm going to Japan. The boss organized a new assignment of imports." He held his knife and fork as if they were chopsticks. "We've got an agent over there, but he likes to keep an eye on the market, to make sure we're not being ripped off by those with local knowledge."

Greta's eyes spat Ninja stars. "So, I'm just the perfunctory little lady, lucky to be consulted at all." She tossed her mane with the ferocity of a lion on the attack. "Didn't you know the show's due to open in a week?"

"Don't worry," Goose said, smirking. "I'll be back by then."

Nate watched from the lounge as the last rays of sunlight vanished from the barren fields of the headland. Saturday turned to night. He picked up the binoculars slung around his neck and turned his focus to the cove below, where the moon was already casting slivers of dappled light on the water. The breaking waves formed foam braids across the bay.

In the car park behind the dunes, beams of light rotated. He trained his binoculars, and saw a circle scribed in the grass. It was the bikers from earlier in the day.

Putting down the binoculars he strode down the hallway. "Give my dinner to Daryl," he shouted in the direction of the kitchen, and closed the front door. The trusty VW awaited, Nate climbed in and roared off in the direction of the cove below.

He stopped the VW by a battered Ngaio tree at the edge of the car park. The bikers were showing no signs of boredom or dizziness. Enough moonlight penetrated the cloud to enable him to read their patches: *Pariah Dog MC*, written in black letters on white cloth. An image of a pitbull-like dog formed the centre.

The girls, in leathers and denims, rode pillion.

He observed from the car. They idled round a few more circuits, while he breathed in a cocktail of petrol and exhaust fumes. Sensual deep-throated vibrations rippled his solar plexus. Now he understood women's romantic attachment to these throbbing multi-horse vibrators. Clouds fermented around the moon and the night became purple dark and combustible.

The car park lay empty except for a battered HQ

Holden with three surfboards atop, and the bikers' late model Falcon XR8 utility, crash truck, which carried barbecue and beer supplies.

The bikers backed into the edge of the sand dunes, tired of going around in circles. Two hairy guys grabbed a 44-gallon rubbish bin and set it on fire for light and warmth, feeding it with discarded Macdonald's and KFC packets, and driftwood. He counted the bikers – thirteen men and six women. The men mooched, guzzled beer and talked. The women unpacked barbecue food.

"… low-down slut," said Queenie, the woman he'd seen with the big guy at the Oasis pub. "Out of my way you poxy bitch." She elbowed her way past the woman he'd defended earlier in the day. No one responded.

Wolf, the president, fired up the barbecue, at the foot of which was a plaque that read: *Courtesy of Castlemere Roading Corp*. Until yesterday, Nate had worked for them.

Two girls in tight denims plopped fillet steaks on the top plate. Two more, with scruffy hair, took a sheet of plywood from the ute and placed it across the back, forming a makeshift table. The girls buttered the bread. But the girl who'd been playing pool kept her distance. The two guys who'd set fire to the rubbish bin dealt cans of beer like playing cards. The women got their own.

The weathered ngaio tree hid him from view. The bikers now settled into hard-core eating and drinking. If not for the plethora of big bikes and patches, it might have been the engineering shop staff picnic.

One of the rubbish bin guys shouted, "Fire's goin', Wolf. There's a cold bottle a piss waitin' for ya."

The bikers warmed themselves around the fire. Nate shimmied out of the car and made his move. Within seconds he materialized from the dark into the firelight; into the inner sanctum of the Pariah Dog MC. He breathed deep, then addressed Wolf and his two lieutenants. "Here I am."

"Who the hell are you? And what the fuck do you want?" Wolf had shaggy hair and a full beard, and was a full head taller than most of the bikers.

Nate moved in closer to the firelight to see their faces. "Remember? At the pub – you offered me a job."

Wolf's eyes shone red, like a possum's caught in headlights. "The kid with the solid right hook."

"Damn right, boss," said the ugly paunchy one Nate had dropped in the fight.

Wolf swigged his beer. "When I said see you round, I didn't mean the next fuck'en bend in the road."

"Well I thought I would get in before you changed your mind."

Wolf introduced the paunchy one. "This big fat bastard is Tank. You're already acquainted."

"I'm Shane," offered a tall muscular guy with sleek black hair, to Wolf's right. His forearms were heavily tattooed in dark yellow, orange and blue.

Nate saw they all wore shiny steel-toe-capped boots.

"Have a beer, meet a few of the bros." Wolf slipped him a can of Heineken. "We never talk shop and party. Know what I mean? Loose lips." He motioned to where the women were preparing the food. He placed his hand on Nate's shoulder in a fatherly way. "There's a job here if you want it." He raised his can. "To old foes and new prospects."

Chapter Three

"Arbeit Macht Frei" – Work will free you

Nazi slogan at the gates of Auschwitz

OUTSIDE THE office of the Republic of Pluto Employment Services, the wind blew with the velocity of a hairdryer on turbo. Seagulls tested radical aeronautical manoeuvres and hip-hop squawks. Playful tornadoes of sand whirled into funicular shapes on the road.

Nate languished inside the office building, clothed in the universal uniform of oppression – blue jeans and black T-shirt. He was influenced more by budget restraints than political affiliations. The familiar roadway and Norfolk pines wilted in the hot bellows of the wind, and the beach over the road was screened off by a high rock wall.

In the waiting room, he had plenty of time to ponder. How did this place manage to stay atmosphere tight? The automatic doors were so efficient that no particles of ozone from outside exchanged with the closeted air the workers had to breathe from inside and he wondered if they ever experienced the sun on their skin or the wind in their hair. Did they ever feel the sensual sting of salt spray crusted on their face in the heart of an effervescent tube, or that magic feeling of being blasted into the pastel blue and gold of a watercolour summer's day.

Over the years the place had become familiar to him, and he knew the drill by heart. If you found a job you were interested in on one of the various boards, you wrote the number down, along with your name. Then you queued for an interview, sometimes for hours. Hours that were warped of time and personality.

A game of *my shit don't stink, does yours?* played by menial officials of the Republic to keep the status quo. Those with jobs worked harder and learnt not to ask for more, like good little Oliver Twists. The officials received bonuses for not advising clients of their entitlements, and the government saved more money to throw into the abyss of overseas debt.

It raised important questions for him. Did these officials learn on the streets, walking over drunks and kicking derelicts into the gutter? And with gravy-train-impassive eyes, they pulled their thongs harder up the cracks in their arses, and said without speaking: *you don't have a chance fella – why would a boss employ somebody like you?* Someone they couldn't use to make money.

He and three other clients were sitting on a bench seat running along the wall to reception. He watched the first, a young woman with a toddler who was destroying the job cards within his reach. "Stop that!" said the mother, a teenage bag lady, hair a tangle, fingers chewed and tobacco stained. "Stop that, you little bastard! Wait till I get you home."

He shuddered to imagine the little one's fate.

He turned his gaze to the receptionist. She had spiky blond hair and wore a red power suit. The mandatory spiral bone carving, guaranteeing health, wealth and happiness and a safe journey across water, dangled from her thick neck.

She gave him the look. The one that said, *You are a sub-female entity*. Her name badge said *Jools*. With a name like that she had to be a card-carrying leso. Her smug expression was the result of twenty years of public service conferences, seminars, and budget blowouts. It said: *I don't care how many destructive little buggers you bring in here to tear up our job cards, you shall wait. Wait. Wait until your name is called. I may appear not to do much, but let me assure you I am busy – very busy, with protocol and the self-preservation of my rather substantial arse.*

Busy-ness had to be seen to be done, preferably by someone else – it had become a close relative to the law. So in Pluto's Republic, whether you waited for a job, your petrol to be pumped, your groceries to be packed or your hip to be replaced, you would be asked, "Are you busy?" This implied only one satisfactory state of being: busy-ness. If you were busy you could feel smug and justified, and if not, well, you could wait until your number was up or was called – whichever came first.

Nate's mother always said, "If you want something

done, ask a busy person." He didn't bother, because anytime he wanted something done his mother always did it. Other times he visited the Employment Service. He wanted something from them a job. And they told him he did not have a lot of options because his work experience amounted to using a shovel on road works.

"Would you like to retrain?"

How to retrain when you weren't trained in the first place? And if your school record was undistinguished? He bristled with a basic curiosity and desire to learn; in another life he might have been every teacher's dream student. But in this life his curiosity and ability to disrupt the class surpassed his IQ. He showed genius in inattentiveness and in asking interesting but irrelevant questions. For example, where do all the teaspoons and socks go? He sat at the back of the class with the comedians, cartoonists, and sound effect specialists.

It was a matter of record that he'd left school without any formal qualifications. But he had an informal appreciation of schoolboy politics, satire and street wisdom – which his mother spoke of as "a certain native cunning" in the same breath as "illustrious ancestors".

He showed aptitude the way he cut and spliced the waves; he read a wave the way a professor unpacks a doctoral thesis, a politician spins a synthesis into a dominant discourse, or a celibate priest unfrocks a choirboy in anticipation of nefarious practices. But today he would show them he wasn't slow on the uptake.

Today he felt empowered.

The queue moved with the fluidity of a tardy bowel motion. The lady with the destructive child disappeared down a corridor with a case manager, to the interview room.

The young couple next in line were bald and dressed in flowing orange muslin. They shuffled along to the end of the bench like two obedient citizens of the world.

Then the unthinkable happened. His old case manager, Maxine, poked her head around the wall behind reception. She'd case managed him for two years, but still failed to recognize him. Her hair was short and black, cut in a man's style.

She lifted a piece of paper out of the receptionist's in-basket and said, peeking over the top of her glasses, "I will see you now, Mr Crust." She scanned the waiting room to see who'd respond. It gave him an extra kick when he saw the contempt on the receptionist's face at such blatant queue jumping.

He followed Max down the corridor and into her cubicle, one of a dozen or so. She sat at the computer and fluttered the keyboard. His details sprung up, and he sat alongside which gave him a nice view of her legs and upper body. Self-conscious, she pulled the hem of her skirt down.

She studied his details, and it all came back. Her face was evocative of a woman drowning in garlic reflux. "I hadn't expected this outcome. I thought you were happy with the referral to Mathew Construction." Her tone was bitchy gruff.

but he knew her job was to get people into work, any work.

"You do realize, because you have rejected this position you will no longer be eligible to be in receipt of an unemployment benefit – and anyway there's a six-week stand-down period."

"Whatever." He tried to keep his mind on the situation and off her breasts and well-toned legs. Something in her dignity, her poise, and her ripe female flesh held in check by her supportive bra and pantyhose intensified the fantasy.

He bet she and the women on the front desk were an item. They would take turns at being the man. *I'm Max*, the haircut said. *No! I'll be Max*, said the spiral bone carving, *I've got the biggest pudenda. Personal agenda!*

"The filthy slags," he mouthed, and looked at her long, slender, crimson-tipped fingers, imagining liberties taken.

Reality broke the spell when he asked Max if she'd heard about the accidental death at Mathew Construction.

"Yes, most upsetting," replied Max. She shifted her weight from one cheek of her arse to the other.

"Well, I don't want that to happen to me." Nate played with his tuft of beard.

"It was an accident. Lightning doesn't strike twice

in the same place."

"Says who?" Their worlds were so different. He wanted to say: because you live in a world of winged panty liners worn by apprentice lesos more twisted than peppermint candy, and more chance of being struck by a same sex obsession than being squashed by a concrete wall. But he didn't. People never spoke their minds, because that had been legislated against. The world stayed the same or got worse.

"I left my CV with the other contractors," he said, smugly. "See you around." He turned on his heel and walked out.

He left the office. – with an uneducated contempt for officialdom and a wry smile that said he could be on a promise – well, if he got a job.

How long before somebody went mad in an RPES office? It was a philosophical question asked with the tenacity of his mother – with an AK47, bazooka or an efficient but low tech baseball bat, or nipple-fed shovel?

He went silent, and the universe shouted: *Stick to your guns, sucker*. And then elaborated: time – inevitable as gradualism, taxation, death, media hypnosis, lethal safe sex, drive-by shootings, terrorism, exploited human beings, American imperialism, imported trends, Auschwitz, Hiroshima, Nagasaki and nuclear fallout.

He left the office the same way he walked in – a free, but poverty stricken man with nobody to sell but himself. Fuck Dodger Blackwatch and his free market.

"The uncertainty of life is its charm." He relied on his mother for inspiration at times like these. If it hadn't been for the uncertainty of how to raise his rent money, he would have been ecstatic.

He said his good-byes and stepped out into the certifiable crazy afternoon with the sun on his face and the wind in his hair, putting freedom to work.

Chapter Four

Of shoes – and ships – and sealing wax –
Of cabbages – and kings.

– Lewis Carroll

THE ROAD, a rock wall and an elevated track separated Nate from the open sea. Overhead, squadrons of those who ostracized Jonathon Livingstone Seagull screeched in competitive savagery. Anybody stupid enough to feed them got pestered until the food ran out or they moved away.

A late model dark blue BMW caught his eye; he coveted it for a moment. What did you have to do to own a car like that? And who owned it? Traditional surf wagon? Never. Purpose-built for autobahn riders while they sipped champagne and molested the PA.

A thin man with long blond hair cleaned seagull shit off the back windscreen, too absorbed to notice his approach.

"Nice car!" Nate said.

"What?" Goose looked up in surprise. Then with full recognition. "You stupid bugger! I thought you were the boss."

"Well ... I'm boss material," he joked.

"Like fuck!" Goose polished the window. "The boss is doing business in Sunvale." He looked at his watch. "I'm picking him up in half an hour." He stood back to inspect and went around to do the window nearest the sea. "A real babe mobile, eh?"

"For sure," Nate said.

He went back to work on the car. "You don't know. I'm off to Japan next week – to check out the next assignment of cars."

"Big deal. What's the surf like over there?"

"I won't have time."

Two skinny young men in wetsuits with surfboards under their arms danced past on their way to the waves, hopping over the sharp stones under their bare feet.

"What about the missus?"

"Oh yeah, I'm sure her gay friends at the theatre will entertain her in my absence." Goose leaned against the car and rubbed a non-existent mark with exaggerated energy. "I can trust them – they're not interested in what's in her pants."

"Wanna check out the surf?" Nate gazed seaward, craning his neck, but the wall blocked the view.

"After you, old pal," Goose said. "Still on the lookout for work?" They tackled the ten steps to the walkway. Nate didn't answer. They got to the top and sat on the wall side on to the Nor'wester and watched sets roll in about head height. Nate was in faded jeans and T-shirt, hair tousled, and Goose was in a suit, tie at a rakish angle like a leash; an odd couple.

They watched the surfers paddle out in a series of duck dives, being battered by merciless waves. One made it over the top of a wave before it broke. The other rolled underneath.

Nate broke the silence. "The Pariah Dog offered me a job."

"You'd be fuckin crazy!" Goose tugged on his tie. "I never thought I'd say this – you'd do better on the dole."

"I'm not eligible."

Goose turned square on to him." I could get you a job at work, detailing cars. That's how I started."

"Yeah, and no time to surf."

Goose sighed and dropped his arms. "Who wouldn't sooner surf all day? Comes a time to grow up, accept responsibilities. What if my old man dropped out?"

"I don't know why he didn't."

Nate refreshed Goose's memory. "Forty years in the old Post Office, one in Vietnam, and he got two days' notice. You told Mike and me yourself, one night on the piss – they got his name wrong in the speeches, and at the end of the day he didn't even get a gold watch."

"I don't remember saying that." Goose wrinkled his brow, trying to recall what he actually said. "Remember! The same fuckers that sold out to PhoneyCom and the billions a year that used to go into Education and Health goes into some rich cat's back pocket in Manhattan, or maybe Jekyll Island."

Goose put some more polish on his cloth "I'm not going to stand here and argue with someone not capable of understanding free market economics. I'd better get the rest of the shit off the windows before I pick the boss up from the Hays."

Nate knew all about the father and son team of Ted and Jim Hays, owners of Sunvale Services, a typical suburban service station for the past twenty years. They were friendly and efficient, but times had changed, and the market place had become open slather. The supermarket wounded the corner store and the service stations emptied the chamber into them, offering lines of groceries as well, at all hours. Ted and Jim Hays didn't consider a service station to be the right environment to sell groceries, but their parent company and competition did. Ted Hayes took pride in the sale of good-quality second-hand vehicles first registered in Pluto's Republic, and ensured odometers recorded the correct mileage.

And he also knew that since the closure of Japanese automotive assembly plants in the republic, and the lifting of tariffs, the market had experienced an oversupply of cheap imports, whose overall quality and kilometres travelled were dubious. They brought the price of second-hand cars first registered in the republic down.

One time, when they'd been out on the booze, Goose had told him how clever his boss was. That Ted owned the land and buildings, but the oil company owned the petrol tanks. The Company had built a flash new grocery and service station on a high-profile intersection further up the road in Sunvale. The problem was, Sunvale didn't generate enough petrol sales to require two sales outlets. The edict from the oil company was that Ted's tanks must go.

Thanks to cheap imports, the car sales side of his business had tumbled and revenue from petrol sales would soon be non-existent. The Hays had fallen behind on mortgage payments, and the bank had refused them an overdraft to purchase more stock. Their one area of growth was cam belt replacement on low-mileage imports. But it didn't generate enough cash flow, and they saw no real way to increase it.

One man's misfortune (Trenton, Goose's boss), was another man's fortune, and Trenton envisioned a sweet deal. He'd told Goose, "This will be a cinch, Gary me lad." Trenton paid well below the Government value of the land and buildings, fully aware the market bounced his way, for the moment. It would make a good high-profile car yard for cheap imports.

Over the years, Goose had gathered other little insights from Trenton, like how low interest rates preceded a property boom, and that shares plummet in an election year.

Three other part-timers worked for the Hays, including Daryl. If Trenton decided to take over, they could consider themselves unemployment statistics.

Nate watched the two surfers competing for the same head-height wave. They lay flat on their boards, arms locked in frantic unison like a pair of dragonboats thrashing for the finish line. The wave came up from underneath, but only one surfer edged far enough forward to capture the momentum. Fully upright, he slid down its smooth face, picked up the whitewash and rode all the way to shore. The other surfer paddled hard, but wasn't able to catch a ride.

"A lesson from nature." Goose pointed at the surfers. "There's no such thing as a free ride."

"That guy was just in the right place at the right time."

"Yeah, but how much luck, and how much good management?"

"Anyway," Nate ruffled his uncombed hair, "I don't want a free ride. I wanna be free!"

It didn't feel like a Monday afternoon. This time last week he was asphalting footpaths for Castlemere Roading. The sun glinted high in the sky, and he left Goose to his meeting with the boss and went to the supermarket to get something for dinner. He did a few laps of the supermarket car park before he found a park between a battered Toyota Corolla and an old XJ6 Jaguar with the personalised plate: PUSSY.

Saturated fat, carbohydrate, tobacco and alcohol junkies replenished the bread, booze, milk or whatever they had used over the weekend. He knew on Mondays the great unwashed topped up. Thursday's groceries lifted most of their meagre earnings so they could survive until next time the eagle shat on them from great heights.

The corner dairy didn't have a chance – the grocery trade's last-chance saloon for the stupid or the desperate. He reckoned tricky Hindus charged customers whatever they could grab in the name of the sacred cow of the free market. And they milked it for all they could get: "Oh yes! Sahib, it is a most glorious state of affairs, glorious, wonderful, most glorious wonderful." They soon learned the poor made better targets than the rich because they didn't count their change.

He picked out a trolley from a basket jam, made sure it functioned and didn't have a steerage problem. He put the inside seat down to stack veggies because he didn't have a toddler to watch and learn, and pushed through the self-opening door with the panache of a veteran supermarket shopper.

He loved to define character by what a person put into their supermarket trolley. He watched a down but not quite out in a tweed greatcoat, who no doubt lived in a backstreet bedsit, a whiff a' the cork this side of a park bench, ticking off tobacco and cheap red with a pocketknife-sharpened carpenter's pencil. There were uppity thirty-somethings with a penchant for wine and camembert cheeses and fresh-smelling young mothers shopping for baby formula, talcum and disposable nappies. They knew exactly how to tell horny strangers to fuck off with a polite smile. And there were suits with mannequin consorts that sniffed out bargains.

But the most telling insights into character came from Tiff's department. He pushed his trolley over there to get some fruit. She didn't see him, or the mating rituals taking place behind her. He watched as a thin woman in a shiny leisure suit rifled in the bananas. She pulled out the biggest, fattest banana she could find and held it aloft to show her available status, or that she may be open to offers. Inverted bananas meant only females need apply. He was amazed Tiff didn't register these happenings. OK, she didn't have eyes in the back of her head. But why didn't she notice the female couple stepping up to the cucumber stand to inspect the cucumbers for width, length, texture and angle of penetration? Nate saw them go for the ones with ribbed spines. Tiff had told him the knobby ones made better vinaigrette.

A lanky youth with acne angry as sizzling pizza topping was struggling with a bag of carrots on the scales. Tiff came to his aid and he flushed bright red. "They're for my horse."

Nate glanced at Tiff in disbelief.

"Horse's arse!" he heard himself say.

Tiff frowned at his language and threw him a cabbage. "Go – put the dinner on."

It amazed him how evocative a cabbage could be. It brought to mind French and Russian peasants queuing in the streets, cake, guillotines, and death camps – the intensity of Adolph and Eva's last fuck, Mussolini on a butcher's hook and a global Kibbutz. The question presented itself. If a cabbage can be so insightful, why can't we? It was a symbol of basic human need. He must put it to Mike sometime.

Chapter Five

They reckon ill who leave me out;
When me they fly, I am the wings;
I am the doubter and the doubt,
And I am the hymn the Brahmin sings.

– Brahma, Ralph Emerson

"LIFE IS suffering! Can anybody explain this statement in the light of the Buddhist tradition?" asked Chas Blande, Rels 101 lecturer. He wrote the question on the board. The ten students lolling around the tutorial table exchanged quizzical glances.

Mike scanned the posters on the walls: a Hindu temple covered with human genitalia; the monkey god Hanuman, the ghats at Benares with multitudes bathing in the Ganges, the many-armed Krishna, and the familiar pot-bellied Buddha and not-so-familiar emaciated one, and the Taj Mahal.

He was sitting at the far end of the room under an artist's impression of the Tower of Babel. The clock above Blande's head said eleven forty-eight.

The lecturer, a tall thin man with a stooped back, brimmed with nervous energy, like a mantis poised to strike. "Come on now." He thumped his pointer on his desk. "We've covered this in lectures and in the tutorial readings."

A student in Gothic garb, with straggly black hair and a nose ring, took a stab: "Life is suffering because this is Samsara and that's what it's like here."

"Well …" He surveyed the faces. "That's a start. What do others think?" He flexed his pointer into a bow.

The others said nothing.

Mike held back. He was tired of being one of the first to break the awkward silence at the start of tutorials. But now he felt the urge to say something – anything – to fill the black hole of reply. "I think life has to be seen to be suffering for liberation to take place." He let out a dry nervous cough. "If life was deemed to be happiness and an end in itself, Nirvana wouldn't be the goal, we'd be happy with the status quo and would be stuck in ignorance on the perpetual wheel of Samsara".

The lecturer became animated, his eyes alight. "A provocative, if idiosyncratic hypothesis, Mr Willis." Blande's mandibles were sharpened to dismember and he turned them squarely on the group. "I'm not interested in what you think. Does anybody know why life is suffering in the Buddhist tradition? Anybody know why?" He looked at them individually.

The tutorial group kept their expressions neutral, hoping not to be put on the spot.

Blande spoke again. "It might well be prudent to take

in the lectures and the readings and rely less on your own ideas." He picked up his folder. "On balance, university is supposed to be a venue for the exchange of ideas, and you shouldn't be intimidated into silence because your ideas might be thought wrong, silly or both."

He dropped his folder onto the desk with a thump. "You should be aware; it's only six weeks until your essays are due. It's obvious from the lack of performance that you'd better get those books open. My office hours are on my door. If you want to discuss your essay you can see me at those times."

Everyone in the class knew he never showed during office hours, and if you did manage to find him, he turned your essay queries back on you to display your foolishness and his academic brilliance. He would preen and prance, almost to the point of epiphany, when a naïve stage one student expressed a desire to visit an ashram, mosque or a synagogue, or to place themselves under his spiritual guidance.

Blande reminded Mike of the classics tutor who'd taken his stage-two tutorial, who loved to mutilate the modesty in young women by requiring them to read lurid parts of the text aloud to the group, watching them squirm with their inherited hypocrisy.

Blande left his office door ajar when he entertained students. He chaired the academic committee, which took complaints from the sexually harassed. Mike observed him once suggest to a stunning first year with long black hair and an underwear-revealing skirt that they work to raise her kundalini power, or maybe explore tantric sex, or chant mantras so her mind didn't interfere with her thoughts. He could teach her to fly with both feet on the ground with knees elevated. Blande gazed up her skirt and said he saw A+ potential, and hoped she used her intelligence this semester and did not come across like a C–.

Mike became focussed.

Blande wiped the board ready for the next group. Chairs scraped and students blabbered. Bland piled his books on the desk. "Just a minute." He handed out next week's tutorial readings as students filed past, smiling in a supercilious way.

"Just a moment." He held out his arm to stop the exodus of students. "I have a few more pearls to cast. Because nobody knows why life is suffering in the Buddhist tradition, I will add this question to the list of essay topics."

Mike packed up for the next class and soon found himself outside, the warm sun on his black hair and pale face. He dropped his bag on the ground, put his foot on a seat and a fist under his chin he squinted into the sun, filled with questions.

What did he know of university? Not as much as he'd learned about the world along the way. Now almost thirty-two, he'd had plenty of experience of work and travel before embarking on academic study. He'd worked on farms and fishing boats in Pluto's Republic and greater Oceania. He'd grown up on a sheep farm of 5000 acres near the Colossus Mountains up north, and now lived on campus in a monk's cell purpose built for the not-so-gregarious overseas student. His father, Ted, wanted him to come home and manage the farm, but he reckoned his younger brother Greg was more suited to farm work.

But then he met Jocelyn at university. Their eyes had met, and not long after their bodies had merged.

Mike broke his stance and strode over to the law library to meet Jocelyn for lunch.

She was standing in front of the big tinted glass doors talking to three other students. She saw Mike and beckoned him over, lunch bag in hand.

He approached her and the girls dispersed.

"Hi." She flashed flawless white teeth and liquid blue eyes at him. "I was just finalizing a tutorial on the new Employment Act." Her navy blue pantsuit and shiny black bob completed her corporate look.

"Where do you want to have lunch?" Mike hitched his bag over his shoulder.

"Down by the stream. By the way …" The air smelt of petrol and fresh mown grass, like a suburban Saturday morning. She cleared her throat. "Did you get the course changes signed? The deadline's up in another three days."

They followed the winding path around the side of the law library, under the flowering cherries to the river.

Mike sighed and scratched his head. "I know."

They found a seat under a pin oak by the river. He didn't relish an interview with the old bitch department head who'd signed them. He regurgitated a vivid memory of their last interview, in which she'd insisted, like Blande, that they left the office door open.

Did she cherish visions of him going down on her? She wished. Or perhaps she didn't trust herself? The flaccid cratered skin disappearing under her tweed skirt didn't excite him.

"There are angels in Hell, too," she'd told an impressionable first-year girl in a tutorial. How would she like to spend the vacation with her, reading Sappho?

Jocelyn brought Mike out of his dream. She gave him a mantra: "You can expand your mind after your bank account."

Mike took a deep breath and imagined her naked.

Her jacket pocket rang. She took out her phone and answered it.

"It's for you" She pointed the phone at Mike as if it were a remote control.

It was Nate.

"Surfing? At the weekend … Can't say for sure … Why don't you come over here, now? My next lecture isn't till five."

Jocelyn bit her bottom lip.

"See you main library steps, two sharp."

Chapter Six

They who hold the torch should shine the light

– Plato

NATE LEFT his car on the main road and walked in. He didn't want to be nabbed by the fascist car park attendants whose worlds were so small they measured them out in parking tickets.

The university registry clock allowed him five minutes to get to the library, strange he usually worked Tuesday afternoons.

Mike stood one foot up and one down on the library steps, chatting to Jocelyn as Nate approached them. He looked around at what appeared to be remote-controlled beings programmed to know where to be at what time. Did they carry books or rechargeable batteries in those backpacks? Their faces were neither happy nor sad; they displayed well-adjusted conditioned responses, at the mercy of negative and positive reinforcement and the free market.

He and Mike had talked about that, and had agreed to disagree. The students didn't sway from side to side, like circus elephants tied with huge chains, learning that escape was futile but that soon a piece of flimsy twine would hold them. The students had learned their enslavement to the system gradually, and were willing to pay through the nose for it. To his mind they were cash cows fed on bullshit, milked until their hefty loans were paid off – the arts students, anyway. And Mike had told him that the law was that flimsy bit of twine that chained up their personal will.

"Hi, guys."

Jocelyn looked him in the face. "How nice to meet again."

But he knew she didn't mean it. "And you." He tightened his lips.

"I'm sorry, Nate, I can't stay. I have to go and talk case histories and precedents to some first years."

Everything about her sparkled in the sun, and she smelled of jonquils in spring rain. Pity she was such a stuck-up bitch. In terms of class, they were galaxies apart. *Class* – a word not used much now, but one of his mother's favourites. "Even though our place is not high in the world today, Nate, we come from good stock. The pity is, in this commercial world the reputation of our illustrious ancestors isn't enough. But you can always hold your head high knowing you come from class – real class."

It was a pity she'd fallen in love with Don – such a classy shyster. Love and class had a lot to answer for.

Mike placed his hand on Nate's shoulder. "C'mon.

I'll show you around."

"Bye, Jocelyn," Nate said.

"I hope to see you again," she replied, "but in the meantime I'll leave you to your boys' talk." She walked briskly away in the direction of the law library.

Cranes bobbed and turned and buildings rose like asparagus spears from decomposed carcasses. Mike pointed out the new accommodation units for the overseas students, the Commerce Dept building, lecture theatres, the new Physical Sciences library. Nate knew space on campus abounded, especially in the humanities.

"That's where our student fees are going," Mike said.

"You reckon?" Nate peered at the latest construction.

"Administration and lecturers' pockets." Mike coughed. "Funny how university teachers have been one of the few groups to survive the reforms with a strong union and a generous retirement scheme."

"Sounds a bit sus." Nate kicked a pebble out of the way.

"Academics are supposed to be our watchdogs." Mike's face hardened. They walked against the flow of students. The pair jostled to the side of the crowd and found a way forward.

"I didn't know that," said Nate, surprised.

Mike's mouth hardened. "It hurts me to say this, because I have such a respect for the scholarly tradition." His face grew red and his eyes watery. "They sold the cloak of academic freedom to a naked emperor."

Nate narrowly avoided colliding with two cute Asian girls, who laughed. He did too. Then he said to Mike, "What good is freedom if it's only academic?"

His words hit a raw nerve, and Mike clenched his fist. It became the one that held the hammer inside the sickle. "They built a lofty foxhole while the students held the mortar."

They flowed into the university bookshop with a surge of students. All the books were pristine – not a beverage-stained cover, a cocked spine, or scurrying silverfish in sight. Mike casually explored the shelves.

Nate was drawn to the girlie magazines, unthumbed in their plastic wrappers. The Republic and the power elite had wrapped them and called it user pays where they could, but it was open slather on the internet. That was beyond their power for now. The Republic insisted the payer got what they deserved. And when it came to education, the punctuation must be correct and the right words used in the right order. As Daryl had said to him once, it was all about gradual indoctrination – they'd always been hot on spelling, from hieroglyphics to the Cabbala to the birth of the Republic.

He had also learnt that the first years of the new millennium had seen the last hurrah of the pedantic muddle of the failed data and symbol system, which could imitate and calculate but not feel, think, see or learn. But used for the manipulation and management of human thought processes. Nate wondered where his thoughts started and his conditioning ended – everybody and everything wrestled for his heart and mind. This bookshop smacked of ink and glue from thousands of freshly minted books. The incense that wafted from the music section made him rub his eyes.

A female pop singer belted out a song with quirky angst-laden lyrics. A herd of undergraduates clicked through the CDs. Mike still browsed the shelves.

An acne-faced student with a spiked Mohawk browsed the art prints, stopping at one Nate recognized – an elongated maudlin portrait of Modigliani. He loved the sound of his name, an artist who'd died in poverty and obscurity.

The student flicked through a series of Van Gogh's in close succession like a silent movie. He remembered *The Starry, Starry Night* from school art classes, the vivid purple and blue whirls and swirls of a tortured soul who suffered to give expression to a vision others couldn't grasp. He'd also been a victim of self-harm. The words of the Don Maclean song came to mind. Mike picked up a sociology text. "Third edition," he said. "Did you know, you can pay mega dollars for a text, only for it to be superseded the next year, usually by the addition of a new chapter or two? Writing new chapters for textbooks is how academics boost their airline pilot salaries."

"I didn't know that," Nate said.

"Sad but true. The problem is, they're often more

involved with research and publishing than with students. The jury's still out: what's more important? The research or the student?"

"That's a hard one."

"The professor! Have you any idea how much they can earn in the private sector?"

Mike picked up a small volume of Ginsberg's *Howl*. "Ginsberg broke through barriers and challenged the establishment. He captured the anger against capitalism, exploitation, repression and subjugation."

Nate held up a book of poems by Maya Angelou and said. "Who's she?"

Mike didn't answer, instead asking, "Do you know why the caged bird sings?"

"I might," replied Nate. He scratched his dishevelled hair. "I think it's got something to do with mindless oppression, in this case of black people."

"Well done."

Nate's mind went back to old "Woody" and year eleven English. Woody had liked words and poetry and saw through the Republic's constitution: The Vagina is Sovereign. He knew that in the Republic, the truth was always opposite, and that in fact women were everyman's servant. He gave it lip service, but advised his students to always question, never become too respectable, and to remember that if you're going to tear down and criticise, make sure you have a fairer and more equitable system to replace it with. He realised

Woody had to say that, as a teacher, but he'd hated the treachery of the system.

Mike shook him by the shoulder. "Hey, wake up, dude. I'm impressed."

Nate picked up a poetry book and broke into 'Jabberwocky' – *the jaws that bite, the claws that catch … shun the frumious Bandersnatch!* For him it summed up the paranoia of the Republic in a few words – the fear of a backlash of revengeful, rampaging man eating vaginas. Woody saw through the constitution, which stated women were morally superior beings because their portal opens for altruistic reasons, like the continuance of the Republic, but a man's staff rises in self-interest. Translated, that meant women were earthy sex objects, and men the big shakers and movers – superior beings who worshipped the phallus away from the public gaze.

This may have explained Nate's classmates' perverse but spontaneous desire to flog each other under the prefabs on sports day. And to explore more user-friendly genitals, with an urgent hand around the warm throb of a painfully earnest virgin cock, more like a secret handshake than the snap of an opossum trap.

Mike took his head out of the book. "Pity you didn't go on at school."

Nate shrugged. "Nah! I only went to disrupt the class, smoke and feel up Joy Sheriff and other scrubbers in the cricket pavilion at Holyoake Park."

Mike glanced at his watch. "I've got a lecture on Zamyatin and Bolgokov. What did you want to talk about?"

"What do you think about – me and the Dog?"

Mike focused on the air above Nate's head. "Well, I can't say I support the idea. I understand the urge to get off the treadmill – you could go back to school."

"I wanna make some easy money."

"I think you'll find easy and money don't belong in the same sentence. But good luck! Catch you in the surf."

Chapter Seven

Cave Canem – Beware of the dog.

– Petroni Arbitri Satyricon

Found with the picture of a dog on a Mosaic
floor in Pompei

Petronius d.c. AD 66

NATE HAD an appointment with Wolf. He was at the
front fence of the Pariah Dog Motorcycle Club which he
reckoned contravened the local bylaws and the lookout
turret didn't have a building consent. He could just
about guarantee that. He figured a passer-by may have
been persuaded this was just another suburban villa, if
they overlooked the two-metre-high concrete block fence
topped by three strands of razor wire and roof lookout.

And if you asked the next door, they would no doubt
say they couldn't ask for better neighbours. In fact it
had been on the local TV news – before these guys had
moved in, burglaries had abounded. The only issue
was the sound of high-revving bikes, and this was soon
accepted by locals as a variation on lawnmower noise.

Shane opened the gate, unlatching it with his right

hand while his Doberman strained at his leash in the other. Nate didn't know whether the dog was grinning or grimacing at him, and had no wish to find out. It had an impressive set of teeth, and Nate didn't care to imagine the damage they could inflict on human flesh.

He spoke to the dog, having learned from the dogcatcher at the Council that this put them at ease, and to let the dog sniff the back of his hand in formal acceptance, or rejection. The dog calmed.

"Fang's not going to eat you." Shane patted the dog on the head. "But who knows – if I wasn't here."

The dog fixed Nate with a beady, furtive stare.

He and Shane walked down the south side of the house, a track wide enough for cars and bikes. The concrete wall followed the house until it reached the back yard, where it met corrugated iron topped with barbed wire.

Shane tied Fang to the rail of a ramp leading to the concrete patio at the back door. The ranch sliders were wide open, exposing the clubrooms inside. The ramp presumably enabled the guys to ride their bikes onto the patio, to take them inside. Three bikes were parked beside the ramp – Wolf's Harley FXRT and a couple of stripped-down Harley FXR choppers. Most of the guys rode Harley FXR's.

The clubrooms reminded him of a public bar dedicated to motorcycle memorabilia. There was a group photo of the gang maybe from other years, and a banner over the top of the bar announced *Headquarters of the Pariah Dog Motorcycle Club.*

They walked through the bar, and Shane knocked on the second door on the left down the hall.

"Okay, bring him in," came Wolf's voice.

Nate was surprised to see Wolf in such a corporate setting, with a computer, phone and two mobiles on his desk. Filing cabinets and the desk filled the space of the bay window, with views of a two-metre-high block wall. A monitor for the surveillance camera showed the street.

Wolf had been working on spreadsheets, but he hit a key and a screensaver of tropical fish appeared. Behind them, a boardroom table filled the rest of the room, providing seating for the male members of the club.

They sat down at the table, Wolf at the head, between Nate and Shane.

"So you want to come work for us. I'll tell you what's on offer and lay the ground rules."

"I'm all ears."

"We got interests in clubs, pubs, parlours, a bit of debt collecting. No tellin' what might come your way. We're an outlaw organization but we're still mainly about the bottom line. Some bosses might get you to sign a contract to say you'll keep it in house; we'll just break your fucking head, no worries. If you're a good dude who knows? You might make prospect."

"I'm not looking for a broken head," Nate said.

Wolf went on. "We won't tolerate narking or

inefficiency. See no evil, hear no evil, got it?" Nate could have been dealing with Dalton, his old boss at the council. "The job is security and driver for our outcall girls, and some parlour work."

Nate frowned.

"No, ya' fucking knot head! Not that sort of parlour work. A glorified taxi driver. The pay's better than construction and you'll have more time for playin' in the waves. And if I think you're doing well there will be bonuses. The hours are seven p.m. till one a.m., seven nights. He held out his hand for Nate to shake on it. "Deal?"

"I'm no bodyguard." Nate scratched the tuft on his chin.

"Don't worry." Wolf threw him a cell phone. "Any problems, just call me. I'll have the boys around pronto – to bust a few heads. My number's in the phone. "

"I'm no hero, either," said Nate. He shook Wolf's hand.

"Deal," Wolf said.

"Deal."

Wolf issued Nate some last-minute instructions. "Start Thursday night. The parlour's Felines, in the city. Go upstairs and ask for Queenie."

Chapter Eight

"Vox Populi, vox Dei."
The voice of the people, the voice of God.
Text of a sermon delivered on Edward III's ascent to
the throne, 1 Feb 1327.

– Walsingham, Historia Anglicana

ENVELOPES WITH windows come once a month, like periods and full moons. Sometimes Nate heard women call their periods the curse, and other times a blessing, because their old man rolled over and went to sleep.

He plucked three letters out of the mailbox. There was a handful of junk mail – or junkie mail – toilet reading for compulsive consumers. He shuffled the letters. A phone and internet bill, a power bill, both exorbitant, the other inviting him to apply for an American Express Gold Card. He screwed it up, knowing he didn't meet the requirements.

Sandy, the golden Labrador from next door, nudged him and sniffed his crotch and backside. "Fuck off." He kicked the dog away. "The lady of the house isn't home."

Everybody wanted money, much of it to finance their libidos through more and more things to flash around like peacock feathers. That's what kept them on the wheel. Dogs got by on loyalty, and he had to admit people could learn a lot from their unconditional love. Cats were smarter and colder. They colonised the human race with cupboard love.

Humans were at the mercy of their unbridled urges. Poor suckers.

Meanwhile, the great unwashed couldn't afford to live and couldn't afford to die. They bailed a sinking boat with a plastic teaspoon left over from KFC potato and gravy.

The dog came back. Could it be gay? Nothing surprised him anymore. Not even the successful sale of bottled water to dedicated tap drinkers, which promised to be a bigger rip off than not landing on the moon. And who ever dreamed of oxygen bars? Or cans of air to go? His head spun.

God help them if they ever put a tariff on surfing – if there was a God? Meanwhile, the politicians dealt the race card from the bottom of the pack, and raised the spectre of who owns the beach. Could this be a window of opportunity to fast track euthanasia along with justifiable homicide? Or were they preparing for more asset sales?

Daryl burst out the front door. "You had a phone call."

"From who?"

"Jude."

"What the fuck does she want?"

"She wants you to ring the landlord."

Nate ambled down the hallway, dumping the mail, and picked up the phone to dial Abe Solomon's number.

Daryl picked up one of the brochures, from a megastore, and leaned in the doorway, reading it. Before Nate could punch in the numbers, he let go a verbal barrage. "Did you know politicians worldwide are working in support of an elite group? They've removed tariffs, which have increased cheap imports and profits to nationwide retail monopolies, funded by the dollar-a-day labour of Third World workers, and everywhere the megastores set up in the Republic go small to medium retail outlets are closed. The politicians call it healthy competition but in reality, it's plutocratic monopoly."

"Shh – can't you see I'm busy? Hello, Mr Solomon. It's Nate, your tenant."

"Thank you for getting back to me so soon, Nathaniel." He heard Abe say.

Nobody ever called him that – not even his mother.

"That's alright."

"This sale of the house business. I promised you first option, and I want you to know it still stands."

"Thanks." Nate fiddled with the phone.

"There's no hurry, Nathaniel, but I would like a firm decision."

"Cash flow is the problem."

"I'm sure we can come to a mutual agreement in time.

I take it this is a genuine expression of interest on your part, Nathaniel?"

"I'm stoked." He thanked Abe and hung up.

Abe Solomon was nothing more to him than a disembodied voice on the end of the phone. All the flatmates' dealings happened through Whitney's Real Estate. Judith, Abe's agent, came around every three months with a detailed checklist to do an inspection on the property. She checked the fixtures, fittings and the state of the garden. Last visit she'd discovered a couple of blown light bulbs, and rogue potatoes in the flower garden. The rent cheque went to Whitney's, usually in advance.

Daryl was reading a piece of junk mail. "Look," he muttered, pointing to a 29-inch TV. "Made in China. See the price?"

"They buy cheap, and in bulk," said Nate.

"The Republic can't compete with those wages – not yet."

"Mike says it's because of tariffs."

"Part of it." Daryl straightened up.

Nate shrugged. "What then, smart ass?" A devilish twinkle flickered in his eye.

"It's just that the greedy capitalists can make more money manufacturing in China. What used to be government funds from assets are going overseas, industry has all but gone; more debt has to be sourced to run the disintegrating republic."

"What's that supposed to mean?" Nate sat down on the seat beside the telephone table. "What are you on?"

"Sodium Pentothal," Daryl shot back, trying to out-manoeuvre Nate. "Remember Paul White?" He didn't wait for an answer. "Paul White was a second-hand computer dealer who bought ninety floppy discs from Citibank. They had international banking information on them. He suffered intense harassment, his house was broken into. He was beaten up. He received a fifteen thousand cash settlement. He died the same day in a car crash and the money was never seen again."

Daryl leaned back against the wall, passing the brochure to Nate. "Do you know how high the overseas debt is? We're told the economy is in the black, unemployment is way down and the Republic is growing. They don't say it's malignant growth." Daryl's mouth became as animated as a pooch gnawing a favourite bone. "When you get your mortgage document, read the fine print: the borrower is a slave to the lender."

Nate browsed the Chinese goods he could have bought if he'd had some money. He snapped at Daryl. "Give it a rest or go into politics."

"That's exactly what they want … us to become one of them." Daryl scratched his back against the open kitchen doorway.

Nate stretched his legs out in front. "You're overreacting – things aren't that bad."

"No?" Daryl spat saliva in Nate's direction. "You

have one vote, and it's a vote for Paul Warburg and Associates. We are turkeys voting for Christmas."

" Who the *fuck* is Paul Warburg?"

Daryl's eyes lit up. "It's all on the internet. He was the mastermind of the Federal Reserve, the Central Bank of America that's controlled American governments since 1913, giving international bankers like the Rothschilds, Rockefellers and JP Morgan power to run the national debt to the sky, making enormous money out of interest, and gaining control over US governments."

"You're a fucking fanatic."

Daryl waffled on. "Later, through the Council on Foreign Relations, they used the same method internationally, including the Republic of Pluto, to gain power over individual governments." He beamed as if he knew the answer to the Sphinx's Riddle. "The CFR was designed to lead to a potential One World Capitalist Dictatorship through central economic control of the world's money supply."

"For fuck's sake!" Nate threw his hands up. "You're paranoid. What about the large corporations that help control the world and have a mega influence by government lobbying?"

Criticism fuelled Daryl. "Well, they are a component too, but Warburg is the fiscal alchemist who turned gold reserves into paper dollars. The Federal Reserve controls international interest rates, inflation and deflation, boom and bust cycles, the rise and fall of the stock market. It's been rumoured their control might even increase if they went back to the old gold standard and society became completely cashless."

"You're losing me. You mean unless you have gold you have no purchasing power."

"Exactly, but that might not happen. Maybe if our Treasury started to print a new legal tender and got rid of Reserve Bank notes, we could pay off our debt in one swift transaction". He laughed. "But as long as private foreign bankers control the reserve banks of almost every nation, economies and politicians will be subject to their control and their demands."

"Who gives a fuck? What can we do about it? It's all a bit paranoid and abstract for this guy," said Nate. "I thought next you were gonna say they control the phases of the moon and women's periods."

He was aware consumers pigged out on cheap imported goods and ignored the job layoffs in the Republic. And people believed everything the media and Hollywood told them to think say or do. A ribbon on your lapel did not mean an agenda up your sleeve. It meant the vagina ruled and enjoyed a gay sashay on the catwalk alongside other designer labels and share indexes. And everybody was happy, if you discounted the unhappy ones.

And he didn't give a fuck about Paul Warburg or international banking conspiracies. His mind turned to more exciting things: the new job, the prospect of owning a house. Most of all he longed to surf with the guys: all this crap about conspiracies was side-tracking him. It was just like Mike had said, "If you wanted to disprove a conspiracy just follow the money."

"I start with the Dog, Sunday night."

"No shit!" Daryl grabbed himself in the crotch like a superstar. "You're pulling my thing? The same guys that piss on each other around the campfire?"

Nate flushed red.

Daryl burst into a raucous laugh.

Tiff came through the front door. "Hello guys, having a good day?"

They didn't answer right away.

"Good news." Daryl took the bag of groceries out of her hand. "No, no – don't get excited. Not the Second Coming. Nate has a job with the Pariah Dog Motorcycle Club, in their massage parlour."

"I don't believe it." Tiff's mouth dropped. "Is this true, Nate?"

"Is the Pope a Christian?"

Tiff took a deep breath and went into disgust mode "The Pope's spiritual state is a question for him … associating with a band of harlots and fornicators … the Devil himself. Whatever were you thinking, Nate?"

"About Catholic priests and other brotherhoods."

Tiff and Daryl moved into the dining room, and Nate went to call Mike with the news. He dialled Jocelyn's number but there was no reply. He didn't like to call her cell phone, but thought his news worthy enough. Of course, he wouldn't tell Jocelyn who he would be working for or the nature of the work. His income would be mostly from prostitution and drugs, which was unearned and parasitical, but entrepreneurial by free market standards. Just unlawful, that was all. He'd say he worked nightshifts. If she pressed him further he'd say *I drive taxis* and hope she'd swallow it.

He called Jocelyn's phone but there was no reply.

Mike and Jocelyn were enjoying a few drinks with Greta and members of the cast.

Greta was proud of this house, nestled at the end of a driveway off a tree-lined cul-de-sac. It looked out across a shallow tidal stream to the open fields of the Boy's High School. Brown trout and big blue-black eels slid through the current.

"Goose will be back tomorrow," Greta called to those within earshot, as she played the genial hostess from behind the breakfast bar.

As people partied, Greta slid the ranch sliders open to enable flow onto the balcony. Others moved into the lounge. Someone played chopsticks and fragments of *Fur Elise* on the piano, yahooing and camping it up.

Greta banged a mug on the bar for attention, and waited for quiet. "Goose rang last night," she shouted again, over the hilarity. "He's very happy with the latest line-up of cars. He's managed to get some rest before he gets back into it at this end."

"Well well, darlings." Lance, a slight, blond man in his mid-twenties, his crimson cheeks smudged and rouged with blusher, guffawed. He played the part of Bassanio, and was wearing mascara and a chunky gold chain. "Aha! If I were you, darling, I'd worry about him getting his end away over there." He made a risqué face, salivating. "Ooh! I know what hotties oriental girls can be, darling. Such smooth, boyish bottoms …" He gyrated his loins in a suggestive way and sucked in a huge breath of air. "Enough to turn a gay man straight."

Greta feigned hurt. "And I thought you were safe."

"Oh, I am, darling – where you're concerned." He chuckled.

She laughed. "You bastard. I'll have to review my next party list."

Mike and Jocelyn stood on the other side of the bar, amused by the banter.

Lance pursed his lips. "Won't you introduce me to your civilian friends, darling? I do tire of talking shop. Please somebody agree." He turned to Mike and Jocelyn.

"Everybody's charming," Mike said.

"Flatterer," purred Lance. "And who is this beautiful lady?" He moved his focus to Jocelyn. "And what is your interest in this little crime scene, my dear?"

"Goose and Mike have surfed together since school."

Lance got into a crouch as though riding a surfboard. "Always fancied myself a beach-bronzed Adonis in a crystal tube."

Greta broke into derisive laughter. "You may have fancied many a beach-bronzed Adonis, but the rest is stretching the imagination of that one-eyed thing you think with too much."

"You're so last millennium, darling." Lance waved an empty wineglass in his limp hand. "Time for another drinkie-poo."

Greta went to get him one.

Mike and Jocelyn nursed their drinks and watched.

"What do the pretty lady and gentleman do?"

"Always the gnarly one, isn't it?" Mike looked to Jocelyn for moral support. "We're both students. Jocelyn's fourth-year law and I'm doing stage two – a couple of personal interest papers."

Greta handed Lance another bucks fizz. She always enjoyed her little soirees, but not when Lance got drunk.

"Well, I'm no match maker, darlings, but isn't that a union destined for oblivion?"

"I don't see why," said Jocelyn. She caught Mike's eye. "We both have interests in common. We believe in law and order and justice and–"

"Mercy?" Lance finished.

"Of course!" Jocelyn puffed out her chest and her eyes flared.

"I'm not so sure about the law." Mike rubbed the stubble on his face.

Lance held his empty glass ceiling-ward so Greta

might see it and refill it. She grabbed his glass and went off to refill again, thinking Lance was heading in the direction of trouble.

"What are you saying, darling? You don't believe in the government whip and the flagellated people?"

"I have come to believe the law is the will of our masters and determines our behaviour," said Mike."

Lance did a peculiar dance. "Boring! Boring! The party's getting bor-ing. That argument came down with the Berlin Wall, darlings. Now the values are unashamedly bourgeois – stiff … I was going to say stiff upper lip, with the invisible hand of the free market up the Statue of Liberty's dress." And in his best Arkansas accent: "I did not have sex with that woman. Don't you have an internet connection "Aren't you curious about the variety of porn available there?"

Jocelyn flushed. "We never look at porn, do we Mike?"

Mike coughed. "I don't need any extra stimulation when you're around, honey."

"Now why can't Goose be more like that?" Greta called from across the room. She could do with him showing her more interest, now that her biological clock was ticking at such a frantic pace.

"Crawler! This is a political broadcast on behalf of the undergraduate bicycle seat sniffers' party." Lance picked invisible lint off Mike's jacket. "I do wish Isabelle hadn't left so early."

"And why is that?" Jocelyn's tone suggested she didn't wish to meet her.

"She could have introduced you to your masculine side," Lance said, "and I could have taken Mike for a stroll. She might have enjoyed your legalese and you her dictation."

Jocelyn flushed. "Mike enjoys that type of discourse. I do not."

"You go girl," shouted Greta.

She brought back his drink just in time to stop Lance turning the conversation irretrievably out of the politically correct zone. "Here's your drink." She handed it to him. "Don't choke on it, darling." Her tone suggested she wished he would.

"Thanks Greta, darling." Lance cracked a broad sleazy smile. "It's called oral fixation."

Jocelyn put her glass down and preened her silken black hair in preparation to leave. "I like to spend my time in more constructive endeavours than divisive theorizing and lurid contemplation."

Mike lowered his brown eyes to Lance and Jocelyn. "I've decided to major in Religion and Philosophy."

Lance jumped in before Jocelyn. "Why?"

Jocelyn pretended not to hear.

Greta broke in – she couldn't help herself. "I guess you can kiss good bye to your contract for Joce's sexual favours." She smiled at Jocelyn. "I doubt she'll negotiate a roll over."

Jocelyn looked like she'd bitten into a lemon.

Lance prompted Mike. "What about acting?"

"No. I'm too transparent for that." Mike pushed his hair off his forehead.

"Gullible!" Jocelyn puckered her moist red lips and unwound the phallic lipstick she'd grabbed from her bag. "Nate shows more sense than you without the benefit of education."

Greta lifted a pretend glass as if to toast her. "Hear, hear," she said.

Chapter Nine

Laissez faire, Laissez passer

Francois Quesnay 1694–1774

No interference and complete freedom of movement.
Of government interference. Also attr. To
Marquis d'Argenson,

Memoires (1736)

NATE WOKE from his nap after a full day of surfing, shivery, stiff and sore. His face glowed hot from exposure to sun and abrasive salt wind; his eyes stung. His phone said six thirty six – work was at seven. Catching the aromas of the dinner Tiff had prepared, he called to her that he wouldn't bother. "I'll grab a burger on the run."

Tiff didn't get the chance to protest. By the time she'd raced to the front door he'd backed the VW out of the drive.

Felines Escort and Rap Parlour stood three blocks from Castlemere city centre, in an older part of town. He knew this area well, having hung out in its burger joints and bookshops.

Over the years he'd watched the area go through

many social, economic and cultural changes, made worse by cheap imports and the explosion of suburban malls. They were death to the city centre and traditional family businesses.

The area had once had major department stores, warehouses, movie theatres, and clothing and footwear manufacturers, all destroyed by the new thinking. Old stores changed into strip clubs, pubs and sauna parlours. Warehouses became upmarket apartments, movie theatres, fundamentalist churches.

The shops had been individual and quirky, based on quality rather than row upon row of cheap throwaway goods. Now, sex shops, antique stores and dying second-hand bookshops co-existed with used clothing boutiques, and open air cafés sat next to grand hotels regal in their original splendour, against a backdrop of glass towers that veered skywards over the city reflected in their giant convex mirrors.

He knew the street scene didn't stir till after seven thirty in the evening. At one time he'd sit in his car watching the streetwalkers in micro-minis clutching slim shoulder bags, emerging moth-like from shop doorways. The queens or gay prostitutes worked separate blocks to the female hookers, and relied on them to help if they got into trouble. The queens sold themselves cheaper than their sisters on the street, but if a client wanted something more exotic, they obliged. Cars pulled in and after a moment's negotiation the john would be whisked away, to a room or a secluded spot where the deed took place. This might happen in a car, up an alley, behind a shop or under the branches of a gracious tree.

He clattered up the dingy staircase of Felines Escort and Rap Parlour. The stairs came straight in off the street, turned left to a landing, left again, and up. He inhaled the smells of musty old wood and cheap perfume.

Queenie was on reception. "You've cut it fine, sweetie. Veronica!" she yelled in the direction of the girls' rooms, which he noticed occupied most of the floor. Two guys, one black and one white, watched a screen in the clients' lounge, and Veronica, who was about twenty-five with blue eyes, wispy blond hair, dark at the roots, in crevice-hugging jeans and a coloured vest, appeared from one of the rooms.

"You've got a client at eight," said Queenie. "Can you hold things till then? I've got to brief the new chum."

Veronica took up her position on reception. Nate followed Queenie, puppy-like, into the staff lounge.

Queenie patted the settee in invitation. He sat down. They watched the back of Veronica's head through the window. He felt Queenie's overwhelming female presence, in her low-cut silver pantsuit, hair up, twisted into a knot. Her breasts heaved like an ocean swell, their tattooed snakes swaying, obeying the pipes of a phantom charmer. His breathing fell in step with hers in subtle sexual rhythm. Her perfume struck him deep. His penis unfurled slow, like a fern frond kissed by the sun.

She burrowed her ample arse into the couch. He noticed the fullness of her mouth and experienced the urge to be swallowed by it. Heat flew to his cheeks – she was old enough to be his mother.

"OK, sweetie. To start, this is not a massage parlour, it's a rap and escort service. The girls just talk and wait for the client to ask for sex, whether hand relief, oral, full sex or whatever takes the client's fancy." Her voice droned on. "This is negotiated with the girls themselves. The client pays a forty dollar fee to the parlour and outcall escorts. Felines run fifteen girls, five in the parlour and ten work from home. You'll be responsible for getting the girls to their job and collecting the parlour fee."

He watched Queenie cross her legs, which emphasized her mounded crotch.

"The girls will get taxis to and from jobs to hotels and motels, but you'll take them to private addresses where they might meet trouble without back up. If you don't like the look of a client or a scene, get the girl out – never mind the bloody fee. Wolf will sort that."

He moved in his seat. Veronica's eight o'clock arrived, a man in his late forties, paunchy, hair ginger and receding. Veronica led him to her room, and Queenie regained control of the desk. The two men were still in the lounge watching TV.

"I don't approve of that." Queenie pointed to where the men sat.

"Of what?" His eyes followed her finger.

"Porn lowers the tone. The girls don't like it – it puts impossible ideas in the clients' heads. Wolf insists – it's supposed to get them in the mood. Are you ready to go?"

"Sure." He looked directly into Queenie's eyes.

"Pick Monique up from the city." She slipped him a piece of paper. "And drop her here." She pointed to the other address out west. "Do you know the area?"

"Not really." He studied the piece of paper.

"I'll give you a street directory, and I'll phone the rest through."

"Right." He took the paper and directory. "See you at one." He glanced over at the two men still in the lounge. The black man got up to get a drink from the dispenser.

"Check out the gash on that!" the white guy said.

Nate descended the stairs on his way to his first job, wondering what it would be like.

From his position on Goose and Greta's balcony, Mike could see all activity inside, as well as the view of neighbouring houses. The party had got a second wind. The booze loosened tongues and inhibitions, thespian cliques cackled all over the place and the discussions were animated and varied. Backstabbers questioned why certain actors got the lead roles, or at least bigger-speaking parts, the acting skills of Portia and Antonio were deemed inadequate.

The director favoured a certain blonde female type; they didn't go into specifics, and insinuated Propp recruited lead men for their sexual preference rather than their acting ability. Many thought Greta a more appropriate Portia than Isabelle. Isabelle at the moment partied with Propp and gay friends in his penthouse flat.

Mike sauntered over to where Jocelyn stood waiting patiently for a break in the conversation. Jocelyn had found a small group of women in the lounge to talk to. These women weren't actors, but friends and partners of the cast. Jocelyn talked to Gwen, a small vivacious woman in her mid-thirties with red hair, cut in a Cleopatra style. "Yes," Gwen said. "I was once a legal secretary and worked for your father. That was six years ago. Nowadays I work at the City Mission part-time on a voluntary basis, and part-time at the Castlemere Law Library." She waved to where her husband stood on the balcony. "Jim plays shylock in the Merchant."

"That's really interesting," Jocelyn said.

Failing to get a word in he refilled his glass from a bottle on the table and walked over to Jim.

Mike turned to talk to Jim, a dapper man in his early forties, medium height with a brown- and grey-peppered goatee. They were the only ones on the balcony, so Jim could speak confidentially. He leaned on the balcony and looked over the opulent neighbourhood, then turned to Mike. "I guess you realise by now my wife works for the mission."

"I find that interesting. I've toyed with the idea of voluntary work there myself."

"The City Mission completed my education. The

sharp rise in unemployment and foodbanks are the direct result of decades of neo-liberal government policies: user pays and trickle down economic theories."

"The government intends to close more schools," Mike replied.

Jim looked over the rooftops of the affluent. "It's disgraceful. I'm glad I've done my turn."

Mike didn't answer, instead reflecting inwardly on the state of the Republic. It stole the livelihoods of tens of thousands of citizens and gave them a benefit. It sold the people's assets to service more government debt; it closed schools, hospitals, and opened up state house rentals to market rate. It abandoned the destitute, the poor, the alcoholics, the drug addicts; it lowered the drinking age and laced soft drink with booze so youngsters could kill themselves or innocent parties in high-performance Japanese imports.

The tax burden on the poor increased, while tax relief was extended to the rich. The Republic introduced all the efficiency cuts imaginable at the bottom end, but the debt accelerated with the torque of a boy racer. The wealth accrued by generations of Plutonians was spent to supply overweight bankers with svelte mistresses, antique Scotch and Cuban cigars, and to finance nuclear arsenals and perennial skirmishes. Surely the day of reckoning loomed. The Republic of Pluto wouldn't be able to exploit enough revenue to meet its debt, and its citizens would be forced into more austerity measures to meet the payments.

Mike thought that Jim, who played Shylock, the grasping, merciless moneylender, showed consummate skill, because Shylock's and Jim's values couldn't be more different. Jim had headed a local primary school, recently closed because of a falling roll – uneconomic, in the words of the technocrats. The school had been rationalised to merge with another one ten kilometres away, which had resulted in the loss of many skilled staff.

"Can I have that paper for a second?" Jim broke Mike out of his trance and took hold of the morning copy of the *Plutonian Press* that had been ransacked for the sports and business section. He read the motto on the coat of arms, which displayed an inverted triangle inside a lotus flower. The motto was also on the nation's flag – it was a yoni symbol, otherwise known as a vagina, and underneath was the phrase: *All you need to know*.

Mike remembered where he'd heard it before. "That's Keats, but it omits *beauty is truth, truth beauty*. My interpretation is that art conveys human knowledge and insights better than science, perhaps, or better than music."

"Your student fees weren't wasted." Jim folded the paper in half and put it back on the table.

Jim on the balcony reminded Mike of a musician on *Titanic's* bridge, in the middle of a freezing Atlantic, minus a violin. Jim turned to Mike, his face grey. A tired, faraway look came into his eye, and he said, "I'm glad I'm not teaching anymore."

Nate plucked Monique from outside the Victorian mansions, in an older suburb two blocks east of the city, near the river. The area had been one of low rents that attracted beneficiaries and students. Now, young professionals had moved in and rents and property values had inflated. The suburb was enjoying a comeback – shops sold organic foods, herbal medicines, deli foods and arts and crafts.

The air had chilled, and he pulled the collar of his denim jacket up. Monique quivered in her red shift. She wore her blonde hair in pigtails with a fringe, a ready-made fantasy, a twenty-five-year-old high-school girl.

He didn't recognize her at first, then it clicked – this was the girl in the bar, the one he'd fought over, who Queenie had abused at the barbecue. She didn't recognize him. He supposed she saw so many lusty male eyes and spunky backsides in a typical day. The cold was making her nipples stick out, and it wasn't hard for him to imagine her naked.

"Well, you're a new face," she said, stepping into the car. "You are from Felines, aren't you?"

She smelt of violets. His hormones raced. "You'd be in trouble if I wasn't. I'm Nate."

"The last driver didn't stay long."

"Bills have to be paid."

They started for the West Side of Castlemere. Awkward silence reigned until the concrete and glass of the city gave way to the road, which followed the river west. Nate felt her eyes roam over his boyish features. Then she said, "Not curious?"

"About what?"

"Why I do what I do?"

"That's your business."

She told him anyway. "So many think it's because I love sex, or have a habit, or have been forced by a pimp or boyfriend. Surprise, surprise! I'm in it for the do-re-me." She watched his impassive face.

"What I thought."

They passed over the railway line that cut the city in two.

"Did Queenie explain to you the difference between a rap parlour and a massage parlour?"

"No." Nate checked in the rear vision mirror.

"They aren't licensed to do massages. It isn't legal for the girls to ask the customer for sex. They have to talk him round till they ask for what they want – without giving a massage." She didn't take her pale blue eyes off Nate. "Wolf and Queenie can't get a massage parlour license, because they both have convictions – I bet she didn't tell you that."

"No biggie." Nate indicated and moved into the right-hand lane.

Monique touched up her make-up in her handbag mirror. "I got out of the parlour once they started asking for rent money for the rooms. They're talking about charging for your services."

"Are they?" Nate concentrated on driving. "I guess it's user pays."

She zipped her bag shut. "I like it better this way. As long as they don't legalize it, I'll be quite happy. There are enough single mothers cracking it. There's some at Felines. If it becomes legit, every girl in the world will be hocking her hole. The price will come right down."

"Then we'll get it wholesale." Nate spoke in a deadpan way, catching her gaze. Monique burst into laughter, and punched him affectionately on the arm. "Very witty. Shouldn't be too far from here." She studied the directory. "Next on the right, after that set of lights," she said, pointing.

Nate indicated and moved into the right turning lane; the light stayed green and he swung into Luxor Crescent. They looked for number five and soon found it, fronted by a wrought-iron monstrosity of a gate. Two huge coach lamps, one on each ivy-covered post, dispersed light, and there was an intercom. The house was out of sight. He pulled up at the intercom and they got out of the car.

"You can do the talking," said Nate.

Monique pressed the button. "This is Monique, from Felines. Could you open the gate, please?"

Her variation on *open sesame* had the gates opening automatically.

Nate drove through the sinuous avenue of oaks and rhododendrons to the cobbled courtyard. He was blown away by the house, a neo-Georgian-style mansion of stark white symmetrical lines, with a portico and columns and capitals. The front garden boasted a Cupid fountain, water spurting out of his soft immature penis. A Range Rover was parked in front of steps, which swept up to the mansion's portico with its chequered floor. The back end of a Porsche protruded from a four-car garage; the plate read LAWMAN.

Nate rang the doorbell. A man of about sixty opened the door. He wore grey slacks, a blue blazer, and a maroon shirt open at the neck with a gold cravat. Italian shoes; hair white and close-clipped; Roman nose.

He ignored Nate and addressed Monique. "So this is the charming Mademoiselle the agency has sent me. Do come in, my dear." No way would he let Nate through.

Nate craned his neck and glimpsed more chequer-board tiles in the entranceway, beyond which were cubic metres of red carpet and antiques, and a staircase themed on *Gone with the Wind*.

"I'm here for the agency fee." Nate held his hand out for the money.

"Your purpose did cross my mind." He made a face as if he'd discovered dog shit on the sole of his shoe.

"Forty dollars, please," Nate insisted.

"Here." He peeled off two twenties from a billfold wad. "Take your grubby little commission."

Nate took the money and retraced his steps. Back at the car he checked his phone for messages – Melanie wanted to be picked up. He drove down the drive and stopped outside the gate. Two bikes roared up behind him. He looked around and saw Wolf and Shane.

Wolf walked towards him and stuck his head in the car window. "No probs, dude?"

Shane waited on his bike. Nate watched him in the rear vision mirror.

"Not so far."

Wolf passed him a package in a *Republic of Pluto Post* plastic envelope. "Drop this on your way."

"Sure." Nate tossed it over onto the back seat.

Wolf got back on his bike. The engines burst into a rumble and two red taillights disappeared into the night.

The party at Goose and Greta's was still raging at twelve thirty-five, when Nate drove past. He delivered the parcel to a state house area on the other side of town. And he dropped Maya, Felines' curvaceous Eurasian beauty, at the Globetrotter Motel. It was his last job of the night, apart from returning to Felines to cash in the night's taking.

His mind already frolicked in tomorrow's surf, and he wondered how he would survive waiting another week to be paid.

Chapter Ten

Go, wondrous creature! Mount where Science guides,
Go, measure earth, weigh air, and state the tides;
Instruct the planets in what orbs to run,
Correct old time, and regulate the sun.

– An Essay on Man, Alexander Pope

NATE ASKED himself why the general public equated surfing on a Friday, a working day, with the worst excesses of the Roman Empire. He left that one with the universe. Swells rolled in around head height. The sun's rays were hot on his face and neck, and there was a slight onshore breeze.

Six surfers competed in the line-up, their rides short, dumping them in the churned-up shallows. He reasoned they must have been grommets or strangers, because of their performance and the fact that they didn't know the best waves happened around mid-tide. Maybe they were desperate?

He placed his board, towel and wet suit on a rocky bank and went to investigate a group of people huddled in the sand. The whole expanse of shoreline belonged to them, except for one other gravity bent lonesome figure on the elevated path between the beach and the road.

The sun lay low in the sky. He guessed it must be nine thirty or ten. Three gulls soared on the thermals high overhead, and he took a deep lungful of sea air and sniffed. *Ah! Nothing like it.*

He approached the group, two males and two females, about nineteen or twenty years old. They were crafting magnificent pyramids, sandy miniature copies of Cheops and Giza, an avenue of sphinxes, and a bust of Tutankhamen; the Acropolis. The architecture featured Greek post and lentil construction, buildings with more Latinate arches and domes, square-sided obelisks, but no twin towers. Nate had always been interested in Egyptian stuff and classical architecture, and spent time in the library reading about it. It must have been Mike's influence.

"What's the go?" Nate spoke to them in general.

The guy in camouflage shorts looked up. "I couldn't possibly comment."

The red-suited woman said, "It's called architectural sand sculpture."

They continued to work as if he wasn't there.

The butch lady in blue placed a cardboard capstone on her pyramid. "Isn't it wonderful people have such short memories and are so long suffering?"

The brown guy finished a sand bone carving. "It's about people, people, people, but get me drunk on money and I'm a two glasses of wine whore."

"I'd be tempted if you were a girl, but I'm broke." Nate got an uncontrollable itch in his right foot. "Hope some kid doesn't kick 'em over." He grinned like a Doberman stalking a burglar.

"That would be like, so divisive," said the blond guy in an apron.

Nate was wide eyed. They worked with the intensity of children in a sandpit, just below the high tide mark. The last full tide had left a line of seaweed, driftwood, broken nets, fish bones, and bits of plastic.

He retrieved his surfboard, wriggled into his wetsuit in a sort of reverse striptease, reached over his shoulder and pulled the back zip up snug, and headed for the waves.

He stopped before he hit the water and fastened his leg leash. He wanted to show these grommets some local tricks. Seven surfers languished in the line-up, all astride their boards, patient for a half-decent wave. He watched the intervals between the sets of waves and paddled out during the smaller sets. Once out the back, a right-handed, hollow, head-height wave came up from behind, and he spun around, lay flat on his board and paddled like a galley slave on chipmunk. He and two grommets caught it. He slid down the face into the trough and did an unscheduled one-eighty-degree turn to avoid one of them, straight up the face, through the lip and into the air, exhilarating but dangerous. He should have just shoved him out of the way.

"Stupid bastards," he yelled, and paddled up the beach to escape them.

The waves frothed larger now and spread their skirts on the shore. He went to take one but was too late; it broke on him. He pushed his board through the white water and came out the back of the wave.

The day heated up. The warm salt wind stung his face and the sun singed his neck. He straddled his board, rising and falling in harmony with the swell, when he recognized Mike's distinctive fluid strokes paddling out. Mike came up close, and sat on his board facing him. "Some good sets forming."

"I reckon about head height." Nate sat holding the rails of his board. They both glided over the top of a wave, which threatened to break on them, and waited for a better one.

"I swung past the Goose's last night, round midnight," Nate said.

"Cliquey bunch." Mike looked directly into Nate's eyes. "Know what I mean?"

Nate nodded. "First night last night," he blurted.

Mike didn't get a chance to respond. A big surly wave crested above them.

"This one." Mike paddled into position. "Go, girl-friend," he kidded.

The wave barrelled and peeled to the right.

"Yee ha!" they yelled, waxed to their boards. Mike hug-crouched in close to the peel and took a big slice right down the face into the trough, which turned beige and collapsed in dirty inshore water, dunking him hard. Nate rode far enough ahead to stay in front of the break. He crouched and rode the dirty water until it caught up with him and gave him a murky sand bath. He paddled over to where he'd seen Mike go down.

Mike stood in chest-high water. "The Pipeline will have to wait," he said, laughing.

"That was a bumpy ride, man." Nate panted with exhilaration. "They're real hard to read." The water lapped against their boards and they undulated with the swell.

"You pick the next one." Mike sat side-on to the swell.

"I started last night." Nate checked over his shoulder for waves.

"With the gang?"

"Motorcycle club, they're businessmen."

"Now I'm worried." Mike laughed.

"It's a job," said Nate, "and I'm free to surf during the day." He turned out to sea, sitting on his board. "If Jocelyn asks, just say I'm driving taxis – true in a way."

Mike began to lecture him. "If you must associate with those guys, don't do anything to break the law!"

Nate knew Mike worried about what Jocelyn and her family would think.

"What do you do at work?" Mike scanned the horizon.

"I drive the out call girls around."

"Why not get a respectable job?" The tide was now

about two thirds in, and the wind picked up a gauntlet of spray and sloshed them in the face.

"Respectable?"

"A lawful occupation."

"I'm a fucking taxi driver." His hands wrinkled at the fingertips and he began to shiver.

"Yes, but you're paid from immoral earnings."

He thumped the nose of his board. "I'll tell you what fucking immoral is – a country founded on slavery and trading trinkets for land or making war with another country because you want their oil."

"Take it easy. I'm not the enemy." Mike smoothed the bristles on his face. "I only want to help."

Nate shook the water out of his hair. The waves flattened out and the sea began to chop. He grabbed the rails of his board for stability. "Sixty per cent of workers in the Republic are paid a fucking pittance while the other forty per cent creams it." His eyes flashed wide. He wobbled and almost fell off his board. "And half the world gorges and fucks itself silly while the other half starves and dies of AIDS." They perched astride their boards with the noses out of the water facing the shore.

"You worry me," Mike said.

"Why, because I want to be free?"

"No, because you're going to end up incarcerated." Mike put his hand up to avoid the back spray. "By not desiring, you steer a middle course between the extremes of action and reaction that create suffering and keep you in karmic bondage to this world." The offshore wind increased the back spray and slapped them with the ferocity of a scorned woman.

"I've gotta fucking live, mortgage is better than rent," Nate said. He expected a knee-jerk reaction from Mike.

"Ever looked up the definition of mortgage?" Mike checked out the time on his diver's watch. "Imagine the karmic reaction if the whole world stopped working. Goose should be coming through customs about now."

"Talking of slaves." Nate smiled at Mike in a smug way.

Mike's face rebuffed him. "Is it possible to be happy and free?" He hummed a few bars of "Me and Bobby Magee."

Greta didn't recognize Goose when he walked through the arrivals gate at Castlemere International Airport. In fact she walked right past him, and if he hadn't touched her on the shoulder she might still have been looking for him. A polished bald head had replaced his long blond locks, and an air of seriousness had replaced his usual sunny countenance.

"Darl, what have you done?" Greta ran a pampered hand over his smooth head. She really didn't like it.

"I'd have thought that was obvious?'

"Come on," she teased, "maybe I can get to like it. Let's get your bag off the carousel." He hadn't been away long, but she'd missed his annoying habits.

As they waited by the conveyor, Goose gave Greta a run down on his trip. "The agent presented a good line-up of cars: low-kilometre sedans, wagons and four-wheel drives to replenish the stock in the yards."

Greta smiled. She wasn't particularly impressed. "Aren't they really just Japanese hand-me-downs for our middle to lower classes? If the middle class still exists."

Goose scowled. "They're good quality vehicles. Why do you have to go on the attack all the time? We're also upgrading our European marques, for those who show enough nouse to earn them. I might even get the job of setting things up in the European division, because of the success of this trip, if the boss's plan to expand still goes ahead at Sunvale."

Greta gave Goose a big kiss on the cheek. "I'm so glad to have you home again, darl." In the same breath she added, "The play opens Wednesday night." She hoped he'd get over the excitement of his trip in time to work up some enthusiasm for the play.

"Great." Goose rubbed his bald head.

They watched the bags go round several times before Goose's black suitcase and brown leather overnight bag arrived. He grabbed them and placed them on the airport trolley. "I know it's Saturday, but I told the boss I'd look in as soon as I got back."

"That's not fair." Greta pouted. "That bloody money grubber Trenton Jones."

"It's business. We'll have plenty of time for each other later."

Goose looked at Trenton Jones across the substantial leather-topped desk. He'd just turned fifty-three but looked forty-five, a head taller than Goose, bald, with a horseshoe ring of brown hair round his scalp, grizzled at the temples. He played squash three mornings a week and tried to squeeze nine holes of golf in at the weekends. He had the air of a general practitioner rather than a car salesman, and reeked of power and financial success via the free market. Maybe Goose could be like him one day.

Trenton stretched out in his chair and took a bottle of Johnny Walker Black Label from the bottom drawer of his desk. He threw ice cubes from his office fridge into two tumblers and poured a two-finger measure of scotch into each, placing them on the desk, then leant back in his chair, lifted his glass and said, "Cheers, Gary lad – here's to a successful trip."

Goose sat down, took his glass and raised it. "Good to be back," he lied.

"Good haircut, son. Like mine – low maintenance." Trenton pulled the venetian blinds open and they looked out over the lot. "A few gaps to fill out there now, but we got a good deal on your consignment."

"It makes a difference." Goose sipped his whiskey. "When you're on the spot you can do a bit of tyre kicking and leg pulling to get the price down."

"Exactly." We can bang a decent mark up on them and we'll be laughing." He winked at Goose. "Might even be a bonus in there for you. I know you and Greta can use every cent since you moved into the new place."

"Thanks." He played with the Corvette model on Trenton's desk. "We appreciate that. How is progress on the Sunvale deal?"

"Looks good." Trenton poured Goose and himself another scotch. "I've put a cheeky offer in," he said in a conspiratorial tone, "because I know the owners are desperate to sell. The agent should get back to me any time now. And if it comes through I'll be looking for a manager."

Goose nurtured dreams of trips to Europe to set up an agent at that end, and all the fringe benefits. He tried hard to curb his enthusiasm.

"Did Yoko show you some Tokyo night life?" asked Trenton.

"Yes."

"I'm glad. You can fill me in later, for now you'd better get home to the wife." Throwing Goose a bunch of keys, he said, "Take the blue Z three roadster off the lot."

Goose caught the keys and couldn't get out of the office and into the car fast enough. He felt at home behind the wheel of the Z three, cradled in the firm seats and surround sound.

The afternoon was so warm he took the top down.

The breeze ravished his bald head and his thoughts drifted on glassy waves. Mike, Nate and surfing hadn't entered his head in all his time away.

At Sunvale, from the sea wall, he watched puppy dog waves lap the full tide mark. A colourful smudge of bathers were enjoying the balmy conditions at the east end of the beach, where a small bay had been formed by the action of the water over many years.

He turned his attention to the boogie boarders, surf skiers and surfers who'd made the beach too populated for Mike and Nate. He spotted the pair as they caught the next wave and rode it all the way to the shore. They took off their leashes in the shallows. A number of sand sculptures had survived, despite the numbers of people now on the beach.

Mike and Nate unzipped each other like cats in mutual toilet, peeled their wetsuits down to the waist and towelled themselves. He walked over to them and they waved.

"Welcome back," they said at the same time.

"What do you think these mean?" Nate said, nodding at the works in the sand.

"Nothing," Goose said.

"They're symbols." Mike pushed his wet fringe out of his eyes.

"Symbols?" Nate frowned.

"They stand for something else," Mike said.

"Not just sandcastles?" Goose ran a hand over his

bald head.

"No," Mike replied. "The ability to process data and symbols, to use language, is what distinguishes mankind from the animal species."

"Really," Goose said. "Are you guys going to the theatre tonight?"

"Yes."

Goose smiled wryly to himself as the tide rolled over the sculptures, whatever they represented, in the way history rolls over everything in comic-tragic pantomime. They were gone. He checked himself – too much philosophy was rubbing off on him. He needed to get back to market forces.

Chapter Eleven

Tell me where is fancy bred,
Or in the heart or in the head?
The Merchant of Venice, 111, II, 63

William Shakespeare

NATE WATCHED the Friday night queues of women waiting in line for the toilets in the foyer of the Hound and Hare Theatre. Would true equality of men and women ever exist? The women's queue was twice as long as the men's.

A crest over the box office read *Otium cum Dignitate*, but he didn't have a clue what that meant. The place babbled with theatregoers and amateur critics.

"Isabelle – such a fine Portia."

"Statuesque."

"Bassanio obsessed with Antonio?"

"You think so?"

"Is it a gay play?"

"Jessica's mumsy."

"Shylock doesn't cut it." [Laughter.]

"Awesome sets."

There was standing room only in the increasing

murmur, which worked itself to crescendo. Nate saw Goose and Mike threading through the crowd towards him, three lagers held head high.

He'd persuaded Queenie to give him part of the night off. She agreed, if he could make it back by twelve to tie up any loose ends. He and the other guys squeezed into a corner window seat with vistas into a courtyard, easing the claustrophobia.

"Phew!" Goose handed Mike a beer and wiped his brow exaggeratedly. "Like a paddle out on a rough day."

"Without the water," Nate said.

"I hear you." Mike slugged his beer. "But it's Greta's big night and she got the complimentary tickets."

"Bums on seats." Goose patted his backside. "They always do that to get a full house opening night. Actors are obsessed with bums."

"Lucky we're sitting on ours." Nate sucked on his can of beer.

"Let's enjoy it for her sake," said Mike. "Thanks for the beer, it hasn't touched the sides."

"What are friends for?"

Mike put his beer down on the glass-cluttered table in front of them. He looked at Nate and Goose and laughed. "Friends are people you don't have sex with or fantasize about. They talk sport and make sure your vote goes to the right party."

Goose chuckled. "No wonder I don't have many."

Nate looked injured. "I should have more friends

than a Lotto winner."

Mike lifted his glass again "But you have to toe the party line."

Goose scanned the crowd. "Where's Joce?"

Mike pointed over to the bar. "She's over there, talking to some colleagues." Goose said, "I know the white-headed old bugger from somewhere."

Nate casually glanced over and recognized the snowy head – it was Monique's French client. He didn't know the tall dark guy in the charcoal suit who was speaking to Jocelyn. "I took Monique to his place the other night."

Goose' frowned. "Now I remember – but it wasn't girls or women. He fancied adolescent boys."

"You got the wrong guy," Nate said. "But anyway, I gotta go."

On his way back he checked out the insurance building clock, an hour before he reverted to pumpkin or a wage slave.

Wolf was slumped behind the computer, reviewing Felines' previous week's turnover. The hallway door didn't shut out the noise of motorbikes, boozy revellers and amplified rock music, which reverberated through the walls and hallway. Queenie shut the office door and looked over Wolf's shoulder. The noise became muffled.

"Numbers are good for last week, babe." Wolf smiled up at Queenie.

"Could always be better, though." She pouted.

"How?"

"If we charged the girls for their rooms and put our commission up to twenty-five per cent of their takings. They can afford it. Remember, it's user pays and they don't pay tax. We have to make a profit."

Wolf swung round in his chair to face Queenie. "Sounds terrific. Do you think it'll be much of a problem implementing it?"

"Knickers off a whore cinch, if … They need the job, some of them have got families to feed. It's also dangerous out there, without our support. There's only one problem – that bolshie little bitch Monique." She smoothed the leather lapels of his jacket, and plucked a grey chest hair.

"Ouch! Fuck you, Queenie." He pushed her hand away.

"I'll leave it to you to deal with Monique."

Wolf punched the expected increase into the spreadsheets and smiled at how it altered the bottom line. "I thought I fixed the Monique problem when she got put on outcalls." He tightened his lips. "Leave it with me." He thought for a moment. "Might have to look at some disciplinary action." He laughed, and Queenie gave him a self-satisfied smile that promised she would be awake when he got to bed tonight.

As an afterthought Wolf asked, "The kid working out alright?"

"Had time off, already."

"Don't let it happen again. Drink?" Wolf opened the door to high decibel ZZ Top and a cloud of marijuana smoke – bedlam city.

Wolf and Queenie joined the rest of the bikers in their bar. The entertainment was a woman of about thirty with bushy dark hair. She was drugged out of her mind, gyrating to the music. Shane slouched at the bar, sucking a beer and a joint, drawn to the action. Wolf pulled up a stool beside him and Queenie joined the other women. The bare-chested barman with a German eagle tattoo poured Wolf a beer.

"The bitch better save some for later." Shane grabbed his handle of beer.

"Later?" Wolf said.

"On the block."

"She up for it?"

"Yeah, no worries. Tank copped her at the Mitre."

"Ain't she kinda slumming it?"

"Unhappy love affair," winked Shane.

"Ah ha!" said Wolf.

"Yuh know what they say?" Shane took a gulp. "Higher the class, lower the tastes. A donkey on Viagra wouldn't satisfy this bitch. Tank reckons she's gagging for it."

Shane leered at her. "Not a bad piece of livestock."

Wolf lit a smoke and watched the bikers' women lounging on couches and beanbags, lost in their girlie chat. They smoked, drank and cackled, like witches round a cauldron. Monique regaled the girls with the sexual habits of her clients. How much easier this was than a forty-hour week. The hours were better and the only qualification necessary was the ability to do a good blowjob or hand job, and lie there while the customer ejaculated like a spastic marionette.

"It comes natural," said Monique, "no pun intended. On a good week I can earn two or three thousand, tax-free." She poked her tongue out. "So eat your powder puff panties out, receptionists and girl Fridays. I'm not working this week, it's rag week, some still do hand and oral."

The delirious dancer showed no signs of tiring or slowing.

Wolf smiled.

Monique lit up a cigarette. "Did you know some fellas will pay big bucks to have you piss or shit on them?"

A girl with spiky peroxide hair spoke. "Man, I'd do it for nothing." She got a chorus of laughter, which encouraged Monique to go on.

"One customer the other night wanted me to–"

"Enough!" Queenie shouted. "What you do on the job stays there! Remember the no narking rule. Revealing who and what clients do is narking, while you work for Felines."

"To justice and true love." Lance raised his glass. He cornered Mike and Jocelyn. "Allow me to introduce you to our leading lights. This is Jed, our sultry Elvis look-alike." Lance wiped imaginary lint from his shirt. His mind raced – *what a travesty, what a loss to the gay world.*

"Thank you very much," Jed drawled in exaggerated southern tones.

"Superb, exemplary my darlings!" said Arnold Propp, the theatre director. He spoke from the breakfast bar to the cast gathered at Goose and Greta's in the wee hours of Saturday morning for the after-theatre party. "I think we're in for a good review."

They all cheered.

Lance continued where he'd left off. "And this is Isabelle." He introduced a stunning Amazonian vision of a woman dressed in a long purple velveteen skirt with a black silk blouse, a hint of lacy black bra beneath. Her eyes were cat green and on her feet were black Doc Marten boots. If they only knew what a tart she was.

She turned and spoke to Jocelyn. "So you're a friend of Jessica's – I mean Greta's."

"Yes."

"Did you enjoy the play?"

"Very much, I have an interest in the law."

"Really?" I just enjoy strutting in men's clothes." She ran a cursory eye over Jocelyn's body.

"I bet you say that to all the girls." Lance was trying to expose her real intentions but failed miserably, so he added, "and removing other women's pants." He smiled at Isabelle, thinking of her amorous history with members of both sexes.

Jocelyn flushed from earlobe to earlobe. Isabelle showed no embarrassment or interest in Mike. Lance smiled. *The bitch doesn't miss a beat.*

Isabelle tossed her hair flirtatiously. "My audience awaits, lovely to meet you." She leant forward and gave Jocelyn a big wet lingering kiss on the lips.

"Tart!" said Lance. He expected a fiery reaction.

Jocelyn was taken by surprise – her face flushed the colour of red wine, her knees buckled, and she struggled to gain her composure.

"That's our Belle, darlings." Lance bowed and extended his right arm.

"Trollope," Jed said. "If I did that there'd be a contract out on my balls."

Tank spurred them on "She told me she wanted to wash her boyfriend away in an outpour of passion, a tidal wave of sex. She wanted to be tossed every which way and left satisfied in a wet patch of lust. She went to the Mitre to pick up a man for that. She said any man would do – one who could fix the humiliation of being dumped for a younger woman, and an oriental one at that."

He reckoned an aqualung might have been the only way to escape the toxic blend of sweet marijuana and acrid tobacco smoke, cigarette butts and bottles strewn like tornado debris, and ashtrays log jammed. Body odour and sweat added to the smelly mess, vintage

Jethro Tull played, Locomotive Breath, quieter now.

Queenie persuaded Wolf to take her into work on a pretext to escape the situation. The Mamas, bikers' women, either moved into a front room or went home.

Shane and seven other bikers shared the room with the woman. She sobered up enough to realize her fate, but too late. The bikers were like a dog pack on the scent of a fox.

To Tank and the other bikers, this women meant nothing more than a cum rag –something to wipe away the stain of their desires and then be discarded like dirty undies. From the moment Tank dropped speed into her claret he knew she belonged to them.

Bikers before, the group of jocular party freaks in black singlets and T-shirts were now one animal force. Shane and Tank cleared the tables and chairs from the central position in the room. The rest of the guys hung around, like zoo animals waiting for the keeper to feed them. This woman would be the chunk of meat he'd throw at them to tear and devour.

Tank lifted her sweatshirt off and revealed two high-riding breasts, gift-wrapped in lavender lace. There was no escape for her now.

"Nice of you to dress up for the boys." Shane yanked off her bra, which released two blue-veined breasts with dark aureoles and nipples like old-fashioned doorbells.

"What's happening? What the fuck are you doing?" Her voice quivered in panic.

Shane held her from behind, unbuckled her belt, and tugged her jeans and lavender knickers to her ankles in one manoeuvre. They left behind an elastic outline and flattened pubic hair that emphasized her dark ravine.

"I don't know if I want to do this." Her hair fell in her eyes and face; her mascara was smudged with tears.

Shane said, "Of course you do, sugar. It's just first-time jitters." He unhooked her knickers and jeans from her feet.

"Tank! I …"

Tank almost felt sorry for her, but he told himself to harden up and be a true Pariah dog. "Be patient, sweetie, we're just getting started."

The bikers hovered like carrion birds in the shadow of dead meat, and squabbled over pecking order.

"She's a bit podgy," said Shane. The bikers leered at her postnatal body.

"She's ready for a resleeve," said Valentino Crass, a slick-back greasy haired biker.

"Her tits have dropped," said Moose, a big square-jawed American.

Pedro Purplehaze, a guy with an Afro, said, "Her thighs have got more orange peel than a fuckin' Californian orange grove."

With buttocks and pelvis squarely on the floor, knees bent, legs apart, she was as vulnerable as a beached mollusc. To Tank and the others she was a female animal who walked erect.

"Where are the other women?" She tried to cross her legs.

"Don't worry about them. We'll look after you." Tank unfolded her legs.

He had picked her up from the Mitre – he would be first. He didn't even know her name. He dropped his pants, then his big rough hands were everywhere over her body, hungry for the touch. She struggled. He held her arms above her head and prized her legs open with a knee. He guided his weapon to her defenceless slit and with a sudden violent lunge shoved it in and thrust.

"Ahh! Ahhhh!" came the sound from her.

He gritted his teeth. It was like a primal cry of pain from deep within. But he ignored it. For all he cared she could go to the limbo before the bum smack of life itself, and in that place she could stay while he did what he wanted. After all, she was just a piece of arse.

He took his weight on his fists and went at her like a dog. His hideous backside quivered until the final spasms of desire left him empty, hot and sticky, limp as a Dalinian watch. He got off and wiped himself on his shirt, inhaling the musky aromas of sex. And the next man took up his position.

"*Otium cum dignatate*. Schoolboy Latin still has its uses, no doubt," Mike said.

Some say it's a dead language," said the snowy headed stranger on Greta and Goose's balcony, illuminated by the spotlights. He'd arrived about twelve thirty, long after Jim and Gwen had gone home.

"It's used in medicine," Mike quipped.

"The law, monsieur," proffered the stranger.

"Botany." Mike gazed skyward at the stars in the clear night sky. "And over the box office in the Hounds and Hare theatre." Mike lifted his glass in a toast. "To the revival of a dead language."

There was something about this guy that Mike didn't like. He was too suave for his own good. Slippery was probably a better word.

"Leisure with dignity, monsieur, is how it translates." The stranger lifted his glass.

"I'll drink to that." Mike swallowed the dregs of his can. He knew Jocelyn would go along with that, as long as it excluded the lower and middle classes.

"So will I, monsieur," said the stranger. He held his glass high. "But first I'll go and find another drink."

Goose approached with Greta and Jocelyn, holding two cans of ice-cold lager. He tossed one to Mike. "Wasn't Greta great?"

Mike tore the tab open and took a slug. It was just as well Jocelyn hadn't arrived a minute earlier. She would have had plenty to say about too much leisure for the plebs.

"Brilliant!" Mike agreed. "She outshone Portia." He blushed red because he knew he was brown-nosing Greta.

"Thanks." Greta wrapped her arms around them both. "But you're biased. I hope the critics agree with you."

"She's more talented than that lanky strumpet, Isabelle." Jocelyn patted her on the back.

Mike blushed red again because he didn't think it was true.

"I'm sorry; I should have warned you about Belle." Greta placed her hand on Jocelyn's shoulder and changed the subject. "I hoped to see Nate."

"He had to be back at work by twelve," said Goose, "or he turns into a pumpkin." Nobody laughed. "He thought you were cool, high praise from him."

"He's working – good," said Jocelyn.

Mike bit his tongue.

Goose looked at his wristwatch. "He should be almost finished for the night."

Nate drove back to Felines to cash in and thought about which casket he would choose if he were one of Portia's suitors. He wanted to believe the lead one (with Portia's picture in it), but he didn't know. He thought Mike might choose lead also, Goose somewhere between gold and silver.

As he went in, Veronica was lounging on the settee drinking Irish coffee. He placed the cash bag on the table.

Wolf peered in. "Not bad for a couple of hours' work."

Queenie passed Nate a cup of Irish coffee.

Wolf landed a huge hand on Nate's shoulder. "Listen, dude, your work isn't unnoticed. I'm putting you up for prospect."

Nate shrugged his shoulders. "When?"

"Tomorrow night."

By the time Nate got back to the car, the digital clock on the top of the funeral insurance building said 1:15a.m.

Chapter Twelve

… The purpose of a rabbit snare is to catch rabbits …
The purpose of words is to convey ideas. When the
ideas are grasped, the words are forgotten.

Chuang Tzu

GOOSE DIDN'T have the luxury of a sleep in. The alarm came on at 6.45.am. His mouth tasted of last night's beer and recycled smoke. He would loved to have got himself a cold coke and gone back to bed, but then he remembered the meeting over the Sunvale deal scheduled for 9a.m.

Greta rolled over on her back and rubbed the sleep out of her eyes. Goose put his hand up her nightgown and felt the warm, firm, familiar mound through her knickers. She pushed his hand away and in a dreamy voice said, "I've been thinking, darl. About a baby."

Goose braked with the lightning reflexes of a driver who has a little child run out in front of him. "Fuck it all, Garbs! I thought we settled that." He turned onto his back, his ardour doused.

"So did I." She sat up, picked up a tiny mirror and explored her face for blemishes.

"That crap about acting being your baby – be a real

women – get a job!"

"Time's running out." She pouted.

"We decided to wait, remember?"

"The older I get, the greater the risk." She rubbed some moisturizer into her pores. It gave her a plausible excuse to make faces at him in the mirror. "One of the few advantages of being a woman – I'm allowed to change my mind."

"Well," he said in a nasty tone. He sat up on his elbows. "I haven't changed mine."

"It's the most creative–"

Goose didn't give her a chance to finish her sentence. "Creative? Changing shitty nappies and three a.m. feeds? Staying in because we can't get a babysitter at short notice? Nuclear fucking holocaust."

Goose was out of bed and halfway to work, crunching on burnt toast, before Greta realized he'd gone.

At work, Goose bristled with agitation as he took his seat, along with Reg, the spare parts manager, and Clive, the sales manager. They faced Trenton Jones across the boardroom desk, shivering in the morning chill. The slimline Venetian blinds were closed and the blazing sunshine outside didn't penetrate. A strong smell of air freshener tickled Goose's nostrils.

Jones addressed the meeting. "Well, guys. I have the news you've been waiting for. Superior Imports now has a European division in Sunvale. I managed to bring the possession date forward a fortnight, so we will have to utilize all our resources if we're to keep the city branch going effectively and manage the move to Sunvale."

Reg stated the staff concerns. "There have been one or two murmurings in the stores, and amongst the mechanics ..." he scratched his head and stared at his feet, "that there may be some cutting of staff."

"I can assure you there will be no cutting of staff – but, we may need to organize what we have more efficiently. I'll talk to them and reassure them later." Trenton held a pen before his eyes as if willing it to levitate.

Clive made a guttural sound. "I'm going to be short of a top salesman when Goose goes."

Trenton put the pen in his inside jacket pocket and eyeballed them individually. "The problem is, the staff have allowed themselves to fall into their comfort zones. It's my intention to spread them thinner on the ground and have them working closer to their capacity." He stood up for effect. "Then, and only then, can we make Superior Imports Japanese and European divisions into a customer focused organization to be proud of. Does anybody have a problem with that?"

"No." Clive ran his forefinger around the inside of his tight shirt collar, as perspiration beaded his forehead.

"None," said Goose. He sat to attention in his chair. He seethed inside and wondered whether Greta or Trenton Jones was the source of his anger. At these times, Nate's freedom-loving lifestyle seemed a more attractive option than climbing the corporate ladder while watching the rear view for the poison-tipped arrows of office politics.

Nate woke up to bright sunshine coming through his cracked old-style roller blind, and the overpowering urge to urinate. From the lounge he looked at the cove below on his way to the toilet, and estimated the tide to be about halfway in. There was a small swell at about waist height – bigger sets of right-handers rolled in off the point.

He spotted a couple of black dots – surfers getting rides. Six grommets mucked around in the inshore break; nice practice waves. The sky was clear blue. The day was hot.

The battery operated clock in the hall said 9.45a.m. The telephone rang and Nate ran to answer it. It was Judith from the real estate agents. "Hi," he said. "So you want to move the sale of the house along?"

"So it's a hundred K. I need to find five K deposit."

"OK, bring the contract around for me to sign and I'll drop it at my lawyer's."

The word *contract* frightened Nate, because once signed he feared an essential part of freedom would disappear out of his window. "Cool," was all he said.

The clock radio in Daryl's room blared out something about the Americans and Iraq.

Daryl shouted it down in an argument with himself. "Innocent blood for oil – twenty to one hundred thousand

Iraqis killed last time. Arms inspections, weapons of mass destruction? They should look in Kansas or Arkansas or the wine cellar of the scarlet White House, or down Monica Lewinski's pants. God Bless America and the free world – keep those cards, letters and body bags rolling in, folks – from shore to golden shore."

Nate knocked on Daryl's door. Daryl opened it dressed in his pyjamas, hair like a young Einstein. The room smelled of body odour and dirty underwear. Daryl never opened his curtains or windows. Conspiracy literature lay open faced on his dresser. More of the same bristled in his bookcase, along with *Hustler* and *Soldier of Fortune* magazines in a stack alongside. A picture of Adolph Hitler graced his wardrobe door under a swastika flag.

Daryl couldn't hold back. Lying on top of the unmade bed, he gestured with arms wide open. "Why don't those Yanks mind their own business? Plenty's wrong in their own country."

"You got me." Nate stood in the bedroom doorway. "I thought you were at work."

Daryl raved. "Do I look like I'm at work? I'm using my sick days while I've still got a job." He bounced on his bed. "And a life, before some button pushing, ten-gallon hat republican enslaves the world in the name of democracy." Daryl's pyjama fly gaped. He didn't wear underwear. "We'll all fry, or worse, survive and freeze our scabby balls off."

"There's no risk of nuclear war nowadays. The big boys have got it covered." Nate verged on laughter. "I can't say that about you – you're old fella's hanging out."

"They're either resigned or in denial. It all comes down to Sankhya philosophy. " Daryl casually buttoned his fly.

Nate thought Daryl underrated the role of the penis in the cosmic plot.

"Or blind Loyal."

"Or under the power of suggestion."

"I never thought of that."

"It's too obvious." Daryl blinked his big puppy dog eyes. "The antidote is simple – don't give your consent to imperialists and mass murders. It's time to hit back."

Nate slid into a dream, a technique he'd perfected during four fruitless years at secondary school. He wanted to clarify a nagging in his mind. "What do ya reckon Tiff meant: 'Water last time fire next time?'"

Daryl sighed. "Every time you see a rainbow it should remind you of God's covenant with mankind. The world was destroyed by water last time, in the time of Noah, due to mankind's disobedience of God. Next time she thinks it will be destroyed by fire. Scary – the reality is we are always on the brink of nuclear war."

"Is it the power of the word and prophecy?" Nate asked. "Like, in the beginning was the word …"

"Alphabet," said Daryl, "but you're onto it. Spelling creates the power of the word and its outcome. God spoke the universe into being. That's why politicians and lawyers are so careful with them. The concept behind this word in Greek is *Logos*, scarily near logo – the symbol for a particular business entity."

"I reckon the real conspiracy, if there is one, is the way parents bring up their kids to fit right into the system."

"Our whole life is fabricated." Daryl raised his eyebrows. "It all plays a part, along with school indoctrination creating spells: using the right letters in the right order to manipulate thoughts and ideas. This can be for the good or the bad; at the moment it's all aimed at the New World order."

He sat up on top of the messy bed, and went dreamy eyed. "David Icke has a theory our history and future is controlled by aliens called Archons in a cabal with human elites who have brainwashed us with subliminal ideas."

"Why aren't you at work?" Nate searched Daryl's pallid face for an answer.

"Because, my dear fellow, I've been fired. I've been given two weeks' notice. I'm using my sick days. Trenton Jones wants rid of all the old staff – we could be cattle or bags of shit for all he cares."

Mike sat in the café, musing over the bovine-like students in op shop clothes conforming in ragged diversity. His hunger gnawed in reaction to the warm sweet smell of fresh baking coming from the kitchen. He wished Jocelyn would hurry, as he watched the students pass, wondering how many of them would find a place in the world; how many would become *well-rounded human beings*. Not only in the physical sense. How many pursued the prerequisites for money making, or to catch a well-heeled mate? How many slaves to student loans? How many foreign students?

Whatever the answers, their lust for knowledge and power reduced Dr Faustus to choirboy status. Somehow along the way, knowledge became confused with information and information with propaganda and propaganda with education and education with data and symbols and data and symbols with programming and programming with the death of the human spirit and heart. The meaning of life wasn't on the reading list as far as he was concerned.

At last, Jocelyn's distinctive French bob made way through the crowd. She put her coffee down on his table and started in on Mike. "I've never been so embarrassed in all my life," she said, intent on stirring the bottom out of her cup.

The fumes from the coffee caused his mouth to water like one of Pavlov's dogs. The scrape of chairs and tables and the chatter of students grated on nerves already set on edge by her tone.

"It was an assault! A violation of my person!" Her pupils became two dark pinpoints.

"Perhaps." Mike pushed his hair off his forehead.

"But don't you think you might be overreacting?" He stared into her mellifluous blue eyes, then at her full sensuous lips, firm breasts and boyish hips. Her type of figure could charm the knickers off a saint on Mothering Sunday.

Jocelyn sipped her coffee. "She kissed me, damn it! Passionately, on the lips – the way a man kisses a woman, and with tongue." She pouted. "And you didn't do a thing."

Mike hunched his shoulders. He was in sympathy with Isabelle's hormones. "Delicate situations call for–"

Jocelyn didn't let him finish. "If Isabelle were a man …" Her eyes narrowed and she pursed her lips.

"It'd be different."

"She assaulted and humiliated me, and if not for the embarrassment I would take her to court. Jason thinks I would have a very good case."

Mike smiled a wry smile. Jocelyn often talked about the virtues of the wonderful Jason, and he tired of hearing it. "Oh yes, your dashing colleague with the hots for you," he said, smirking.

"How dare you!" Jocelyn blushed. "Jason's much too professional to involve himself romantically with co-workers."

"What about you? Would you have fought him off?"

Jocelyn pretended not to hear and carried on. "Jason says that deviant trollop had no right, legal or otherwise, to touch my person."

"She's the vanguard." Mike thought he knew what motivated her. "She thinks women's sexuality has been co-opted by men."

"You mean to tell me," said Jocelyn, exasperated, "that to kiss other women in a licentious way, without their consent, is no different than rubbing noses or thumbing knuckles?"

"A form of solidarity." Mike smiled. "Not unlike belonging to the Law Society, a secret society or any band of mutual back scratchers or hole pluggers pledged to help one another to the detriment of everybody else."

"You leave out the element of choice." She tucked her hair behind her ears.

"I'm sorry." Mike raised his eyebrows. "I seem to be under a conservative illusion that freedom of choice is somehow divisive?"

Jocelyn frowned. "You're twisting the issue. You're getting consent muddled with dissent."

"I stand corrected, counsellor," said Mike. And he prepared himself to prosecute. "I understand to belong to the Law Society you must swear an oath of allegiance or you can't practice law."

Jocelyn would not be drawn into derisory argument. "Jason and I talked about career opportunities for you. He suggested human resources, a growth area, and they are open to arts graduates."

"I'm humbled."

"My sister thinks it 's sound too."

"Whoopee! My future's taken care of." He waved his arms above his head in mock glee, and his hair fell back over his dark eyes.

Jocelyn's face turned red. "Thankfully none of the law faculty witnessed that childish display. You can do your degree then a post-graduate diploma in HR. But Jason thought it might be useful to pick up more points in psychology. He says there's no shortage of work for HR graduates."

"Thank you, Jocelyn and Jason, for the interest in my career. Fortunately I have other plans." Mike got up to get himself a bun and hot coffee. "I'm surfing this weekend."

Jocelyn's eyes flared. "And I'm washing my hair." Which Mike took to mean her legs would be closed tighter than a Scotsman's wallet on a bank holiday.

My brother ..." she said.

"The detective."

"Yes – he says they're crying out for graduates on the force. He's overloaded working on a gang-related drugs bust, but he can't talk about it.

Chapter Thirteen

Reform must come from within, not from without. You cannot legislate for virtue.

Cardinal Gibbons

WOLF CALLED Nate into work Saturday because he wanted a parcel urgently delivered. It took Nate and the VW into old territory, a Dumbarton address – a suburb nearer the city than Seaview, a state house area with dogs and kids running wild in packs.

Evil-looking hombres covered in tats wore heavy-duty security chains across their chests. They walked bull terriers and American pit bulls, which he knew were used for prize fighting, when they weren't being used to intimidate. Many houses lay empty – a result of government restructuring – their windows broken.

The burnt-out carcasses of cars provided sculptural effect in the front gardens, monuments to apathy and free market politics. The grass was long, lank and dry, and grew up through the broken teeth pickets. The shops had concrete posts in front to stop drive-in smash and grab raids. Graffiti-covered roller doors slid down over the windows at closing time.

Groups of skaters in baggies and back-to-front baseball caps slalomed around dog shit on the pavement. Young mothers, children themselves, pushed prams and smoked while defending their purses from stoned boyfriends.

The address he wanted came into view – nine Warblington Avenue. He was glad he no longer lived near here. He felt for the skaters. Warblington Ave, a tidy little street flanked by flowering cherries, very much state house heartland, up a side street.

He stopped outside a tidy brick house with a pink silk tree overhanging a green corrugated iron fence. The scent of Chinese jasmine wafted over from a pergola.

He shoved a hand through the fence to ring a little brass bell – and was glad he did, because two American pit bulls came through a sliding door from under the pergola and answered the interruption with low growls. A dark-skinned man in dungarees and a Stars and Stripes bandana walked behind them. A black Trans Am was parked in the drive.

"From Wolf." Nate slid the parcel through the hole in the gate.

"I's bin expecting yaw." He passed Nate a sealed envelope through the same hole.

Nate grabbed it, slid back in the car and drove away at speed. There was no question a drug deal just went down, and he was an accomplice after the fact.

He didn't know how many of the others were involved

in drug dealing, and he didn't care. If he wanted to succeed he couldn't afford to take the moral high ground. His income was mostly from prostitution and drugs; it wasn't earned by him; it was parasitical but entrepreneurial by free market standards. It was just unlawful, that was all. How else could you get paid a couple a thousand bucks plus a week for virtually nil input? Anyway, weed would soon be legal – lawmakers overlooked anything that made people more manageable.

He recalled how damaging the pushing of alcohol had been to his family. Now they wanted to push drugs as well. He knew to duck for cover and to watch out for his mother if the old man started drinking whiskey. After calling her slag and a frigid bitch all weekend, she'd have to make excuses for why he wasn't at work on Monday. When he began to sober up he'd plead with her and say it would never happen again, but it always did.

One time he'd come home from the pub with another woman, and had wanted both women in bed.

Nate turned back onto Dunbarton Road and a plainclothes cop car turned into Warblington Ave.

It occurred to him: what if police and governments shared a vested interest in pushing drugs to profiteer and make for more docile and compliant citizens? It made him think. He never had trusted cops, or those with power over others. He floored the pedal on the trusty bug and pointed it in the direction of home.

Nate drove around the waterfront towards Sunvale. It brought not only a change in geography, but a change in reality. Moored yachts bobbed, their bows turned into and deflecting the incoming tide. The sun sparkled on the waters, and off the Porsches, BMWs and palatial mirror-glassed houses.

A red Porsche in the yacht club car park caught his eye. The personalized license plate read LAWMAN. He remembered seeing it on his first job, out west with Monique, the back end protruding from the garage – it belonged to Monique's client. He watched his distinctive white-headed body clambering around on a yacht called *Osprey* it was on the side of the bow in cursive writing. Louveteau prepared to take her out on the full tide. Nate envied him – a mansion, a Porsche, a thirty-foot yacht. What else? He sounded like a beer commercial.

He hated the idea of spending hard-won cash to pay some buzzard for the conveyancing on his house, which he'd heard Jocelyn say was usually left to the legal executive anyway.

He looked at the clear blue sky. Hang gliders rode the thermals from high above down to the beach. Traffic mooched bumper to bumper. The restaurants and pubs spilled onto the street, and crowds in different stages of undress ambled between the beach and the shops. The rich smell of cappuccinos and ozone fought for supremacy in his nostrils. A film of windblown sand covered the road.

He took the beach road home. The surf billowed in around about shoulder height in glassy sets. The sun's position about three thirty. He watched the swells rise out in the bay and the car snorted up the switchback and descended to the shack below.

He heard voices coming from inside the house before he got out of the car. The kitchen windows were flung wide open on stays, and from where he parked he could make out every word. He wound the passenger's window down to hear more clearly.

Daryl's voice said: "Because you sit down to piss."

"Don't be vulgar!" Tiff shouted back.

"Indigenous blood, then."

"I do not!

"Screwing the boss?"

"How dare you!"

"How else did you get into management?

"Plain hard work and–"

"The boss lady's in your church?"

"She is ... but ... that had nothing to do with my appointment to produce manager. The directive came from head office."

"I'm not often wrong," said Daryl.

"You are this time."

Nate crept in, pushing open the kitchen door. Pretending he'd heard nothing, he sat down beside Tiff and across the table from Daryl.

"Any mail?"

"Not a thing," said Daryl. "Just the usual. Tiff's trying to shine a light on the dark night of my soul. I hoped to get away without confronting my psyche until I was dead."

"Your soul you should be worried about. You too, Nate," said Tiff, "if you want to be truly free."

"Your idea of freedom," Nate said, "is horse breaking."

"That's not so." Tiff pushed a wayward strand of hair under her scarf. "Even if you are riding with rank outsiders."

Nate went into a dream, and then he spoke. "My father didn't leave me much, but he did say: 'Nate, me boy, never wear an apron or a saddle, and never put on a skirt – your job is to take them off. And he left me with an old chess set with a note that read: *Work your moves out for yourself.*"

Tiff looked to Daryl for moral support, but she didn't get it.

Nate said: "I hope there's plenty of hot water for a shower. It's gonna be a big night tonight. By the way, congratulations on your promotion."

"It just shows where steady, sober and dedicated work habits can get you. The way is open to all taken on their merits." Tiff straightened the scarf on her head.

"Bull-fucking-shit! I worked my ring out at Sunvale Motors. Guess I had the wrong genitals."

Tiff was unmoved. "When you have found the truth that is Jesus Christ, you will know the only conspiracy is led by Satan, who is the father of lies."

"Is he a politician?" Nate guffawed. Even Tiff saw the funny side and used the moment to reload her argument. She sat erect and didn't look very comfortable.

Daryl played with a fork left on the table. "What if I told you that all major world religions are bullshit, created by psychopathic aliens called Archons who feed off human anxiety and guilt and enslave them, stopping them from finding the truth of our oneness?"

"Well that came out of left field," Nate said.

"There is only one truth, and that is Jesus."

"Thought you might say that," said Nate. He couldn't wait to see what Daryl's drug-inspired brain had come up with this time.

"The thing is most religions have a messiah due to return soon who the followers believe will destroy the wicked – that's the reason they don't revolt against the system. But Archons and human hybrid elites are in control. And they believe the religious fanatics will eventually kill each other."

"Well the Bible does talk about wickedness in high places," Tiff said.

"I remember that from Sunday school," Nate said. How could he forget his teacher, a thirty-something professional virgin with a moustache most young guys would have been proud of, who'd banged on about things like that. She'd lived alone with ten cats.

Daryl went on. "What's happening in the world goes

way back, to before the solar system itself." He moved in his chair. "Archons can't physically manifest on earth. But they can affect human beings with subliminal messages. This is how they created our religions and ideologies".

"I don't believe that," said Tiff.

Nate liked to keep an open mind, but not so open his brains fell out. "Go on," he said.

Daryl coughed. "This Babylonian brotherhood lives on earth by drinking menstrual blood and eating human flesh. They live underground. The Holy Grail, or chalices, are symbolic of this, hence the term scarlet women – blood taken from virgins for the archons' hybrids and bloodlines."

"How totally sick and perverted," said Tiff.

Nate had to agree. It was something that had never entered his mind before.

"They're a death cult that loves murder and mayhem, paedophilia, black magic and child sacrifice, misogyny and war. And with their destructive practices, they're set on destroying the planet, raping its resources out of greed. They have no empathy or compassion."

"Sounds very satanic," Tiff said.

"Bloody parasites, probably behind neoliberalism too," Nate said. He found it very hard to take seriously.

"Of course," Daryl said. "The universe is made up of 'vibrational' energy, and these reptilian beings along with hybrid elites manipulate global events to keep humans in constant fear so they can feed off the 'negative energy' this creates."

"Never heard anything like it," Nate said. It certainly did sound out of this world.

"Well it would explain why historically women have been so repressed," Tiff said. "It all sounds very Old Testament."

"Many prominent figures of this Babylonian Brotherhood bloodline, including British royalty and the Vatican, are forcing humanity toward an Orwellian global fascist state, or New World Order," said Daryl, "where truth and freedom of speech is ended. The only way we can defeat them is if people wake up to 'the truth' and fill their hearts with love."

"A bit like Christianity but without Christ or God," Tiff said. "I'd be suspicious of that."

"And remember," Daryl said, "you attract the vibrational energy you put out."

Nate got up to go. "Don't know if I can swallow the reptilian bit, gotta shower."

It could be just another red herring to keep them away from what's really going on. It was all too confusing. Again it was a doctrine of non-action against the powers that be. Love was supposed to conquer all, but in their world it seemed to enslave. He would try and keep an open mind.

Nate stuck out in the crowd, a raw-boned contention, arms freckled and bare of tattoos, waiting on the whim of the Pariah Dog organization for acceptance or rejection. In his hip pocket was an envelope full of money. His eyes stung from smoke.

It was Saturday night and the clock above the bar said eight thirty-five.

Wolf leaned on the bar and talked to Shane, who sat astride a high stool. Wolf waved Nate over. He thumped his mug hard on the bar.

"Quiet!" he shouted.

The barman turned the music down.

Wolf placed a fatherly hand on Nate's shoulder. "Some of you will know Nate. He drives for us. I'm nominating him for prospect. If there's any against, now's your chance."

A murmur rippled through the crowd.

"Once a bald'ead, always a bald'ead," shouted Tank." "I wouldn't trust 'em as far as I could kick him."

Nate knew baldhead was the term for an ordinary citizen.

"Yeah," Shane yelled in agreement. He n and inched up on his stool. "Put him to the test – see if he's got the balls to be a Pariah Dog."

"Yeah!" yelled the rest.

"OK," said Wolf, in the tones of an Indian chief in a low-budget Hollywood movie. "Pariah Dog has spoken." Wolf grabbed Nate by his T-shirt sleeve and walked. "C'mon, dude." They jostled through the bar and past Queenie, Monique and other girls in the corridor going in for a drink.

Once in the office Wolf held out his hand. "OK, dude, let's have it." Nate pulled the envelope out of his back pocket and handed it over. "I guess you've sussed you're not paid big bucks for driving a few whores around and delivering mail." Wolf slashed open the envelope with a letter opener, its handle depicting a naked woman. He pulled out a bundle of hundred-dollar notes and counted them. He seemed satisfied.

"I figured it was drugs," Nate said.

"So it doesn't worry you?"

"If I get busted? First I gotta get caught."

"Shit happens." Wolf threw the money on the desk. "If you do, you know nothing, right?" He bent down and opened a combination safe in the floor under a mat, placing the wad inside. "Prospects have to take the rap for more senior gang members sometimes. How do you feel about that?"

"Jus' part of being staunch."

"Good." Wolf reached into his bottom desk drawer and extracted a couple of joints from a tinfoil stash. He gave them to Nate. "You did good."

They wandered back into the bar.

Nate had no intention of taking the rap for someone else, but he didn't want to jeopardize his newfound lifestyle, either. He'd learned enough to know quality of life depends on the amount of money in your kick.

Your purse in the end is your very best friend. It was one of the most sensible things his mother had ever said, but it was very neoliberal. The old man might have agreed if she'd substituted pussy for purse.

Wolf and Nate sat on the tall stools near Shane and Tank with their backs to the bar.

"You're using them!" Monique screamed, from the woman's corner of the room. "Cause there's no market for your own big wrinkly thing." Queenie's shoulders and back rose and clenched like a corned alley cat in mortal combat.

"You ungrateful little whore!" she hissed, spitting saliva. "Felines have always looked after you."

"They've always looked after themselves–she snarled.

Queenie got to her feet and grabbed Monique by the hair. "You know the drill for bolshie little bitches."

"Go fuck yourself with a courgette." She tried to wriggle free. "Let go you filthy crone."

Queenie landed a back hander in Monique's mouth with her free hand. A small trickle of blood sprouted from the corner of her lips.

Nate felt a natural urge to intervene, but things were different now. Prospects only ever followed orders. Instead, he lit up a joint using Wolf's lighter, which lay on the bar. He took a deep toke and was helpless as he observed the action unfold. Queenie, like a Neanderthal, led Monique by the hair to the centre of the room. Three hairy guys moved the tables back.

You didn't need to be psychic to know her fate. The

action echoed in the distant recesses of his mind. The smoke – good shit – no telling the ingredients. Everything strobed from the real to the unreal and back again down neon-lit space in his head.

He watched as most women exited the bar. The ones who thought Monique a threat to their men stayed to get their kicks and watch the indignities about to take place. Valentino Crass held Monique in place. Puck Uggles and Pedro Purplehaze undressed her while Queenie kept hold of her hair.

When Nate focused again after another deep toke, she lay prone and naked – blond tousled hair, pink and white almost adolescent breasts, golden black fuzz on her pubis. She was like Tinkerbell crash-landed in a tarantula's web.

Queenie had a tight hold on her hair. "Not so street smart now, you little slut."

"Who's the slut? I'm not enjoying this." She spat and squirmed to underline her point.

"No?" Queenie inserted a rolled-up twenty-dollar note into Monique's mouth. "I bet you are now." One of the guys let her hand go and she removed the note.

"You fucking filth," cried Monique. She tried to spit in Queenie's direction. "You and your mates are sub human."

Wolf instructed Nate to begin. "It's your move, Nate. We'll follow."

"Take her like a true Pariah Dog," bellowed Tank.

Nate's head spun. She reminded him of a little red riding hood in a den of ravening wolves. He wanted to help her, but how? He had surrendered to the Pariah Dog. His acceptance and patch membership and job depended on going through with it. Anyway, he told himself, whores got raped all the time. She'd told him herself she only did it for the money. She didn't enjoy the sex. Why the drama? He would make sure she got well paid for his part.

She lay naked, her petalled limbs fragile as a lotus flower entangled in a meat grinder. The eyes of the Pariah Dog guys bore into his back with expectation. In one movement he dropped his jeans and underwear to reveal a six-pack stomach and a bigger than average penis. His head spun and his stomach was twisted in knots. When it came down to it, he just couldn't do it, and there was no way he could help Monique now.

Wolf grabbed him. "What you doing boy? You don't want to partake so you can watch a real dog in action?"

Puck Uggles held Monique's legs and Shane positioned himself between them. His small taut backside and hips filled the valley between her legs.

Queenie still held Monique by the hair.

"Close your eyes and think of how you have betrayed us, bitch," Queenie said. She laughed in hysterical hatred. "Go for it, honey."

Monique spat in her face.

Queenie wiped it off and pulled harder on Monique's

hair. Puck and Pedro held an arm each.

Monique screamed at Shane. "If my hands were free I'd squeeze your balls to mush."

One powerful surge and Shane breached her fleshy portcullis and slid inside her. Nate needed to vomit, but he somehow held it in. His insides numbed. The fog in his mind cleared for a moment, and he wondered how he could live with what he'd just witnessed.

Chapter Fourteen

Roll on, thou deep and dark-blue Ocean, roll
... Man marks the earth with ruin, his control
Stops with the shore ...

– Byron, *Childe Harold*, 1V

NATE GAGGED for a lungful of air. Without it, his life expectancy would amount to a few minutes. The wave flung him deep into its churning bowels, twisted and turned him so he didn't know up from down. It willed him to submit, and he resigned himself to a watery end. Then he hit the sandy seabed and kicked off like a jumping frog. His head popped into the broad afternoon sunshine. He coughed and spluttered saltwater from his mouth and nose.

He lived.

The sun burned into his back; molten gold, it laid low in the sky. The waters glistened and shiny objects reflected inshore. He lifted his hand to shade his eyes and turned his board out to sea. Further out, Goose and Mike straddled their boards, patient for a wave. It was a funny sight, Goose's shiny bald head and Mike's black hair stuck wet to his head like a bathing cap. The swell tumbled in, big mothers, over head height but infrequent. They surfed off the reef at the southern point of the bay, while divers closer in to the headland were after paua. The faraway gurgle of an outboard motor drifted from the shore, over by the surf club, and the irregular wallop of the waves slapped the steep rocky sides of the headland like a woman punishing a man's impudent hand for wandering into her pants.

The wetsuit kept his body warm but the water chilled his bare hands and feet. He paddled towards the others. A fin cut across his bows and gave him a start. "Shit, see that?" He pulled his board around to get in the line-up.

"Yeah." Goose had seen it too. "Dolphins."

The dolphins bodysurfed in the transparent hollows of the waves.

"Won't be any sharks, then," Mike quipped.

Mike's remark made Nate's dangling legs feel vulnerable. "No – only car dealers."

Goose knee-jerk reacted. "Beats dealing drugs."

A wave crept up on them.

Mike made eye contact with Nate. "I told Goose about the deposit for your house. How did you earn that much so quickly?"

They all crested the wave.

"Easy." Nate held his board tight. "I borrowed it."

They plummeted down the other side. That ended the probing questions for now. They paddled further out to the reef where the waves worked better. A yacht nosed round the cape under full sail. It got closer. Nate lifted a hand to visor his eyes for a better look. "That's the *Osprey*. He's going home." Two figures lurched at the helm.

Nate watched a big set forming way out to sea and turned to Mike and Goose. "That yacht's owned by that slimy guy Jocelyn spoke to at the theatre."

The big set was closer now, between them and the yacht.

Goose said, "He used to try to get me into his Porsche when I stayed at Grandma's, in Sunvale."

They glided up the crest of a head-high wave and gazed ominously down into the trough; it collapsed from under them and they missed a major doing over by milliseconds. They flew over the other side, into the path of another howling monster. Nate spun around and paddled fast; he took off on the lip and witnessed the burial of Goose and Mike under tonnes of white water. He didn't envy them the experience of going through a serious wash cycle.

He kept ahead of the break, riding the classic curve, peeling to the right, and huddled into the wave's barrelled effervescent heart. He ducked and crouched and could have been a sperm in a fallopian tube as he watched the world through the eye of the barrel – time was like a fizzy pill soluble in ocean tumult.

Ideas flooded his mind. The sea and the wind, with a little help from the stars and planets, guided the

Polynesians from Hawaiki and the Dutch, French and the English from the Motherland, and the aboriginals from the islands a few hundred kilometres east, before them both. They presided over the signing of the Treaty and the bloodless revolution of the Neoliberals, which saw the ongoing sale of land and state assets to foreign owners, this time for a little more than guns and blankets, but robbery all the same. Business was insatiable, finding new ways to exploit what remained of the natural world to keep the wheels of commerce turning. *Business*. The word betrayed itself. He laughed. It might appeal to Tiffany – busy with sin in the middle.

Daryl had introduced him to the hidden meanings of words, their subtle mathematics, and their full meaning the sum of parts. How funny for the opponents of the free-marketers, if the sun overslept tomorrow. Was it under contract to shine?

He shot out of the tube through a shower of nettled spray and a flourish of surfboard tail into the air and down the back of the wave. Whenever he surfed, his worldly cares disappeared and he merged with the eternal if only for moments. Unlike the land or its people, nobody owned it – yet.

He straddled his board, pulled the nose out of the water like a shark on attack. Where were the others? He scanned the surface. They walked out of the shallows. He caught the next wave in and sidled up to them, their wetsuits were down to their waists, and they dried off.

"Hey, guys." Nate was puffed from running.

Goose rubbed his head with the towel. "Fucking wave should have come with a hurricane warning."

"You're telling me nothing." Mike tousled his hair.

Nate threw down his board.

They sat down, their backs against the sand hill, their boards littering the sand. The sun glowed hot and the wind caused goose bumps to sprout on their sunburnt forearms. They focused out to sea. The *Osprey* disappeared round the northern headland.

"Louveteau's twisted." Mike and Nate listened. "He takes young boys out on fishing trips."

"I know." Nate fumbled in his clothes for a pack of cigarettes.

"He gains the parents' trust first," Goose went on.

"That's what I've heard too." Nate found his lighter and smokes and lit up.

Goose spoke in a detached way, as if he was talking about a film or a TV programme. "He takes the boys out a few times to get their confidence, usually one at a time, and then overnight …"

"And?" Nate and Mike said in unison, eager to hear more.

Goose obliged. "He plies them with dope and booze and then has his way with them." He eyeballed them both. "The next day the boys know something happened, but it's like a bad dream."

"There must be evidence." Mike leaned back with his

hands behind his head.

Goose shook his head. "They're too embarrassed and scared to tell. Next morning it's sketchy."

"Somebody must know what he's like." Nate kicked sand on his board; it made funny patterns on the wax.

"He's an expert barrister and his reputation is impeccable." Goose brushed sand off the leg of his wet suit.

"Jocelyn never mentions him," Mike said.

"Why doesn't that surprise me?" said Goose. "He hates women. My friend Joey Paterson told me he calls them split arse mechanics, in French."

"You're shittin' me." Nate blew smoke.

"Joe was about fourteen," said Goose. "He couldn't tell me what happened when he slept on the yacht. Big tears welled in his eyes; he bit his bottom lip and said he didn't remember. But it was sore going to the toilet."

Nate blew a final puff of smoke in Goose's direction and snuffed his cigarette on a piece of driftwood. "What about the fact I dropped Monique off at his place?"

"Fucked if I know! Don't blow that shit in my face!" He wafted the stray smoke away.

The sun glinted high over the northern headland. They packed up their gear in preparation to go home.

The *Osprey* motored into the mouth of estuary under its own small diesel power. Squawking seagulls shadowed in her wake. A following sea threatened to engulf the stern, an illusion, the yacht was a safe distance ahead.

A white-haired man at the helm wearing the captain's hat didn't pay it any mind. He busied himself issuing instructions to the dark- haired man at the bow. "*Ça roule.*" Everything was going well. Jason, his little queer fish, had no idea that he'd picked up drugs. Soon they broached calmer but fast-flowing water.

"Open your eyes for the buoy," Louveteau shouted. Jason was his ultimate prize. Louveteau watched as he grasped a grappling hook in one hand and the bow rail with the other.

"Nearly there ... approaching ... get ready." His lean body stooped over the wheel. The *Osprey* now cruised well into the confines of the harbour. "Ready grab ..." shouted Louveteau.

Jason hooked the buoy, tied the boat to it and dropped the buoy back in. "All secured," he yelled aft.

Louveteau breathed a sigh of relief and muttered, "*Très bien.*" His mind went back to where they had been. It was the end of a successful trip from one hundred kilometres south to the little fishing village of St Marie. *Magnifique.* Jason traipsed the antique and curio shops while he picked up his little parcel from yachting comrades from the Caribbean. Jason bought an exquisite piece of Clarice Cliff for two dollars.

Jason loaded the luggage into the dinghy. "Where did the extra bag come from?"

"Let's just say I collected it along the way," Louveteau said.

They buttoned the cover over the cockpit of the *Osprey* and stepped down into the dinghy. The last tentative rays of sunshine sank below the jagged line of the monolithic Alps while darkness spread black tentacles over the estuary. The sky was full of stars, which twinkled and beckoned from galaxy hillsides.

Jason rowed them to shore.

They were lulled by the steady burble of the outboard motor. They dreamed, and their conversation turned to a girl in a red shift with blond bangs and pigtails.

Nate arrived at Felines five minutes early, around seven twenty-five. He spotted Monique and was ashamed to look in her defiant eyes. Monique flaunted her abundant charms to the customers outside Felines. She drew hard on a cigarette, obtaining maximum satisfaction, a hybrid of Marlene Dietrich and a twenty-first-century demimonde. Her shaggy blond hair, short leather skirt, crimson lipstick, sheer blouse and fishnets were alluring bait on a seductive hook.

He went to rush past her but her foot came out and he fell heavy, his head coming down hard on the metal edge of the second step. He lay shocked and dazed, but remained conscious. Blood oozed out of the wound on his forehead.

Monique towered over him, menacing. "How does it fucking feel?" She arched and hissed like a tormented cat. "I should strip you now and fuck you up the arse with the bent end of a hockey stick. On second thoughts, no! You might enjoy that."

He lay on the floor, bleeding and humiliated, his head a fairground whirlygig on full throttle. He tried to get a word out. "I'm s-sorry, Monique. There was nothing I could do."

Her face was crimson. "If I'd had my way I'd have cut your balls off, and would have tipped off the guys from C-Block that there's a nancy boy on his way who wants a good rummaging."

His throat was dry and his stomach sank. He would have done something if he could.

"I want … to see you and them behind fucking bars," Monique said.

"I'm sorr-sorry." Her words filleted his insides with a blunt knife. "I was stoned – off my head."

"Tell it to the judge." She chucked a handkerchief at him out of her sequined shoulder bag. "The cut's not too bad."

He folded the handkerchief and padded the wound, stemming the flow of blood.

Monique's lips tightened. "Imagine being slapped around and forced by eight or ten big hairy men. Think about the scratches and abrasions between your legs."

"There was nothing I could do."

"Well, you would say that. Now go and get that treacherous bitch upstairs to stick a plaster on your head. If Melanie's up there, send her down."

He walked into the parlour. The place contrasted with the carbon dioxide and burnt rubber of the streets – it had a musky, sweaty, animal sort of smell. Maya, an elegant Eurasian with the sophisticated air and charm of an Asian airline hostess, was on reception. Another of his mother's quotes came to mind: *While appearances deceive, they may as well deceive for, rather than against you.* How right she was. Maya's aura didn't hurt.

The doors to the rooms were all shut – business was going down. The TV blared in the lounge without an audience. Melanie and Queenie were in a meeting in the staff lounge. He didn't need to eavesdrop to hear Queenie say: "It won't affect you outcall girls."

"Good," replied Melanie.

"I don't think twenty dollars a night is unreasonable, do you?"

"No one likes parting with money."

"What … happened?" Queenie watched Nate amble in holding a handkerchief to his head.

"What's it look like?"

"Are you OK to work?"

"Jus' a scratch – got a bit of a headache."

"Come over here." Queenie reached for the first aid tin from a shelf above the kitchen bench. "Let's have a look." Nate bowed his head for her to see. She put antiseptic on cotton wool and dabbed the wound.

He winced. "Fuck that hurt."

"Hold still." Queenie grabbed a handful of his hair to

keep his head still while she applied the first aid. "You'll have a nasty bruise there by tomorrow. After the fiasco Saturday night you're going to have to pick up your game if you want to be a patched member of the Dog. That's if the rest of the guys think you've still got what it takes."

"Yeah, I was just too stoned."

"Maybe you can prove yourself some other way. Now I want you to take Melanie out on a job. It's over in your territory: Ocean View Terrace."

"I know it." Nate touched the bump on his head.

"Ring if you feel too sick to work."

"I will. Come on Mel," Nate called. "We're outta here."

Nate and Melanie clip clopped down the stairs. They met Monique at the street entrance.

"I'm coming too." Monique placed her arm around Melanie. Nate didn't protest. They clambered into the trusty VW.

"They won't be charging outcall girls rent," Melanie said from the front passenger seat.

"No, but they want to charge you extra for the taxi service," replied Monique from over the back.

"She didn't mention that."

"She wouldn't, would she?"

"Working tonight?"

"I quit – Saturday."

"That was fast."

"Fancy a job at M&Ms?"

"Never heard of them."

"Monique and Melanie – stupid."

"I'll think on it," said Melanie.

"Don't think too long," said Monique. "If they change the prostitution laws, every woman and her pooch will be charging admission." They all laughed at the image that conjured.

Nate kept quiet the whole way. He stopped the VW outside Melanie's job, took her in, came back with the forty dollars and flopped into the driver's seat.

"That was a weird job – the guy's in a wheelchair." He should have kept his mouth shut.

"Well, hel-lo, Mr Sensitive. Men in wheelchairs do not necessarily have disabled cocks. They have needs, same as anybody else. And it can be very satisfying for them – and us – to give them hand relief, oral or whatever they can manage."

"Yuck!" said Nate. "It doesn't seem natural."

"Is it more natural for a woman to be forced by eight or nine degenerates?"

"If you put it that way."

"Drop me at the Mitre!" demanded Monique. Nate complied without a word.

On the way, they drove past Sunvale Services. Nate could see the dynamic hand of Trenton Jones oozing from every structure. Jones had transformed the buildings to a tasteful medium blue; the signage was glacier white with two maroon racing stripes trimming the base of the building. They must have worked all weekend. The windows gleamed and the yards were spread thick with new asphalt. It was now officially the European division of Superior Imports Ltd. The signs said so.

Chapter Fifteen

Please Sir, can I have some more?

– Charles Dickens, *Oliver Twist*

GOOSE DIDN'T like Mondays, but his hate stopped this side of shooting the boss. He knew who buttered his bread. His eyes examined the new premises. He breathed in paint fumes, enjoyed a mild chemical high, and wondered how to fill the immaculate asphalt yards. A million things to do and no time to do them. He shouldn't have surfed yesterday – he should have been working. It didn't help to have Greta around the house dribbling like a filly in season, afraid of missing out on baby making and being less of a woman for it.

He knew what to do, whenever he panicked: prioritise. Make a list, not an option in the surf when you were steering down the barrel of a huge killer wave. He needed to move cars, spare parts and tyres – and check with Casey, the mechanic, to ensure all workshop facilities were up to scratch, and what to take with him. Goose's office supplies and documentation needed to go, but what else?

Trenton expected him to make do with one mechanic,

a parts assistant who also handled retail and car sales, and one manager-cum-car salesman – himself. When the dust settled he'd hit Trenton up for a tasty little intern. Goose believed every business organization needed at least a token bit of fluff – someone to infuse the place with oestrogen and be useful up a ladder at stock-taking time. A pretty little accessory to tag along with him and take down the details at car auctions, while he mused about seduction strategy. She needed to be youthful, enthusiastic, and idealistic enough to follow orders and hold him in awesome respect. He didn't expect her to lay down her life for him – simply lying down would be enough for starters. Goose didn't envisage any trouble convincing Trenton about the need for a bit of fluff, especially after a few Johnnie Walkers.

If only Mike and Nate were so easily persuaded no alternative existed to free market policies. At least Mike showed sense enough to get himself a woman with her head screwed on, rather than one others screwed the arse off.

Jocelyn's phone rang. "Let me guess." Mike's dark eyes peered over the top of his coffee cup. "The prodigal Nate?"

Jocelyn held her hand over the mobile phone and nodded.

The cafeteria echoed in its emptiness. The sulphur smell of egg sandwiches under construction and the sound of food processors in top gear and utensils banging in the stainless steel sinks assaulted her senses.

"It's Nate I'll put him on speaker."

" Cool," Mike said.

"Hello, Jocelyn? Nate Crust speaking."

"Did you want Mike?

"No, you."

"How can I help?

"I'm buying a house – I need a lawyer."

"I could ask Dad to work on your behalf?"

"That'd be cool."

"Do you have finance arranged?"

"Don't lawyers do that?"

"Interest rates are better through the bank."

"Sweet."

"Get your finance arranged. In the meantime, I'll talk to Dad. Bye for now, keep me posted."

"Thanks," said Nate. He hung up.

Jocelyn's face was expressionless. "He needs a lawyer."

"I heard hallelujah, another convert to the propertied classes," Mike said, pouring on the sarcasm. "He's almost respectable."

Jocelyn frowned. "Perhaps I underestimated him." She flicked her black hair out of her eyes, and the end of her nose moved a millimetre skyward. "It shows how far you can get with determination and energy and not much else."

Mike forced a grin, showing even well-maintained teeth.

"I'm supposed to feel inadequate, right?" He put his elbow on the table and leaned on the palm of his hand.

"No, but he is focused on what he wants. Just … sometimes, I wish you'd take a leaf out of his book. You have so many advantages." She opened a text on the law of torts and read silently.

Mike focused on the canteen assistants filling the display stands with sandwiches and cakes. He estimated their wages to be similar to those of their counterparts in international fast food outlets – minimum wage, and they liked to employ school kids. Youth rates were more competitive.

He knew Jocelyn's father drank at the gentlemen's club, where he could ridicule the working class with impunity.

He also knew it was the disparity in wages and conditions that ensured class division, which was ordained from on high with the precision of a draughtsman's compass. Workers were supposed to accept the status quo in the interests of harmony.

Mike clapped Jocelyn's book shut to get her attention. She jumped. Her mouth tightened and she blinked hard. Mike revived the discussion.

"Yes, I'm fortunate." He explored Jocelyn's mask-like face. He hadn't noticed the hint of a moustache before.

He proceeded. "I will eventually have a half share in the old man's farm. People like us have a responsibility to use our advantages to help those without the wherewithal or the opportunities – don't you think?"

"Precisely why I want to be a lawyer."

"Is it really?"

"Look!" Jocelyn's mouth stayed tight between words and her soft blue eyes changed to beady pupils. "The rich and the poor have always been with us."

"Exactly." Mike adopted the beaten-down persona of a wage slave. "But the attitude is hardening. There's a feeling the poor deserve to be poor. And the rich deserve to be rich, a sort of free-market karma. The invisible hand of the market has become a sort of social justice. So there's no need for conscience or the will to change the status quo."

Jocelyn's eyes narrowed and crows' feet showed at her temples. "Don't put yourself on a guilt trip. Society has always been organized that way." Her eyes pleaded. "The fact remains; you and I have more in common with the rulers than the rabble."

"There's so much injustice." Mike dropped his eyes..

"It only seems that way," said Jocelyn. "The rulers have created the beliefs and legislated for the behaviour of the rabble to protect them from destroying themselves and others. Don't let your class or your intelligence down by thinking they're badly done by."

"It isn't fair." Mike set his mouth hard.

"That may be your experience." Jocelyn pursed her lips and spoke as if cooing to a baby. "Poor, poor, Michael. I'll just get my violin out."

"Everything's reduced to the profit motive," said Mike.

Jocelyn's face coloured. "Grow up, Michael! Do you want to work for nothing?"

"No, but I want to enjoy what I do, and help others – our jails are full of the desperate, the frustrated and uneducated … and the mentally ill–"

Jocelyn didn't let him finish. "Maudlin rubbish! They have the same choices you or I have." She fidgeted with the collar of her blouse and fingered her pearls as if they were rosary beads.

He kept on. "The poor and the unemployed scratch like fowl in a dust patch while government and corporate greed is legally sanctioned."

"Save your sermons for the poor and the meek."

"I can't help it …"

"You won't, you mean."

"I might volunteer … for the Mission."

"Are you nuts? My mother works there."

"At least she cares." Mike knew how to enrage her.

"Are you are suggesting I don't?" Jocelyn thrust out her chin and her chest; her eyes were on fire.

"Volunteer with me – put your money where your Tory mouth is."

"I've got lectures, and I've already explained the facts

of life. If you want to continue to enjoy my favours – get a life." She picked up her bag and click clacked her way out of the canteen, leaving Mike to ponder on what she'd said.

Mike gathered his gear together and saddled the Vespa Grandturismo 125, nicknamed *Rosinante*. He'd bought it for a song at the mission and put in new rings. As he wove through the streets he saw the city's homeless begin to stir from the parks and under bridges. Castlemere was a beautiful city of waterways and gardens, marred only by the smog and the derelicts that lived in obscene little groups wrapped in newspaper or army surplus greatcoats, snuggled into their mammary bags of glue or wine colostrum. They moved camp from one scavenger source to another, feeding out of rubbish tins, begging from passers-by, or doing squalid sex for food.

He wound the throttle back in anger, and overtook a black limousine. The disappearing middle classes and those above didn't see them, or skewed them out of focus. If confronted by them, they'd explain them away as the authors of their own loser destinies – druggies, glue sniffers, alkies, or the useless.

They had no market value; hence they had no human value – a whipping-boy minority, like the old, the fat and the ugly, who could be happily discriminated against in Pluto's Republic. At the same time, did it never occur to Plutonian consumers that a billion workers in Third

World countries worked for less than a dollar a day so they could buy glitzy trinkets at giveaway prices?

This policy had put large numbers of Plutonian workers out of jobs and made huge profits for the retail sector – but the liberal consensus agreed this represented the true entrepreneurial spirit of the free market and Pluto's Republic.

A one-time piece of inner city suburbia cordoned off with high mesh gates and barbed wire loomed in front of him. As he scootered through the wide open wrought iron gates he mused that this was a sort of benign concentration camp. A series of old houses renovated into an office block, clothes and opportunity shops, and a drug and alcohol rehabilitation centre.

He'd visited before, with student friends, to buy stuff cheap to set up student flats. Concerned citizens from all walks of life donated goods, volunteered their time or both. They might be horrified if they knew where some of it ended up. He pulled up in front of the op shop and walked in.

He flicked through a dog-eared copy of Kerouac's *Desolation Angels*. It seemed to him these people shared an extra dimension – call it soul, or what you will, which added up to the bottom line not being their chief concern. They were motivated by empathy for their poorer brothers and sisters who struggled to survive.

His watch said ten fifty-eight; his appointment with Gwen was fixed for eleven. He strode over to the office block and knocked on her door.

"Come in … welcome." Gwen ushered him into her office, once a living room for a gentleman's residence – bay windows, wood panelling, lead lights – the whole character drama.

"I remember you from Greta's party. How's Jocelyn?"

"Fine," he said. "She is very focussed on her law papers at the moment. The university year is really just getting started".

"And how are things with you?"

"I can't complain," said Mike," no one ever listens anyway." He laughed

He slipped his CV across her desk. "I'm keen to become a social worker and would even consider some voluntary work in the meantime."

She glanced his CV. "Well, you could well be the sort of calibre person we're looking for. I'll let you know in due course."

"Well I really appreciate that. I would like to do what I can for the less fortunate."

"Some would disagree but I too believe that's what life is all about."

"Thanks again," said Mike. He was already halfway out the door. "Remember me to Jim." They locked eyes. Mike noticed for the first time her attractiveness, her red Cleopatra haircut, big brown eyes and full lips.

She averted her gaze. "Jim went missing on a photography trip, to the West Coast. The searchers found his equipment, but not him. Not a sign."

"I'm so sorry." Mike averted his eyes. "I hadn't heard."

"It was on TV and in the papers for a week."

Mike flushed. "When I'm studying, the world passes me by. I am sorry." He was in fact apologising because her desirability interfered with his sympathy for her loss. He went for the door.

He sat on his scooter, helmet on, and viewed society's rejects ambling past. Did he have what it took to deal with such people? A skinny red-haired girl in dungarees with tattoos and self-harm scars on her arms walked by. A drunken guy drinking out of a bottle was following her, shouting, "Wait up you fucking bitch."

Over in the corner of the car park were two scruffy looking young women sharing a joint, kissing passionately between puffs. There was an old guy lying on a bench by a shop door, sound asleep and snoring with a half-drunk bottle of whiskey in his hand. He looked like he hadn't showered in a year. In front of him, two dark-skinned guys were pushing each other, shaping up for a fight. He thought he'd better get out of there.

In the shop he'd seen incognito dealers cruising, looking to acquire an antique or a rare first edition for a few cents. They were easy to spot. Part of him understood Jocelyn's reluctance to be associated with the place, and another part of him was outraged.

"Williams, Walter & Smith, Jason Wright speaking."

"Hello Jase, it's Jocelyn." She hoped he wasn't going to spin the conversation out.

"To what do we owe the pleasure of your sweet voice?"

"No time for foolery! Can you put me through to Dad? I'm between lectures. " There, that told him.

"Consider it done, sweet lady." Jason dialled Tom's extension.

"Walter."

"It's me, Dad. A friend of Mike's, Nate Crust, wants some conveyancing done."

"I have no objection." He coughed down the phone. "I presume his money's as good as anybody else's. Get him to make an appointment when he's ready to proceed."

Jocelyn was glad that in this world, it was more about contacts and who you were than what you actually knew.

A knock resounded on Tom's door. He put his phone down and Francis Louveteau burst through the door. "Didn't interrupt anything did I, Tom?"

"No." He held his hand over the receiver.

"Good. I'm out for a long lunch. Jason will cover."

Tom lifted his hand off the phone. "Where were we?"

"I'll let Nate know." Jocelyn hung up the phone.

Wolf was slouching in a corner at the Black Swan Hotel when Francois Louveteau walked in. He saw Wolf and sat down opposite. It occurred to Wolf that a stranger might think they were two architects discussing a project.

Wolf drank double bourbons. He noticed Louveteau wasn't drinking. The heavy beamed ceiling and lattice windows infused an Old World ambience. The first of the early eaters queued at the smorgasbord counter.

Louveteau broke the ice. "I have delivery, monsieur."

The aroma of roast lamb and beef filled the restaurant and gnawed at Wolf's digestive juices. "Good."

Louveteau straightened his tie. "It's now a question of quantity and price, monsieur?"

"We could corner the market." Wolf ruffled his greying bush of hair. He would play it cool. "But it's not a big market." They were careful nobody moved within earshot. "Methamphetamines are the new big thing, and acid is still a good mover." His eyes swivelled.

Louveteau lowered his voice. "I'm talking coke, monsieur. Four hundred a gram."

"And wholesale?" Wolf gave him a wry smile.

"A competitive price." He sharpened the crease in his pin-striped trousers.

"Supply won't dry?" Wolf eyeballed him with the question.

"I get regular shipments, monsieur."

The booths around them filled up, so they took their drinks to the tables outside, beside the river. Wolf kicked at the ducks waiting to be fed, and looked on as they pecked at a duck with an injured leg. They showed no mercy, only malicious intent to kill. They quacked in hot pursuit as it hobbled along the riverbank, trying to escape into the shrubbery.

Wolf laughed in the direction of the ducks. "The dynamics of the market place."

Louveteau raised his glass and proposed a toast. "And may the devil take the hindmost, monsieur."

They sat down under an umbrella advertising Smirnoff Vodka, in white aluminium filigreed chairs that matched the table.

"To the essentials, monsieur. My wholesale is one fifty K a kilo. You should recoup another one fifty."

"Perhaps." Wolf rested his glass on the table. If he didn't, something was wrong. He smiled to himself.

Louveteau emptied his glass in one gulp. "There are reservations, monsieur?"

Wolf lowered his voice. "Coke is hard to unload. To stay high you need a snort, or top up, every half-hour. Ecstasy is cheaper – for a similar buzz that can last all night, but it's not without its health risks."

"I always have a quantity in stock."

"My capital is limited. I would sooner invest in meth, the poor man's coke. It's more popular and I get a quicker and better return."

"How?"

"Local labs can supply us within a day or so, and the street price is lower than coke at two- to three-hundred a gram and we still cop a hefty profit. You never know what coke has been cut with."

"Rest assured, monsieur, I have not interfered with it."

"No? I bet some link in the chain has. How'd I know the ratio of talcum powder or laxative to one gram of cocaine?"

"Does it matter? As long as the customer's happy. I've had no complaints so far, monsieur."

"I would need a sample."

Louveteau played with his empty glass. He sighed. "Are you interested or not?"

Wolf shot him a quixotic grin. "At a price. What say you, monsieur?" He paused for extra impact. "A hundred big ones – after I check the quality."

"One kilo, monsieur, is worth hundreds of thousands on the streets."

"A little word to the wise." Wolf checked his watch. "The cops estimate street values can be divided by ten." That should turn the tables his way. He grinned.

Louveteau cleared his throat urgently. "Let me say, monsieur, I represent criminals in a court of law and they are forthright compared with you."

Wolf curled his bottom lip. "Business is business. The market will dictate what your one kilo of cocaine is worth."

Louveteau got up to go. He didn't shake Wolf's hand. "You realize, of course, I'll go to the opposition."

"For sure. Tell my brown cuzzies I asked after them."

They wouldn't be interested. Meth was their thing.

Louveteau's cell phone rang in his pocket. He picked it up. "Louveteau. Robins? I can't talk. Make an appointment." He put his phone away in disgust. "There's no escape from these infernal contraptions."

"Yeah," Wolf said. "But they come in handy."

As an aside, Louveteau said, "We live in a new age, monsieur. Of cell phones and do what you will. We are our own God."

He knew of Louveteau's reputation. "Well … I draw the line at pederasty," said Wolf. He was only too aware there were laws for the compliant masses, but a few were slimy enough to slip through or were well connected enough to be immune. That's why he'd chosen the outlaw life. It was less hypocritical.

"You have fallen foul of hearsay, monsieur. My role with my boys is purely platonic and all about their education. I encourage them to question everything, especially authority. This is the Aeon of Horus; we've had the gods and goddesses. This is the time of the crowned and conquering child God."

Wolf could see why this man was such a good barrister. He was able to turn his fucking nefarious practices into a testimonial of concern and excellence of character. "You sound like you truly believe that," he said. It sounded like high-blown bullshit to him.

"I certainly do monsieur. I try to do my bit. I have seen some horrendous treatment of children at the hands of the Republic."

Wolf couldn't look at this man. He was such a mixture of half-truths and deceit. He was just too cunning and conniving, an excuse for a human being. But Wolf would have to grit his teeth and deal with him. Business was business, and that was the bottom line.

Chapter Sixteen

The destructive urge is also a creative urge.

– Mikhail Bakunin

A BATTERED orange Beetle, surfboard on top, rattled into the curb.

Nate threw the passenger door open. "Going my way, lady?"

Charlotte Robins, AKA Monique, put her cell phone in her shoulder bag, took out a lighter and a pack of cigarettes, extracted one, put it between her lips, flicked her lighter, and the cigarette glowed into life. She drew hard and took a lungful of noxious air.

The traffic was a steady flow both ways. "Fuck," she said. "I'm going to be late. I'm due in town in fifteen minutes. I've got an important appointment. If it wasn't so urgent you could stick your ride."

"Get in." Nate patted the passenger seat. She did. Her fresh flowery scent brought back the horror of her rape. The tension in the car was suffocating, but he'd have to put up with it for the ride to town.

The cigarette smoke didn't help. "Put that fucking smoke out!" he said.

She stubbed it out in the ash tray.

Monique looked straight ahead. "I have to do an important client from up north, a politician, so busy he can only ever fit in an hour or so for recreation. He's ugly and fat, but he does have a magnetic personality and wit. A powerful man, but underneath he's a sad, pathetic, narcissistically wounded little boy, as are a lot of my clients."

"I almost feel sorry for him. Nearly there," Nate said, pulling up at an inner city set of lights.

She ignored him. "It's a fair deal; I give him physical and emotional release and he keeps me up with politics, as well as being very generous with his money. He pays much more than other clients, and I enjoy being so close to wealth and power, and the sumptuous hotel suites with floor to ceiling views over the city, back dropping to the Alps – it's like you could reach out and touch them. I'm high in the sky and above all the cares and woes of the battlers scurrying like ants below."

Nate changed the subject. "I've been feeling bad."

"So you should."

"Jus' couldn't think straight."

Monique kept her focus on the road ahead. "You want to be accepted."

"Jus' to belong, for once!"

"Well, you almost made it to patched status."

Nate went quiet, only to be blitzed by the fleeting *burr … um, burr … um,* of big FXR Harley Davidsons overtaking close down the centreline between them and the oncoming traffic. They were Pariah Dogs. They must have been doing ninety kilometres an hour, laid back on their choppers, hair and beards parted and blown back against their matt black helmets, their old ladies on the back holding on tight to scrotums.

They were full of contempt for citizens, who they called baldheads, and society ruled by the boss and the clock. A brotherhood of freaks living to ride their bikes with the fuck-the-world arrogance of the outlaw, dangerous and untamed – yet oddly friendly. Sometimes they helped stranded motorists, leaving business cards that said *The Pariah Dog Motorcycle Club has assisted you*. And on the other side a quote from Shakespeare: *The evil men do lives after them; the good is oft interred with their bones.*

He thought of them like modern cowpokes or gunslingers, memories of a romantic past lifted from the pages of old-time cowboy books ready to hand out their cruel justice to the disloyal, rivals, or those that lay down a challenge. They were heroes to those who didn't have the courage to break free from a dead society, and a beacon of freedom and brotherhood to outsiders and those broken from family who faced the ever-increasing torment of modern life. Wherever the men and their bikes gathered, a certain adventurous, insatiable type of woman followed, to indulge in orgies of drink, drugs and sex. Accusations of rape and drug pushing were often made against them, but they always denied it. Their standard answer was they were a motorcycle club, but he knew better.

They turned into the street where the hotel was. "Real sorry, 'bout what happened," blurted Nate.

"Words are easy! But I know you didn't want to hurt me. You saved me from them before."

"I'll try to make it up."

"How?"

"For starters, I'll taxi you free to your jobs."

"OK." Monique frowned." But you're still not off the hook. If it wasn't against my principles I'd go to the cops, and you'd be an accessory after the fact."

He winced and swung the car into the Grand Hotel forecourt. A uniformed doorman guarded the entrance. The VW and surfboard projected a surreal vision of a deformed pelican into the mirrored plate glass of the ground floor restaurant.

Monique fumbled around in the glove box for a pen, and Nate read out his cell phone number. She wrote it on her forearm, underneath a dragonfly tattoo.

"Ring when you're finished," he said.

The doorman flicked Monique a knowing wink and she slipped past him in her sexy little black dress, pigtails, bangs and bright red lipstick. Nate thought she looked real hot, and he blushed with the knowledge of her every contour and crevice under her clothes. She seemed to float through the pink plush marble foyer and disappeared into a waiting lift.

"Charming, my dear," said Lewis Chambers, member for Harbour City East. He cupped each breast in his hand, weighing them for authenticity. "More exquisite than I remember, almost pubescent. Do come in and get more comfortable." He lowered his hand. "I am a man of great appetites, as you know, and I do like to savour what I am about to consume."

Monique screwed up her face. She moved out of his grasp. "I hope that doesn't mean you're planning to go down on me."

"No, my dear, but I do find the idea extraordinarily tantalizing."

"I bet." She did not.

"Be a dear; let me see your Brazilian."

She watched as he donned a white hotel bathrobe with a blue Grand Hotel insignia on it, wobbled over and shut the curtain. He shuddered with anticipation, and let his dressing gown fall. He pranced in front of her, naked except for a pair of socks monogrammed with a compass and square. His unremarkable penis was exposed – a small, pink acorn beneath his white overhanging belly. His man boobs were voluptuous, and his belly and chest were thatched with sparse black and grey hair with pink erect nipples, like a chimpanzee peeking out of a thicket.

"Let me see it!" he said, his impatience increasing.

Monique began to disrobe and pulled a coquettish young girl face. She didn't have a choice if she wanted his money. Rhythmically, she hoisted her dress off over her head. She undid her 34b bra, and stepped out of her red silk French knickers, which displayed her darkening mound.

Chamber's penis popped like a wound-out lipstick. "You've let all that filthy hair grow back."

"You naughty little boy." She rolled her eyes in a coy way and went down on him, thinking of the three hundred bucks.

"Yes, I'm naught ... very wicked ... ah. I want to eat your thing but it's all hairy, like a mummy. It's no good, must keep going, don't bite me ... harder ... faster, oh you ... Oh! Oh! Your DNA's worth cloning. Oh! Oh, Ahhhhhhhh!"

Lewis held Monique's head with both hands, as delicately as if it were an egg. She removed her mouth and continued with her hand. He ejaculated in short spurts. "Oh! Ah, you bitch ... beautiful slutty little bitch."

When he finished she went into the bathroom to clean herself up and wondered about putting her rates up. The cost of living was always on the rise.

When she returned, Lewis had composed himself and was reclining in a chair in singlet and y-fronts – a middle-aged sixth former, minus his cap, black hair flopping over his brow. She slipped back into her clothes.

The musky smell of semen and body odour pervaded the room.

She didn't like to encourage pubescent fantasies, even though she'd learned that fantasies aren't erotic thoughts, they're not necessarily repressed wishes. Many of her client's would risk being locked up and having the keys thrown away if they'd ever acted out their fantasies. She liked to think of herself as not only a prostitute, but also a therapist. She hoped to provide a constructive outlet for what could be destructive urges if not managed creatively. Maybe she overstated it. This didn't mean she intended to shave her pubis for Chambers or anybody else – she wasn't a young girl, and it wasn't healthy.

"I feel oddly calm and detached." Lewis lay back in his lazy boy chair. "The world has stilled. The French call it the little death."

Monique tidied up her things.

"The feeling you get after you've come."

"I'll take your word for it."

"Death may not be such a bad prospect then," joked Lewis. "God knows we know how to complicate life. I have so many appointments scheduled for this afternoon with corporate businessmen who contribute munificently to party funds."

"So that's how it works," Monique said.

He rocked in his chair. "These same gentlemen waste no time in advising me how my influence could best be used in return. I much prefer Saturday morning surgeries, where I can resolve the problems of the great unwashed." Chambers got up from the chair and slipped his dressing gown on. "I would like to still the world just long enough for us all to see where we are going."

"It won't happen, though, will it?" Monique sat on a bedside chair and brushed her hair.

He pranced over to the window and opened the curtains, and held forth on his high-rise soapbox. "I went into politics with a desire to change things for the better for everyone." He looked into the distance. "But the system has gathered a momentum of its own; it has become a great Leviathan swallowing everything in its path by stealth and deceit. It's become a plutocracy in the guise of a democratic meritocracy, but then the few of us that have read our Plato know the end result of democracy is tyranny anyway."

Monique fell back in her chair with hands behind her head, braced for a state of the nation speech. "I thought you believed the Three Year Plans were for the better."

"Neoliberalism, the political theory that dare not speak its name, was designed to transfer control of the economy from the public to the private sector, under the belief that it would produce a more efficient government and improve the economic health of the nation. We sold assets to pay debt in one-off payments." Lewis gazed out the window. "At least, that's what the plebes were told, but we never had a mandate. You could put it down to noble lies."

"The cause of revolutions." Monique sat upright. "The bloodletting type."

Lewis blathered on. "It was party policy to lie about the nature of the Three Year Plans to enable them to be fast tracked, sold as a substitute for the welfare state. But it was really socialism for the rich, financed by the plebes."

"One day the people will wake up," Monique said.

"I hope that never happens," he said. "It only ever benefited the top end. Wealth was supposed to trickle down, but it never did. We relied heavily on propaganda and censorship rebranded as political correctness."

"So all the reforms were in vain?" She couldn't bear the indifference of this guy.

He turned around to look at her. "If you discount the irreparable suffering and damage done to the social and economic infrastructure," he said. He took his wallet from his jacket, which lay crumpled on the bed, and peeled off three one-hundred-dollar notes, counting them into Monique's open palm.

She felt like she was taking blood money.

Chambers frowned. "Till we meet again." He gave a raucous belly laugh. "Or not, if technology can improve the experience – it's going to be robots and artificial intelligence eventually. We won't need the human hordes or natural reproduction." Chambers smiled at Monique with a hideous grin.

"That's depraved," Monique said.

"Just a tip: remember, democracy isn't safe if the people tolerate the growth of private power to the point where it becomes stronger than the democratic state itself. That's fascism, which can lead to totalitarianism."

She ignored him. He was preaching to someone who'd already sussed that out through bitter experience. She slipped the money into her purse and snatched out her cell phone.

"Thanks." Bastard was too good a word for him.

"Thank the long-suffering taxpayer." He laughed again. "They're a diminishing breed. "I must shower." He disappeared into the bathroom.

"I'll ring a taxi and let myself out." Monique sprung off the bed.

"Fine," he shouted from the bathroom.

"Nate? Monique. Get over here. I'm ready."

"With you in five."

Nate parked the VW alongside the river, over the road from the hotel. The garish orange car was a relic from more egalitarian times, a battered proletarian between its bourgeois Mercedes and BMW cousins.

Monique came out of the hotel foyer.

"That was quick."

She burrowed her bum into the passenger seat and looked sideways at him. "Tell you what." She adjusted her bra. "It's two hours till my next job. I'll buy you a drink."

"You're on." He peered into her eyes and felt a pleasant twinge in his penis.

"My makeup alright?" She turned face on to him.

"Sure." He played down the erotic effects, her slightly parted lips moist and bright red, her teeth chiselled porcelain. There was blusher on her cheeks, but they were natural looking. Black eyeliner and eyelashes tarted up the effect.

They got out of the car. He clunked an hour's coins into the meter and they wandered a block, alongside the river, following the scent of espresso coffee and fresh baking marinated in carbon dioxide. The pair crossed over to where a clutch of up-market pubs and restaurants spilled tables and chairs into the street. They perched opposite each other at a wooden table, alfresco, under a pin oak splattered with bird shine. He fiddled with the laminated menu, watching the punters on the river and the pretenders on the street.

She gave a big sigh of relief and said, "I could sit and watch people all day." The sun was hot and no wind stirred to cool the air. He relaxed in his faded jeans and black T-shirt; she was plain but elegant in her little black dress. They were out of place amongst the trendy voyeurs and consumers who wanted to see and be seen by their peers in café society.

Nate was a little envious of the conspicuous consumers with their low-riding chromium-rimmed cars, fine wine and food, fashionable clothes, and beautiful playmates. He reckoned they were products of the microchip – digital this, cellular that. Children of the silicone valleys and mirrored towers; PlayStation techno freaks, cell phone holstered cybernauts, surfers of the information wave with fibre optic genitals and binary eyeballs set deep in sunglass-reflective bald heads.

He forced himself to look away from the white triangle of Monique's knickers, exposed when she uncrossed her legs. He felt mellow enough to confide in her.

"I'm buying a house." He fanned himself with the menu.

"How you going to do that?" She looked around and shaded her face with her hand.

"I've raised the deposit – just. Gotta get finance."

"The tricky part.'

"Shouldn't be a problem."

"It can be."

A waiter stepped by and took their order – a lager for him, and a white wine for Monique.

They continued their discussion.

"Why can it be a problem?" he said, frowning.

"Well, you work, and you're well paid, right?"

"Yeah. Spit it out."

Monique noticed her dress had ridden up and pulled it down. "Well, there's no record of your earnings. And you don't pay tax."

"So?"

She sighed in frustration. "The bank manager's going

to want to know where you work. How much you earn? Etc. etc. Dumbo!"

"Never thoughta that."

"I've been there." She pushed out her chest. "Got the tits and the T-shirt."

A buxom, woolly-headed woman in her thirties brushed past their table.

"Kathy!" Monique shouted. The woman turned and recognized her.

"Charlotte." Kathy seemed fidgety and nervous, averting her gaze, not pleased to see her. She didn't even look at Nate when introduced. His face was a study in disbelief.

"I'm still not sure about this entire court case thing," Kathy said to Monique. "Perhaps sleeping Pariah Dogs are best left alone. Anyway, I can't stop." She ruffled her curly mane. "I've got an appointment at the hairdresser, or should I say, magician!"

"Who's she?" asked Nate.

"A friend."

"How come she called you Charlotte?"

"That's my name."

The waiter arrived with the drinks. "Sorry about the delay, guys, but it's been crazy in here today."

"That's one uptight lady," said Nate, slurping his drink.

"What did you expect? The Pariahs raped her too." She paused, and her mouth hardened. "I want you to help us bring a conviction against them."

Nate felt himself turn pale. "I wasn't even there."

"No, but you were there when they raped me."

"And you want me to testify against myself?"

She let go an impatient sigh. "No, silly. If you give evidence against them I'll tell them how you couldn't go through with it." She smiled full and sunny. "And I'll testify I witnessed Kathy being raped and heard her say: 'I don't want to do this.'"

"Do you know what you're asking?" Nate sucked his beer like mother's milk. "If I betray the guys, I'm dead." He pulled a pack of cigarettes out from his T-shirt sleeve, but he didn't have a match. He eyed the surrounds for a fellow smoker to bum a light. "I'll be skinned like a machine-peeled spud." The cigarette wobbled in his mouth. "Have you ever seen a body dragged down a metal road behind a car?" He shuddered involuntarily.

Monique showed no emotion. "If you're convicted of being an accessory to the Dog, you could be doing quite a long stretch too."

The waiter walked past, and lucky for Nate, offered to light his smoke. Nate took a lungful.

"If you help me put them away you could be home free," said Monique.

He clenched and unclenched his fist. "You mean back to being a hamster on a wheel." He tugged at his bush of brown hair and fingered the down on his chin. "How the fuck did I get into this mess?"

Monique didn't answer. She didn't need to. He put himself through the third degree: could it be that he didn't play organized sport, and he didn't waste his days, like Goose – licking the boss's ass – especially when the surf was up.

Chapter Seventeen

My Teachings are like a finger pointing at the moon.
Do not mistake my teachings for the moon.

– The Buddha

IT WAS Tuesday morning, the first week in April. Goose reclined behind his desk and stared at the chrome-plastic, tin can and rubber displays on the showroom floor. They were automotive additives, accessories, manuals and magazines – a sparkling Jaguar XK8 coupe, Mercedes Benz SL 500 and Porsche 996 C4 Carrera. Two browsers mooched through the showroom and two customers slumped at the parts desk – nothing the other staff couldn't handle.

He let his mind off the chain and retraced his morning trip to work in his mind, cruising past dole bludgers on the beach with the climate control on and the radio tuned to the share index. He explored the sparkle of the rolling surf, and soaked in the sun's rays, coming through the XJ Jaguar's sunroof onto his polished baldhead. He wondered why the Republic didn't harness the power of the sea to make electricity – an obvious resource going to waste.

He loved the sensual seats, the plush smell, the

lacquered trim, snarling Jaguar logo and the low growl of the eight-cylinder motor, and the guttural throttle responsive to every accelerator tweak.

This brought to mind another feral cat – the ginger-hued Greta. He'd learned to obey her every whim with the relish of a slobbery dog responding to the bell-shuttered dong of her tolling clitoris.

He shut the louver windows to the showroom – the smell of engine degreaser had spread from the workshop to his office. His attention focused on a couple in the car yard. They disappeared between the gaps in the four-wheel drive vehicles. Were they tyre kickers, dreamers, or serious cashed-up punters? They required further investigation. But first, he sweet-talked his reluctant backside into severing its relationship with his office chair.

When he did go and look, he got one hell of a shock to see Greta's fiery mass of hair pop up from around the side of an X-type Jag, with Lance in tow.

"This is a turn-up," he said, bemused. "I only saw you a couple of hours ago and you didn't say anything about coming to see me."

Greta's face fell at his dispassionate greeting. "We wanted to surprise you. Lance inherited a sum of money from his grandfather and wanted to put some of it towards a quality European car."

"Why didn't you say so?" Goose smiled a wide toothy smile. "A good choice, mate," he said, resting his hand on Lance's shoulder. "What sort of money do you want to spend?"

"No more than twenty-five biggies, darling." Goose removed his hand quickly, in case Lance's effeminacy rubbed off.

"You realize," said Goose, matter of factly, "at that price you'll be looking at the bottom end of the quality market."

Lance shrieked with high-pitched laughter. "It has never deterred me before, dear boy." Greta joined in laughing.

Lance tossed his golden head. A chunky gold necklace encircled his neck.

Greta and Lance leaned against a V8, forest green Land Rover Discovery. Goose frowned. "Is this a thespian joke, or can anybody laugh?"

His attempt at taking control made things worse. Lance shrugged. "I'm so sorry, darling; it's so … funny, so … bloody hilarious." He took on a mock-serious tone. "It's certainly not …" he broke down, cackling, "a lesbian joke." He burst his sides. "I blame your dear lady. OOh! OOh! She's incorrigible, darling."

Greta gave Lance an affectionate punch on the shoulder. "No! She's the cat's mother."

Lance and Greta rollicked against the Land Rover.

Lance shouted over Greta's laughter. "I take it dear husband and partner, the expression *bottom end of the quality market* wasn't a pun or a Freudian slip?"

Goose flung Greta a look that said *What the fuck did you bring him here for?* But instead he said, "I don't like being called Greta's partner. I thought you were here to buy a car."

"You're a bloody pervert, Lance Pierpont." Greta straightened Lance's collar. "Let's go car hunting."

Goose led the way.

"I want to look at beamers," Lance announced.

Goose showed Lance three in his price range.

"I like the red one," Lance said. "But I'll let you know about my decision. Twenty-five thousand is a lot of opening nights on a struggling actor's wages. This is a better buy – a 318. It's the new E46 shape, leather seats, silver paint, ten thousand less k's for a few extra thousand dollars – twenty-nine thousand nine-ninety."

Goose tried to tempt Lance. "The keys are in the office, if you want to go for a test drive."

Lance threw him a double entendre look. "Later, darling," he said with a saucy grin. He wriggled into the driver's seat, pawing the gearshift, then got out again, and he and Greta inspected the outside panels.

Goose eyed Lance's hindquarters and felt himself going hard when he thought of some of the more lurid things gay men might do to each other.

Greta brought him back with a bump. "Did you know there are another three plays in the offing? *Streetcar Named Desire, Death of a Salesman,* and *The Changeling.* We don't know which is to come first, but rehearsals are in three weeks."

"So the baby making is on hold," teased Lance.

Greta bared her teeth, and gave Lance the foulest look. Goose wanted to ensure Greta remained focused on the theatre and off the baby-making idea.

"I like the car – but I'll be in contact." With a wicked grin he joked about Greta not being pregnant: "You must be doing something wrong, darlings." Then he gave Goose a smouldering eye.

Trenton Jones and a mousy looking female motored into the yard.

Goose waved Lance and Greta off and welcomed the others. He could read Greta's period symptoms with more accuracy than a gynaecologist – she was a premenstrual Jekyll and Hyde who went from bubbly and available to surly and remote in one ovulation. She thought oral sex meant talking dirty. Her period usually meant no sex for five days, and she wondered why he got surly and remote. Greta accused him of having too much testosterone and not enough self-restraint, and during her period complained about his desire to try alternative orifices.

The woman stepped out of Trenton's car in her leather mini skirt. He noted her firm uplifted breasts. He held his breath for the obligatory flash of pants and she didn't disappoint. He examined her exquisite legs and imagined the ripe plum conjunction of her crotch. He mused, was she a raw recruit in the Machiavellian world of human resources? Or did she possess enough life experience to know a flash of knickers, firm young tits, and the hint of a promise and natural savvy could take her further than an honours degree from Clever Clit College?

He loved her soulful brown eyes, which at different angles took on a hue of ocean green. Her mousy shoulder-length hair was parted at the side and there were braces on her teeth – testosterone killers – but, it could be worse imagine if she had a similar contraption down below.

Trenton moved around the side of the car and introduced them. His bald head protruded through his horseshoe band of hair. "I promised you an intern, Gary. This is Tracy, the latest addition to Superior Imports."

"Welcome aboard, my dear." All the time Goose undressed her in his mind. "I'll show you around. He placed a hand on her shoulder. She didn't seem to mind – always a good sign. "There are only three of us. You're the only female, mind you."

Tracy listened unfazed. "Oh I'm quite used to being around males. I come from a big family of brothers."

Trenton took Goose aside and left Tracy looking at a new era VW Beetle.

"You're not offended," – he moved square on to Goose – "by my employing of Tracy? Once things settle, the decisions will be yours."

"I did have someone in mind."

"Would you like to talk?" Trenton's face was one big

question mark.

"That won't be necessary." Goose led Tracy with his hand on her shoulder.

"This is Nate Crust; could you put me through to Mr Solomon, please?"

"Just one moment," came the automatic response.

Nate waited, as instrumental guitar elevator music played in one ear. He lolled against the wall of the hall at home. In the other ear music drifted from Daryl's room, a primal scream from John Lennon's *Working Class Hero* album, from another time and reality – long before the destruction of the Twin Towers. It served to introduce a blues song Daryl made up as he went along:

"My bus arrives at midnight / ship sails the morrow morn'
Left home when I was young / lookin' to be free
Heard an exiled prophet say / first you must learn to be
My bus arrived at midnight / ship sails the morrow morn
Bus arrived at midnight / ship sails tomorrow morn
Life is but a riptide / that leaves the dock at dawn."

Nate knew all about this music, because Daryl press-ganged him into his room over a beer or a joint to listen to the lyrics of certain songs on his father's old LPs – music, conspiracy theories and mind-numbing substances the only interests Daryl and Vince, his old man, shared. Vince created in Daryl a nostalgic thing for 60s and 70s music – Pink Floyd, Led Zeppelin, Beatles, Jethro Tull, Cream, Deep Purple, Uriah Heap, Hendrix, and Ozzie, long before the existence of reality TV.

To Vince's mind – and he passed it on to Daryl – the CIA rubbed out John Lennon because of his political agitating. What better way than have a mad person do the shooting? Lennon had to be stopped, in case everybody decided to get off the merry go round and mind games, called the free world.

A mature female voice on the phone said: "Through now."

"Nice to speak to you again, Nathaniel. I trust there are no problems?"

"One or two – can't get the money."

Abe was quick to rally him. "Only a slight hiccup in the big scheme of things, my boy. Do you have a lawyer?"

"Yeah."

"And you have the deposit?"

"Nearly"

"I am quite prepared to leave ninety-five thousand in as a first mortgage.

"That's very generous."

"Get onto your lawyer and tell him to go ahead, and if he wants more details tell him to contact me."

He couldn't believe his good fortune. And again he thought of his mother – she would have said: "When fortune smiles, distrust her most." And, of course, fortune had to be a woman. "Why are you doing this?" The question nagged.

His voice quavered. "Shall I just say I have very good

reasons, my boy."

"I don't know what to say. I'm stoked."

"That is unnecessary. farewell for now, Nathaniel." He hung up.

Nate reeled – double, triple, quadruple stoked. Did anybody ever experience such generosity and goodwill, and from a complete stranger? It made him suspicious. What could he want from him? Apart from a beat-up V dub and a dinged twin-finned pin-tailed surfboard, and his house deposit, he owned nothing a wealthy man might be interested in. And then he thought of Francois Louveteau and his habits. Did this old guy want him for a sexual plaything? He cringed, and felt himself blush red, but he'd learnt to expect the unexpected in this world. The question remained, what did he want? Anyway, whatever, the green light to go ahead with the purchase flashed on the grid.

The muzac still boomed from Daryl's closed door. He thought of Tiff, who toiled at the supermarket, but left her door open in the hope of converting the heathen world with her tracts and posters on the wall. She bible-bashed even in her absence. He picked up the phone handset and at the same time his eyes caught a poster of grazing sheep on rolling downs with weeping willows and a river winding through them. The words read: *The Lord is my Shepherd: I shall not want.*

It annoyed him. He wasn't a bloody sheep, the dumbest animal in the world, and he set his mouth, more determined to get what he wanted. He punched out Jocelyn's phone number. He couldn't wait to tell her the news.

He knew Jocelyn and Mike often studied at Jocelyn's architecturally designed flat. It was a marriage of complex angles of smoked glass, stained cedar, idyllic surrounds of native bush, rhododendrons and exotics plants set to the music of a trickling stream. It nestled up a leg in a section far from the road that serviced five or six other similar properties. This little house had been put in a trust for the Walter offspring, so Mike told him, and the family owned many properties in Oceania, Asia and In Pluto's Republic.

He tightened his lips. Jocelyn and her siblings didn't know the anxious, stomach-in-mouth wait for the next pay packet, or benefit day, for life's little essentials. Their money didn't grow on trees, but it did sprout in a certain privileged soil. The Walter siblings could now concentrate their full energies on achieving, or mucking about, because their material needs had been taken for granted for a long time.

After about seven or eight rings, and just when Nate thought the answer phone was going to kick in, Jocelyn picked it up.

"Oh, hello Nate," she said in a tired voice. "How's progress?"

He tried to stay earthbound. "Finance is through."

"Oh, that is good news," she said, trying to sound

enthusiastic.

"Could you let your father know?"

"No, Nate, I think you should do that yourself. He's been advised. Just ring and make an appointment."

Nate somersaulted from dizzying tokes of self-esteem. Did he dream? He felt accepted, treated like an equal, initiated into their world. Did being a future property owner make the difference? He began to feel ashamed and resentful about his gang connections. But he was also amused that the girls not only serviced their clients – they would also service his mortgage. He was being entrepreneurial. He lived in fear Jocelyn might find out about his underworld connections.

"Would you like to speak to Mike? He's here – right beside me."

"No time, tell him … I'll catch him later." He wasn't in the mood for a sermon on the horrors of capitalism. He thanked Jocelyn and hung up.

Mike lounged on the floor parallel to the coffee table he used as a makeshift desk. He read his essay out loud. *"In conclusion, it can be seen with reference to the Four Noble Truths, life is suffering in the Buddhist tradition because we are influenced by our past karmic inheritance, which leads us to transmigrate to Samsara, the cycle of rebirth, old, age and death. This is because accumulated harmful karma keeps us coming back. There is no hope of achieving permanent release from this world.*

"Suffering ceases, as we have seen, by way of the Eightfold Path when we extinguish the fires of desire (Nirvana) that keep us on the wheel of rebirth. Nirvana is not a place but a state of, nothingness, where no harmful Karma can be generated and is the ultimate end of rebirth or suffering."

Jocelyn stood in the doorway, listening to Mike's essay. "That was Nate," she said when he paused. "The house sale is going through."

"I'm pleased." Mike tossed his essay on the table. "The poor guy could do with a break."

She sat down beside him with her back to the coffee table. "You don't actually believe that rubbish, do you?"

Mike said nothing, not wanting to cause a rift.

The sun shone directly on them, causing a pleasant drowsiness. Jocelyn yawned and stretched in her a little tailored pleated skirt and white top, to emphasize what lay underneath.

Mike admired Jocelyn's tanned, well-toned legs and yielded. Animal desires kindled in his chest and loins, his breath and heart rate were hyper-tense. She was so cool and doll-like; he, a lion bathing in the sun.

"Finished my essay," he quipped.

"I heard." Jocelyn threaded her fingers through his hair. "Now you can concentrate on me."

Mike pushed the coffee table back and Jocelyn fell against the couch. He cradled her head in the crook of one arm and slid the other hand down her knickers. Jocelyn shut her eyes and sighed.

He knew her well enough to read the signs. A smile played on her lips. Aroused, she became meek, mild and cooperative, and yielded like a flower to a nectar-crazed bee. She slithered his fingers to the magic spot. He remembered the time she came to learn about the joys of the clitoris. It had been quite late in her life, after much self-exploration. She exhaled sweet beautiful sighs and worked her vagina against his hand slowly but with teeth-clenching intensity. She head locked him and held him in a lingering kiss. The contortions of their tongues tried to give voice to indescribable physical sensations in the constricted caverns of their mouths. They closed in on each other, but still a sense of distance existed, somehow.

In his imaginings he was possessed by the lanky strumpet, Isabelle, and he envisioned Jocelyn surrendering to her impertinent lips and outrageous fingers – but to confess that? To tell Jocelyn of the images he harboured of her and that wanton dyke, Isabelle, in torrid acts of cunnilingus and cucumber tribadism? His penis throbbed and hurt after being erect for so long without relief. He watched Jocelyn convulse in ecstasy on the end of his hand. His mind was far away, what chance did he have of achieving a spiritual state higher than a cockroach?

We (he chose to implicate as many of the silent majority as he could in his thoughts) are slaves to sexual desire in its myriad forms because it's a fix, a drug-like rush, a temporary escape from the tensions and frustrations of the mundane world, and the social engineers take advantage of that fact. Desire spins the Wheel of Dharma, and power mongers broker by centrifugal force. And rich American women go to Ashrams to debauch; but it was a long way from his spiritual home.

Jocelyn heaved and groaned in the final throes of her desire. She was a double for Whoopee! Barbie. Her usually pristine hair was askew, her classic skirt lifted up, revealing black lace knickers.

His hand gathered speed, plucking her concert-pitched clitoris to exquisite strains of funky flamenco. He didn't know what sounds played in her head, but her pelvis bucked in ecstatic frenzy, whipped and whirled, a bucking bronco bent on unsaddling its rider.

The pressure on his hand increased and her face contorted. Little *ooh! aah!* rhythm section sounds merged with the strings. Her back was an erotic bow tensioned by the crotch string rhythms of naked lust spasming on the balance beam of primordial orgasm.

Three flourishes of the vaginal rosette, a crescendo and prolonged finale "*Ooh Ah! Ooh ah! Ooh-Sah-belle.*"

Mike removed his hand slow. Jocelyn sagged like a sponge at the slamming of the oven door. She stood up and regained her composure, straightened her hair and skirt, and planted a perfunctory kiss on Mike's cheek. Mike frowned. "Did you say Isabelle?"

"Orgasm speak for lovely release." Her cheeks flushed.

"Happy to oblige."

"I love you." She grabbed his hard penis. "Let's go and get rid of that. C'mon, there are new sheets on the bed."

Mike flashed her cheeky smile. "Replicate your genes time?"

"Cynic." She led Mike to the bedroom by his belt. "I'd sooner get into your jeans." She unzipped them, and tilted her head to the side in a silent invitation to ravish her. "Take the sox off too."

Mike got into bed, and the phone rang in the study.

"It'll be a student," said Jocelyn. She threw the covers off and slipped into a pink towelling dressing gown from a chair.

"Hurry back."

Jocelyn picked up the phone. "Good … you've made a time … He'll decide when the time's right … He's fine." She came back into the room "Two guesses who that was?"

Mike didn't answer.

She flung her dressing gown on the chair, her pelvis level with Mike's head. He got a waft of salmon. It brought out the erotic grizzly bear in him.

"He asked after you."

"I get the gist – OK to dally with, but Daddy doesn't approve of my long-term prospects."

"Your words, tiger." She grabbed his penis. "Daddy doesn't have to approve of you. Now shut up and get on with it before this thing goes down!"

Fuelled with lust and mild anger, Mike clambered onto Jocelyn's nakedness. She positioned him. With a fierce clench of his buttocks and a lunge of his loins he was a divisive force between her legs. In Mike's world, Isabelle and Jocelyn wrestled with him in a tangled ménage à trois.

He withdrew at the penultimate moment and spurted all over her stomach.

Jocelyn screwed up her face and removed it with her dressing gown. "I don't like this coitus interruptus," she said.

Mike wiped himself with her gown. "Tell your old man not ring up in the middle of it then."

"I hope one day you will come to your senses."

Mike laughed out loud. "I thought I just had."

"You know what I mean." Her voice was serious enough to be dangerous. Her brow furrowed and her eyes narrowed. She played with the sparse dark hairs on his chest. She spoke as if talking to herself. "Even Nate shows more initiative than you."

Chapter Eighteen

The life so short, the craft so long to learn.

– Hippocrates

Aphorisms 1.1 Trans, by Chaucer

ON WEDNESDAY morning at 9.15a.m. Daryl skipped down the hall in his pyjamas with his radio blaring. He pushed into Nate's room. "Listen to this."

The voice on the radio said: *"… at four thirty this morning, a Castlemere suburban gang house was firebombed by a rival gang. Police say there had been long-term rivalry between the Pariah Dog Motorcycle Club, alleged distributors of illicit drugs with links to white supremacist groups and investment in the sex industry, and the Culture Assassins, an ethnic group linked to black militant organizations, also known for involvement in drugs and the sex industry."*

"Fucking hell!" Nate sat up, rigid in his bed, and threw the surfing mag he was reading on the floor.

The report continued: *"It's not known what triggered this latest conflagration. Chief Inspector George Waldron, area commander for Castlemere East, said the word on the street was that it was over territory and gang control of strip clubs, sauna parlours, prostitution and the drug trade. The attack happened in the early hours, at around four thirty a.m. The house has been extensively burnt. All motorcycles on the premises were saved from the flames. One Pariah Dog gang member has been hospitalized and is in intensive care from two .22 calibre gunshot wounds. Five more members are suffering from smoke inhalation and minor burns. Others from both gangs are helping police with their inquiries."*

Nate slipped out of his bed in his T-shirt and underwear, reached for his cell phone on the dresser and dialled Wolf's number. Wolf must have been out of range or his phone was off.

He dialled Queenie's. "I just heard."

"Nothing we could do," said Queenie. "Wolfy and I were here. He's at the cop shop now. Tank caught two bullets."

"Is he OK?"

"Too early to say."

"Any work tonight?"

"Come in early – Wolf wants to brief everyone. In the meantime, keep your head down." She hung up.

The turmoil confused Nate. He'd almost forgot the lawyer's appointment at four o'clock. He needed to be on time.

He rang Monique to see if she'd heard anything. The phone rang seven or eight times and then a tired and sleepy voice answered. "Hel-lo. Charlotte."

"It's me, have you heard the news? Turn your fucking radio on."

"I'm not awake yet, what's–"

"The CA have fire bombed the clubhouse."

"I know something, but I can't say over the phone. I'll meet you at Lefty's in ten minutes. Bring your togs." She hung up.

Somebody was showering as Nate walked down the hall; steam seeped from under the door. Daryl must have slunk away while he'd been on the phone.

Tiff cornered Nate in the hallway. In a sharp voice she said, "Tell those friends of yours it's not too late to repent."

Nate laughed, "Yeah, right."

"Well, without the protection of the full armour of God the enemy will defeat us every time."

"We're talking 'bout a different enemy."

"Are we? Take care, Nate." And she added, "You shouldn't talk about your coloured brothers in those derogatory terms."

He gazed skyward as if he would welcome divine intervention. "What galaxy are you spinning round?" He tripped over the step on his way out and almost fell headlong over the welcome mat.

There weren't many at Lefties when Nate arrived, and Monique's blond head stood out in the garden bar. She was a real turn on in tight jeans and a delicately embroidered white top. Her hair was loose. She wore no makeup, and when he got close she smelt sweet and sexy.

"I've ordered for us." She smiled. What once used to irritate him now seemed OK. He sat down opposite and marvelled at her eggshell blue eyes and crimson lips.

They watched the surf rescue boat slide down the slipway backwards and slowly reverse till it managed a clear run out to sea. The breeze was light and from the northwest. It caressed them.

"I wonder what happened," he said, his eyes following the rescue boat. He sniffed the salt and seaweed on the wind; the surf was flat and ideal for swimming. His focus became softer and more intimate. The pancakes and coffee arrived and they began to eat and talk. It was cruisy. He loved breakfasting with Monique.

He wanted the surfers to see them together. Three strolled past and flicked Nate a green-eyed look. He lost himself in her kaleidoscope eyes. "OK. Let's have it."

"I will, but not here." She drained the last of her cappuccino. They climbed over the crazy stone pattern fence to the beach. Monique slid her jeans and top off to reveal a bright yellow bikini. He removed his T-shirt and left his board shorts on.

The water came direct from Antarctica. They dived under a wave to get used to it. The sun shimmered on the water when they surfaced.

"Phew! That's better," he said, "but I'm naked without my board."

"I feel the same in this bikini." She shivered.

"Yuh look great."

In a quiet voice, she said, "I caused the attack."

Nate splashed his face with water. "You're fucking having me on. How?" Small waves lapped and slapped around them, and they moved with the rise and fall of the small swell.

"Easy. I used my feminine wiles." She smiled and poked her breasts out. "I went to see Axe, the president of Culture Assassins."

"And?"

She cocked her head demurely to one side. "I told him of my brutal rape by the Pariah Dog boys, said I wanted revenge."

"Then?"

"I said I overheard them plotting a surprise attack on CA, because their methamphetamine labs hurt the Dogs' drug profit."

"You could have gone to the cops."

"Louveteau said we'd only destroy our own characters and credibility. Anyway, I don't care; street girls have ways to get their own justice."

"So where does that leave me?"

"Driving my taxi – if you want? Come here." She clutched him affectionately by his messed-up hair. "I've decided to give you a break." A wave butted them together. "Do you know …" She gave him a sexy, enigmatic look. "I never kiss my clients?"

"No. I didn't." His eyes were like saucers.

She pulled the strap of her bikini up. "It's much too

personal a thing." She cupped her hands behind his neck. He shrugged. They sank into each other's eyes. Monique tousled his curls.

"I'm sorry I couldn't help. They would have killed me."

"I know. Besides, us working girls have a way of getting our own back. But I'm saying yes to you now, but only to a kiss. What do you say?"

He couldn't say anything. She pulled him close and they kissed.

"I will teach you, if you'll let me." They hugged. "But don't think you've got the key to my heart and knickers. I want a proper relationship." She took her hands from around his neck and kissed him on the cheek.

"I thought you wanted my balls for a trophy."

Her eyes softened. "That's before you started to grow on me. But don't get any ideas. I'm not the storybook whore with the heart of gold – if you cross me, your balls will be mountain oysters for the CA."

"That's cool with me." He slung her a cheeky boyish smile and watched the waves increase in size and frequency. A group of surfers paddled out. He wished he'd brought his board and could follow them, but more important business loomed. He disentangled himself from Monique, and they waded out of the sea and towelled off.

"I'd better check the guys out," he said.

"I want a ride home first." Monique playfully flicked

Nate with her towel. They dressed and got in the VW. The relic rumbled past a group of Pariah bikes outside the Sunvale Police Station, and at the Mitre Hotel garden bar, and he recognized Shane, Moose, Johnny Smallbone, Puck Uggles, Valentino Crass, Finn McCool, and Pedro Purplehaze, the guys who raped Kathy and Monique. Tank wasn't there. By the time Nate had made the return trip to Monique's, the sun hung over the Mitre at about one o'clock in the sky.

The Dogs had been guzzling booze from opening time, he reckoned. They languished over wooden picnic tables, smoking, happily intoxicated. A yahoo went up when he strode in. If they were harbouring any bad feeling about him wussing out on the gang bang, they weren't showing it or were too drunk to care. He didn't really know any of them that well.

Pedro Purplehaze offered him a joint he'd just rolled. "Hey, dude, want a smoke? Heads, good shit."

Nate took the joint and Shane lit it up.

Shane spun around to Nate. "Have you seen the remains of HQ?"

"No, been lying low."

Shane's eyes misted. "The mutt bought it; shotgun blast blew his poor fuck'en head off his skinny shoulders – poor fuck'en mutt. Got a feeling doggie Karma's gonna white line those nigger bastards at a hundred mile an hour."

Puck Uggles put his hand on Shane's shoulder. "They'll

keep, Shane, they'll fuck'en keep."

"Easy brother." Shane removed Puck's hand from his shoulder. "I don't like being touched."

"Relax guys." Valentino Crass smoothed his black brush back. "From what I heard at the pig sty, the law's gonna take care of 'em for us. Rumour has it the filth found a large amount of coke on the premises and Axe could be gonna do serious time."

"I believe harf of what I see and nuffin of what I hear," said Finn McCool, from behind a mass of spiky brown-streaked hair and beard. "I reckon it's a furfer ploy by the CA hopin' we'll turn paranoid and beat ourselves to deaf with motorcycle parts."

They looked accusingly at Nate. "Ya haven't heard any whispers, have ya boy?" Johnny Smallbone scratched his crotch and adjusted his black beanie.

"I don't know a fucking thing about the Assassins." Nate frowned and stroked his chin tuft. A low rumble suffocated the conversation and Wolf rode his cut-down Harley FRXT up the sidewalk through the gate and into the midst of the Mitre garden bar. He sat astride the bike. Everything throbbed to the pulsations of the low rumble. Wolf switched the engine off – all went quiet and still. Nate was all ears.

"I've just come from the pigs," said Wolf. Moose, the big square-jawed Canadian threw him a can of beer. Wolf caught it. "They're not looking at charging us." A unanimous "Yahoo" echoed from the guys. "But the

Assassins are in the crap up to their elbows. Our piggy friends found five hundred grams of cocaine – that's possession of a class A drug – serious slammer time." The dogs cheered from the ranks. Wolf went on, "Which leaves us with the problem of finding a new clubhouse."

Nate didn't intend to volunteer his place, so he changed the subject quick. "How's Tank?"

The question brought a smile to Wolf's hairy face. "Full'a shit and dirty talk. The fat bugger had me in tears and convulsions. He asked an old toxic tits scrubber of a nurse to sit on his face. She didn't take it well." The guys chuckled. "He told her to give herself a chance and take the lemon out of her cunt to make room for him. The nursing staff shook in hysterics and struggled to keep a straight face. The poor bastard took one bullet in the shoulder and the other narrowly missed a lung. It takes more than a nigger's pea shooter to put old Tank down for long."

Nate estimated the time by the sun to be about two thirty, enough time to go home and change and give Monique a ride if she needed it. He buzzed her on his cell phone. Her next client was booked for three p.m. at the Grand Hotel. No time to go home. He stopped off at the local megastore and bought a corporate blue business shirt, and changed out of his tatty black T-shirt in the car – his jeans were OK; faded but tidy.

He collected Monique at two forty-eight going by the insurance clock. She looked like real hormone tucker in jeans and a white T.

She gave him a gentle kiss on the cheek. "I've got a kinky one this arvo – he's a judge and he likes to be humiliated." A light twinkled in her eyes, as though she'd discovered the vaccine for penile arrogance. She whispered to him in a childish conspiratorial way. "Come with me."

He shrugged. "OK. Why not?"

She gave him directions. He pulled the VW up in front of an austere concrete-walled building with a façade of mock columns and capitals. They ventured inside – it looked like a school hall, and her high heels clip clopped on the hard polished wooden floor.

To Nate, there was something eerie about it.

Monique showed him to a broom cupboard from where he could watch the proceedings. He left the door open just wide enough to peep. She placed her briefcase on a side table.

An old, dapper man in white slacks and blue blazer arrived. He might have been en route to a bowls tournament. They disrobed without speaking. The old man was a gravity challenged mass of wrinkles, and age spots. They were both naked except for an apron each. The aprons were blue, white and square. The design included a triangular flap and three rosettes. Two tassels hung at the sides. The aprons were fastened with a snake clasp on the left side.

Their antics mesmerized him. The man bared his left

breast and kneeled on his right knee.

"What seek you?" Monique asked the judge.

"The light," he replied.

She blindfolded him, and led him out of an imaginary crypt and casket that was depicted on a cloth on the floor.

"What is your state?"

"Darkness," he replied.

Monique removed the hoodwink on the judge's head and led him out into the light.

"The lower degrees and the profane are tricked and deceived." He laughed.

"I know," she said. "You really worship Lucifer." He did not reply

. "We are integral in the plot for world domination." He smiled. "You may as well know as no one will believe you."

"What do you desire?"

"The FUCK!" He cowed at her feet. She lifted her foot. He leered up her pinny. "Ah the congenital wound."

She left the cold steel crescent moon of her stiletto on his naked buttocks: "For my sisters."

Nate's eyes popped.

The old boy writhed in painful ecstasy.

She said in a low voice, "You are now a freeman and eligible for the higher esoteric degrees."

Nate listened and watched, hoping to learn something. They pulled on white gloves, held their hands up to form two isosceles triangles. Monique took a velcro patch depicting the compass and square, and placed it on his and her aprons, over top of their genitals.

"The symbol of the heterosexual sex act," he said.

Nate couldn't believe his eyes. They began singing in unison, a tune somewhere between the melody of 'Bohemian Rhapsody' and 'Colonel Boogie'. "All good boys have tits and clits, penis bad, vagina good. That's the party line for the suckered plebs." They sang it three times.

"I wasn't sucked in for a minute," Monique said.

"I'll spell it out. The Square represents the female, passive, generative principle, the earth, and the baser, sensual nature; the Compass represents the male, active, generative principle, the sun/heavens, and the higher, spiritual nature. The vagina is the field of fertile soil; the penis sows the seed, man owns the field."

That was all news to Nate.

"You're a real charmer," Monique said.

The judge smiled like a politician who had inside knowledge. "So called good and evil are complementary. You can't have one without the other. We are beyond the fertility metaphor. Any form of sex is sacred and the penis rules."

Bizarre. Nate opened the door a bit.

"And what about the female penis, the clit," Monique said.

He didn't say a word.

She placed a blanket and her tools on the checkerboard

floor. "Jahbulon," she said.

Nate concentrated on them. The judge laid face down, buttocks elevated in a receptive position, moaning in anticipatory ravishment. Monique clapped on surgical gloves. She picked up his gavel. The handle was smoothed over the years from constant ruling, but still retained its classic phallic shape. She smothered it in Vaseline, held it by the head, which could have doubled as a steak tenderizer. And, as if to give an enema she said, "Lift up!" He did enough to expose the wrinkled target in the foul crevasse.

With one violent thrust she ravished him, handle deep. He screamed all the way to the hilt in an uninhibited primal way. "The lust of the goat is the bounty of God – William Blake," he said. She plunged him a few times and left him satiated, gavel in situ.

Unbelievable. This was definitely a first for Nate.

"Thank you, Lady Justice."

She removed it and took off her gloves. "That will be five hundred dollars," she said. "Would you like a receipt?"

"That won't be necessary," he said in a meek voice. He took his clothes from the floor and went to change in the bathroom.

She took the opportunity to get Nate away, and went back in to get her five hundred dollars.

She joined Nate in the car. She straightened her clothes and hair.

"What a weirdo," he said.

She smiled at him, sage-like. "One thing you learn in this business?"

"And what's that?"

"Not to judge."

They looked at each other and burst into laughter, off and on, all the way to the law courts. Nate found a park between a prison van and a stretch limo full of ethnic gang members waiting for their private helicopter to land. Nate and Monique got out of the car. She went off to get some retail therapy, which she said was better than sex, and he went to his four o'clock appointment.

Chapter Nineteen

Thrice is he armed that hath his quarrel just
And he but naked, though locked up in steel,
Whose conscience with injustice is corrupted.

– Shakespeare, *Henry V1*

TUESDAY, FOUR p.m. The floor-to-ceiling marble intimidated Nate. The mirrors twisted the perspective – his reflection was a barnacle gargoyle on a pristine marble wall of the law. It didn't do much for his shaky confidence.

A pretty young woman with dark eyes welcomed him and said, "You must be Mr W's four o'clock?" And bid him wait.

It occurred to him nothing escaped the shark teeth of reform except the ability to keep you in a constant state of humiliation: Mr V Fucking Important is too busy to see you right now. He's charging an overweight client flesh by the nanosecond. All our lines are busy … but we value your call … please hold while we serenade you with contempt. If you want to talk to a human being it is not possible. To speak to an industry trained parrot press B, an Android C, an inarticulate refugee D, a career politician E.

If you want to scream obscenities or throw a childish tantrum please ring our 0800 number; if it's an emergency, press hash or star, and we will send someone out in a white coat. Thank you.

He thumbed through a *Time* magazine and pretended to read an article about Iraq and Saddam Hussein while his mind did angst somersaults about what might happen, not in Iraq, but in Tom's office.

Tom Walters came in, introduced himself and ushered Nate into his inner sanctum. Nate smiled at the receptionist on the way past.

He was impressed by the files on the desk, in manila folders, tied with rubber bands. To him the office smelled of aged paper and young, fertile women. Tom, a huge grey-headed man with a bulbous red nose from a love affair with the bottle, was a dinosaur in an increasingly female profession, but women were wasted on him, Nate thought. Walter's affairs were the type you have with the mini bar, and the silver hip flask in the inside breast pocket.

Photos of his wife, kids and grandkids and racehorses abounded. His degrees hung on the wall behind his desk. Replica models of classic cars were displayed on a wall shelf: a Jaguar XK150 roadster, an MGTF and a Mercedes Gullwing. It was just another day in the tick tock world of Tom Walter LLD, so different to Nate's.

"Our Joce tells me you surf with Michael."

"Yes, sir," Nate heard himself say, brown-nosing it.

Tom picked up a new manila folder and opened it. "Well. As I've said to Michael, it's a healthy pastime – but you wouldn't want to make it a vocation. He needs to pull his socks up, for Joce's sake. Now, documents to sign." He indicated where. "I'll get Nicky in to witness."

Nate attempted a comprehensive read.

"Don't worry, standard stuff." Tom passed the documents to Nicky and she witnessed them with a lovely smile, leaving a trail of hormone-disturbing scent as she returned to reception.

Nate noted his monthly outgoings to Abe Solomon and the interest rate. A mortgage seemed to him like an employment contract – a legal parasite on his young life and labour, his flesh and blood wrapped in a death pledge, to feed the ever-hungry Archons and elites. What did Daryl say? A con/tract was a trick and a treatise and, by signing, you gave your consent to being totally ripped off to the conditions laid down.

Well if he wanted the house he didn't have a choice; that was how the system worked. But Abe was giving him real energy-backed cash, the product of work. That wasn't how the Archons, the dark Lords, and the elites wanted it. They would have preferred he went to a bank where they could create his mortgage out of thin air. He would actually borrow nothing, but a debt would be created for the amount of the mortgage. The only money involved was his: the money and interest he had to pay back. That was Daryl's take on it, anyway.

For the first time in a long while his mother's voice came to mind. Whenever he'd wanted some of the things other kids enjoyed, like a brand new bike, a surfboard, or a PlayStation, he'd always been given second-hand stuff, and when he'd complained his mum had said, "Look at everything we've done for you, and you're still ungrateful. You must be plain bad seed."

And he'd answered his mother back, real smart-ass: "You did say, 'It's a wise child that knows its own father.'" She was furious.

When he'd gone back into the room her eyes had been moist with tears. "I've been peeling onions," she'd said. Then he'd tried to jolly her up.

Tom showed Nate out with a hand on his shoulder. "I look forward to our dealings in the future, Mr Crust. No doubt this is only the beginning of our relationship and your housing portfolio." He waved a document at Nate. "Copy of the mortgage. Our account will be sent out within the week. It's been a pleasure. I'll see you to the door."

"Thank you, Mr Walter."

"Call me Tom. Any problems of a legal nature, don't hesitate." He shook Nate's hand and grabbed his arm, like a politician on TV.

Francois Louveteau and Melanie strode out of another office in animated exchange. They caught up with Nate and Tom at reception. Francois said to Nate, "Excuse me, monsieur, I never forget a face. Do I not know you?"

"I believe," said Nate, trying to be sophisticated, "we have a friend in common."

"Ah monsieur, could that possibly be?"

"Charlotte Robins?"

"Of course, of course, how silly. Is good to meet you again …?

"Nate."

"Yes! Of course, monsieur," Nate said."

"Must rush, meeting at five." He turned to Melanie. "All the best, mademoiselle. Keep me informed. Is good to see you, Nate."

"Small world, Mr Crust," Tom said. "Small world indeed."

Nate waited for Melanie, who gossiped with the receptionist. He overheard Walter saying to Louveteau, "Right, he's a straight up and down sort of guy." He felt invincible. Nobody had ever called him Mr Crust, except old dotty Dotrice, his year eleven science teacher, when he caught him trying to light Fatty Forsythe's farts with a Bunsen burner – but straight up and down?

Louveteau gravitated to the photocopy machine to talk with Jason. Nate heard him say there would be a special court hearing for Axe, president of the Culture Assassins, in the morning. He expected him to get bail, set high – 500 grams was quite a large amount of cocaine.

Melanie, having finally exhausted the scandal, walked to the car with Nate, and he offered her a ride.

She accepted. "The cops busted me," she said. "I asked a plainclothes copper if he wanted a hand job. Don't say anything to anyone."

"Mum's the word." He fluffed her hair flirtatiously.

They nattered as they thumped up the stairs and approached Felines reception desk.

"Just in time." Queenie marched with them to the staff room. Nate was two hours early. Four other working girls were there. He knew them as Kelly, short blond and buxom; Francesca, tall thin and brunette; Ginger, freckly and boyish; Tara dark eyed and sultry. The air was a blend of scent, powder and the residue of snuffed-out cigarettes that stung his eyes. They slouched on any available seat. Wolf and Queenie remained standing; Wolf had his back to reception and Queenie leant on the bench.

The room went quiet as Wolf spoke. "I think you know why we're here – you've heard about the attack on the Dog headquarters. This is just a caution. We expect further gang attacks on our operations. These events have focused the cops on us and they're goin' all out to bust us. Don't give 'em any opportunities … Queenie."

Wolf and Queenie changed places.

"Just to remind you all," said Queenie. "The customer must always approach you for sex. Now a side issue – from tonight, it will be Felines' policy to charge twenty dollars per shift for the rental of rooms. Out call girls will be charged twenty per trip for the use of our taxi.

Our commissions are going up to twenty-five per cent .I know this won't be a popular measure …' she eyed the girls individually, "but I'm sure the cost can be passed on to clients. That is all. To your stations."

The meeting disbanded.

Wolf took Nate aside. "How's that Kraut bucket of yours?"

"It goes."

"Can you fit four in it?"

"Sure, with room to spare."

"I've got a meeting at five. And I need you to drop off Kelly and Francesca, at the town hall conference centre. They're gonna put a dyke show on for the local Chamber of Commerce. Don't worry about the fee, it's taken care of."

"Sweet."

"One other thing."

"Yeah?"

Wolf walked Nate out into the lounge. It was empty. The TV blared. Maya, the Eurasian, manned the desk. He lowered his tone. "There's a meth lab I want you to pick some gear up from. They know about you. They used to supply the CA."

"Sweet."

"Remember, no heroics! Any sign of trouble – at all – lock yourself in your car and get the fuck away, if you can. If not, get a call through and I'll have the boys there. Shouldn't come to that."

"Thanks. That makes me feel a lot better." Nate got drawn into the porno on the TV.

Wolf rounded the two girls up and next thing they were kicking them out at the conference centre. Wolf's parting shot: "If you can't put your heart into it, make it believable. Remember, they're paying good money to see a couple of dinkum dykes." They gave him a look that said they'd like to stick something into him, and it wouldn't be hard and warm. Wolf didn't pick up on their attitude, but Nate did – he wasn't bad at reading atmospheres.

He let Wolf out at the Black Swan Hotel on the riverbank. The sun was about five thirty, and the streets were busy with commuters finishing work for the day. Francois Louveteau waited in the doorway, standing erect like a tin soldier left behind by some schoolboy who dreamed of the higher-tech theatre of polished warheads and guided missiles. Nate watched them shake hands in the doorway, but the traffic moved him out of sight.

"Monsieur Wolf." Louveteau held out his hand. "Is good to meet you again."

"Likewise," Wolf said. "C'mon." The two men threaded their way through the restaurant to the riverside and sat at a small aluminium table, watching the flotsam and jetsam of leaves, lunch papers, ducks and Coca Cola bottles flow past.

"A lot of water, monsieur, under the bridge since

last we meet."

"For sure," Wolf said. There was something about this guy he didn't trust.

"Would you reconsider, monsieur, perhaps the purchase of five hundred grams of cocaine?"

Wolf looked into the air as he pondered the prospect. He broke the silence. "Tell you what – forty-five grand, if the quality's OK." Louveteau extended his hand.

"As you say, monsieur, you have a deal … with reluctance on my part."

"Don't come the old Gallic soldier with me." Wolf smiled. He knew he'd still make a hefty profit.

"Ah, but the risks, monsieur, for me, they are capital risks."

"For sure."

"If ever proven, monsieur, I am counsel and purveyor of the CA's unfortunate demise. I should never see the light of day again."

The bizarre situation appealed to Wolf's humour. He smiled a wry smile and sat up in his chair. "If you weren't so clever and devious."

"Thank you for your confidence, monsieur."

Wolf leant his elbows on the table. "Slip me a sample of the coke," he said. "And we'll finalize the business from there. I'll send my driver to pick it up."

"Ah, yes, Nate. We are acquainted – the chauffeur of the charming *fille de joi*."

"Yeah, the pilot of the whore's taxi. You surprise me,

dude, a man of your … classical tastes, going for a little slapper like Monique."

"Oh I am not, monsieur. But she is intriguing bait, to catch a juicier fillet that might be sautéed into an exquisite piece of queer fish."

He wished Louveteau would stick to plain language. "Makes sense … I guess"

"I wish to consolidate my business dealings with you, monsieur. I have a client with a considerable amount of real estate. He owns an old villa on half an acre of wasteland." He dangled the key in front of Wolf. "You can have possession right now, rent-free – ideal for the new headquarters."

"What's the catch?" said Wolf, knowing he could really use new premises.

"No catch, monsieur, if you can ensure the neighbourhood becomes an undesirable place to live. The area could be devalued and redeveloped for a song."

Wolf took the key with glee. Disturbing the locals – too easy. "You have a deal, Monsieur Louveteau." He managed to get his tongue around the Frenchman's name.

"And, I trust, a satisfactory business relationship, monsieur."

They shook hands. But Louveteau wasn't quite finished. "I am in the business of law, monsieur, and every day the most heinous murders, sex crimes, and robberies go undetected because they are committed by those above the law, and their fellows cover for them. Prison is for stupid scapegoats, fall guys of the initiated."

"I'm aware of the situation," said Wolf. But he couldn't help thinking how this was all a bit out of left field.

Louveteau continued. "I learnt early, justice is for fools. It is injustice, the self-interest of those that succeed – the strong – you and I monsieur, those not controlled by the moral coercion of the weak. We vanquish them every time. I have no respect for the law or its hypocritical practitioners." Louveteau left the restaurant.

That guy's wacko, thought Wolf. *The same guy who has the word LAWMAN on his number plate.* Just pure deceit, he guessed. He remained seated and dialled Nate.

Nate sat in the car observing the movements outside of the lab – nothing to report at this stage. The lab was hidden away on an unusually wide back street over the road from the rear entrance of a major department store and a multilevel car park. On the lab side of the street the buildings were two level and brick, used for small automotive businesses up the East End of the street, and ramshackle flats on the second level.

He parked in the West. A French restaurant filled the ground floor, with quality flats on top. The lab was up an alley behind the restaurant, where any suspicious running of water was likely to be associated with the restaurant kitchen. He stayed out of sight long enough to be persuaded it might be safe to approach. He ran into the building and out again, in seconds, with the parcel of methamphetamines under his arm. The guy in the lab was a senior chemistry student trying to pay his student fees off quick.

Nate got back in the car, but something in his bones said, *wait*. He went to start the car when an old yellow and grey premiered Chevy Impala sedan full of Culture Assassins screeched into his end of the street. He ducked, and they turned into the alley. Four big guys got out of the car carrying baseball bats and were intent on getting inside. But Nate was close enough to gag from their noxious car exhaust. He would get away before they came out again.

As soon as the last CA guys disappeared through the lab door he gunned the car towards Felines – just in time. In his rear-view mirror he saw the CA guys come out on the pavement again. Dusk set in. He turned his car lights on. He braked hard and missed a black cat by seconds. He was out of the clutches of the CA for now. He weaved through the labyrinth of back streets into Felines' lockup garage.. He made his way up the stairs.

Queenie's eyes were wide. "What's up?" she said.

"Had to get away before the CA guys before they saw me.

"OK still pick-ups for Tara and Ginger," Queenie said.

"Not this fucking taxi."

"You poor guy," said Queenie. "Ring Wolf and let him know what happened."

Nate went into one of the vacant rooms and called Wolf.

"You did the right thing," Wolf said. "Take the rest of the night off. I'll send some guys around later."

Nate was relieved and lay back on the plastic-topped mattress in a spartan room with a cabinet, a chair and a rarely used massage table. He must have dozed off because when he awoke, Queenie was stroking his forehead.

"It could have been quite different tonight, honey." She smoothed his brow.

"Yeah, the pricks could've wasted me. If they spotted me."

"Take your shirt off, roll over and I'll make you feel better." Her hands and fingers kneaded his sinewy shoulders and knobby spine all the way to the junction of his buttocks.

He almost purred. "That feels good."

"You know – I had a son about your age once." She started moving her hands all the way up to the nape of his neck and out to the extremes of his shoulders.

"A son?"

"He died of meningitis." She chopped her hands up and down in no particular pattern over his back.

I'm real sorry to hear that ... Ooh! That's nice."

"He would have been twenty-five. A bright boy – studied to be an engineer. Still makes me cry, it was so sudden."

"That's terrible."

"No, it's life, death and the futility of it. He caught it off a drink bottle. You can put your shirt back on now."

He looked at Queenie and didn't see the snake tattoo on her voluptuous breasts. Her musk perfume and the way her pantsuit clung to the contours of her crotch didn't stir him. He only saw a concerned and loving mother nurturing him. Why did he feel he committed the foulest of incestuous crimes? He blushed to the quick of his soul, or whatever made him feel these things. Why did he have such fine feelings for a woman who revelled in subjecting Monique to such vile atrocities? It didn't make sense. It made him wonder why he didn't accept Goose's offer of a job – at least his mother would have approved.

Chapter Twenty

*… And 'mid this tumult Kubla heard from far
Ancestral voices prophesying war!*

– ST Coleridge, *Kubla Khan*

"EUROPEAN BUYING trips are off in the interim because last month's sales have plummeted and I can't spare you off the lot, Gary."

"I see." Goose cleared his throat.

Trenton leaned on the counter in the showroom. "We've tried all sorts of radio advertising campaigns with balloons and hoopla, thousands slashed off here, no deposit there, and twelve months or more interest free – to no avail. Money's short. Our customers are paying their tax."

"Surely it's only a temporary downturn," Goose said. He was going to stay positive. He required a business strategy – to deliver quality European cars at a better price than his competitors. It didn't help to let your competition know you struggled. He believed Trenton's advertising campaigns may as well have shouted their economic position from the rooftops. He always put on a prosperous face to customers and said business was brisk, whatever the reality. So when Lance and Isabelle pulled up in her 2 CV he played it very casual. He let them approach him. Shame about Isabelle's sexual preferences, but he kidded himself the cure for her condition hardened in his pants.

Lance went through a mock introduction. "Allow me to introduce the charming and diabolical Beatrice – Joanna, darling, the proverbial 'deeds creature' from the play."

"Charmed," said Goose. He was embarrassed in front of Trenton.

"We, or should I say *I*, darling, am here to test drive the automobile."

"I'll leave you in capable hands," Trenton said. He returned to his office.

"Good luck." Isabelle winked at Lance. "Ring if you want a ride home."

"I hope, darling, I'll be traveling home in Bavarian Motor Works style."

Goose snatched a bunch of keys down from the rack behind him. Isabelle took off in the 2 CV like a rough-tuned motorcycle, in a blue-black pool of smoke. Goose knew enough about cars to suspect the rings might be worn or the fuel mixture too rich, but that was a problem for her.

Goose rattled the keys. "We'll be alright for a while. Tracy, the new girl's, holding things."

Lance laughed. "You wish, darling."

Goose didn't see the funny side. "You drive."

"Where?"

"Up to the lookout."

They got in the car and buckled up their seat belts. The sun shone bright in Goose's eyes, and was about one o'clock in the sky. Below, surfers floated like black beans on a rolling azure sea. The car ate the switchbacks to the lookout in several deep-throated bites. Lance turned into the car park. It seemed to Goose the view went on forever, to the Alps in the West, and the Colossus Mountains in the north and down to the undulating ocean below.

"Breath-taking view, darling," Lance said.

Goose tried to keep Lance focused. "You won't get a better car for the money, and kilometres."

"What about at Euros, darling?"

"The kilometres are likely to be higher and the models are older."

"Let's go for a walk." Lance checked his appearance in the sun visor mirror and loaded the suggestion with innuendo. "Maybe I can be persuaded to buy."

"I thought you'd already decided."

"Not quite. Let's go."

Lance and Goose ambled through a rainbow dell of rhododendrons and azaleas while two magpies pogoed across their path to the high-pitched singing of cicadas.

"I used to come here when I was a kid," said Goose.

They followed a rut, little more than a sheep or goat

track, worn into the side of the headland. Gum trees interspersed the path and the back yards of houses cantilevered over the bluffs.

The sun was burning Goose's bare arms and face. The waft of gum nuts mingled with cooking smells filtering through the trees and shrubs, along with sieved ozone.

The men trudged out of the vegetation; there was a sheer drop to the sea a hundred metres below. The salt wind was mild and tousled their hair. The bank above rose at a steep angle skyward. The Pacific Ocean slapped and tickled the bottom of the cliffs, whooshing and sighing like a maiden aunt who dropped her stitches to knit her clitoris.

Lance pushed a ngaio bush aside and revealed a huge cavern. "I'd wager you didn't know this cave existed, darling."

"Somebody did bring me here, once, but I could never find it again."

"Let me guess. One Monsieur Louveteau?"

"Yes!" As they entered the cave, the strangest feeling came over Goose. Thousands of years of civilization crumbled, and there was just him and Lance, the sky, the sea, a cave, conjuring the most basic human instincts in him.

"I'm so lonely." Lance held Goose. "So lonely."

Goose sloughed off all pretence and went with his primal urges.

Lance's audacious hands explored Goose, like a sex-starved nymphomaniac loosed from an iron maiden. He moulded his hands over Goose's penis, and searched for his nipples. Goose ripped at Lance's shirt, belt and trousers. Lance's hands moved inside Goose's clothes like he was shelling a pod of peas.

The two men lay naked in the cave, then Lance crouched on his hands and knees. Goose took a condom from his wallet and unravelled it onto his muscle-bound penis. He went to work on Lance like an oversexed pooch on the nearest leg, but more intimate than that.

The sunlight flickered through the ngaio and silhouetted their gyrating image on the wall by juxtaposition of light and shade. The wind whispered in the early autumn leaves:

> *A Writhing beast with two spines;*
> *Two hounds in ecstasy blind,*
> *Bay at the afternoon sun, and*
> *The ghost of yesterday's moon.*

They squealed, grunted and snorted, quivering pork in a trough of carrots and swedes.

"Hold on ... I'm coming." Goose thrust hard.

"Ooh! Ooh! I want your baby."

The momentum gathered in their loins.

Goose pushed harder and felt the firm flesh yield and the sphincter tighten like a suction pump. "Take that ... you bloody ... faggot!" Goose sneered, with extra penile thrust. They orgasmed together, the same rhythm, and the same muscle intensity.

"Ooh, daddy, daddy," squeaked Lance.

"Don't call me that … you … misfit,' said Goose. He was ambivalent and shamed, yet he enjoyed the surrender to his basest desires. He puffed and thrust harder, feeling in control with his masculinity intact. "Take that, and that." With a series of depraved lunges, he projected any guilt he may have had onto Lance.

"You low life … pillow biter."

Goose spurred himself on to more feverish rummaging and with little warning, enveloped by an intensity of orgasm he had never experienced. "Ahahahah! Ahahaha!"

Goose exploded inside Lance and Lance erupted simultaneously with such force.

Goose withdrew and Lance lay fulfilled and spent in a post-coital, foetal position. And Goose knew there was no faking of orgasm here, as the whiff of sex and the ocean wafted past his nose.

"Get dressed." He threw Lance's clothes at him.

The only words spoken on the way back to the car came from Lance. "Did you know, darling …" Lance batted his eyes in Goose's direction. "Some races believe the penis is made for the anus?"

Goose ignored him, contempt on his face. He waited till they got back to the car to do his collar and tie up. He pulled the passenger visor down and knotted his tie in the mirror. He handed Lance the keys. "You're driving, flower."

"I'm flying, darling," Lance said. He took the keys.

"You'll be fucking flying if this gets out."

"Wow," Tracy said as they returned. "You look like you've been through a gorse bush backwards."

"A ngaio tree actually," said Lance with a smirk.

"Car trouble." Goose blushed red. "We had to get under the car." His bald head glistened with beads of sweat. "It's fixed now," he said, trying to take the heat off the situation. He hoped to hell he wasn't going to have ongoing trouble with Lance using what had happened for leverage. "Anything to report?" Goose asked Tracy.

"Some interest in the navy blue Range Rover, and somebody called Nate wants you to call him."

"By the way, darling," Lance, interjected. "I'll take the car."

Tracy looked quizzically at them, cute as a dark-eyed puppy with its head to one side.

While Goose and Lance had been "fixing the car," thrashing away in the cave with bodies and personal demons, something else had been going on.

Nate and his flatmates were watching TV, with shocked expressions. The Americans and their allies had crossed the Kuwaiti border to attack the Iraqi dictator, Saddam Hussein.

"What bullshit," Nate said.

"Yeah," Daryl agreed. "They want to free the people of Iraq in contravention of international law, and eventually force them into an acceptance of neoliberal democracy. The people in Pluto's Republic and the world are aware of this, and they hunker down with drinks and nibbles to celebrate the democratic freedom to watch the slaughter of innocent Iraqis in the privacy of their own living rooms as if it were a game of football."

"They have to protect us from the Islamic extremists," said Tiff. "This could be the start of Armageddon."

"No need for panic, it's a playground scrap over oil," said Daryl. "Some thought Nero and Caligula were the Anti-Christ and the fires of Rome a sign of the end." He wriggled in his seat. "As it happens, Armageddon is the name of an electronic gamesters' convention and *Big Brother* is a reality TV show." He laughed cynically. "To think people wasted all that paranoia."

All three were squeezed onto the couch to watch as the allied troops invaded the Southern borders of Iraq. "It's certainly a sign of the end times," Tiff said.

"The Archons would have sucked it up," Nate said.

They watched a montage of the build-up of the American military machine, Leviathan aircraft carriers laden with fighter planes, monstrous battalions of tanks with sophisticated systems to repel and alert against chemical or biological weapons.

"God's on their side," Tiff said.

Nate bet her God would have American citizenship

and hold an American passport.

She leaned forward on the couch in readiness to mount the pulpit. In her best prophetic voice, she said, "In the end times the Anti-Christ, Mr 666, a Jew, will head the EU and will bring peace to the Middle East in a seven-year covenant with Israel, the EU –" her blue eyes gleamed, "– and probably with Arabs and Palestinians."

Daryl smiled. "Oh really?" he said. He crossed one leg over the other.

"He will revive Jewish sacrificial worship." She gasped for breath and repositioned her headscarf. "The False Prophet, leader of the World Church and Satan, exercise power over the EU leader and form a satanic trinity."

"Old news, even in Grandma's day," Nate said.

"Mumbo jumbo, upside down," Daryl said.

"The truth," Tiff went on. "After three-and-a-half years the EU leader, Anti-Christ, breaks the covenant and stops the revived sacrificial Jewish religion. The False Prophet builds a life-like image to the EU leader; it speaks and rules from the temple."

"Sought'a like a US president," Nate said. He was getting tired of sitting and felt the need to do something physical.

Tiff eyed him in disgust and continued. "This is not a matter for levity. At the beginning of the Great Tribulation everyone will be forced to worship the image of the EU leader, the Anti-Christ, and take the mark of the beast."

Daryl half-watched the military invasion on TV, and interjected. "A continuing dogma to take your mind off the fact your hard-earned tax dollar finances war and the slaughter of innocents."

"Society will be cashless by this time," Tiff added as an aside. "Those that don't worship the image or take the mark of the beast on their right hand or forehead will be unable to buy and sell. If they refuse to take the mark they will be hunted down by the secret police and put to death."

Daryl's face coloured up. "Well I won't be kowtowing to a fucking statue. But if you keep up the propaganda, who knows what will happen to everybody else?"

Nate was feeling a bit squashed up on the couch between the other two. He had to marvel at how millions of people had believed this sort of thing for such a long time. And he reckoned Daryl wasn't far wrong on his ideas about the power of words.

Tiff couldn't be stopped. "The Jews are tricked. They think the False Prophet is Elijah because he calls fire down from heaven and the EU leader is the anti-Christ because he miraculously comes back to life from a deadly wound."

Daryl's eyes glassed over. "If you keep banging on it'll become a self-fulfilling prophecy."

The phone rang in the hallway and Nate answered it. Goose had returned his call.

"What about the job?"

"We took on a new girl, Tracy. Sorry, there was nothing I could do."

"The house sale went through."

"I wish I did have a job – you sound much more positive."

Daryl overheard Nate's end of the conversation and yelled out. "You'll never get a job at Superior Imports – you're the wrong fucking sex."

Nate hung up the phone and it rang again straight away.

It was Wolf. "Pick up a parcel from Louveteau," he said. "Take it home and put it somewhere safe and tell nobody. The court bailed Axe – expect trouble from the CAs."

Nate still wasn't a patched member of the gang, so he didn't want to refuse, but he was risking everything, not only his house, but also his liberty. He needed to look again at what his freedom meant to him and how to keep it.

Tiff shouted out to Nate: "If you're going into work, can you take me?" She got off early Wednesdays to do hospital visits.

"Sure!" he yelled back. "Give me a mo' to change."

He returned to hear Tiff and Daryl finish their theological discussion and to watch innocent people dying horrible deaths so others could one day live in a so-called free country. He sat back down on the couch and listened.

"This is where your theories come in," Tiff said to Daryl. "The international bankers, the flunkies of the Anti-Christ and the False Prophet form a new Roman Empire, a world government that controls international trade." Tiff got up from her seat and snatched her handbag off the table in readiness for her trip to town. "This period ends in the real battle of Armageddon and Christ's return to the Mount of Olives to execute judgement."

"We are headed for world government, nothing surer," said Daryl, "but I think it's based on a secular love of money and power, more than spiritual depravity and deceit, maybe the same thing." He laughed. "The Archons and elites are having a real banquet on us. It's nothing personal – like the Mafia says, it's just business."

"Yeah," Nate said. "Money rules."

"I've got to go," Tiff said, "but the question is Daryl or Nate – will you join our Lord in the air with the born-again believers, just prior to the Great Tribulation, or will you suffer its horrors?"

They all leaned back in the couch.

That sort of scared Nate. He'd always joked about these things before, but he guessed that was the intention of Bible bashers: preaching a story of love but frightening the hell out of you in the same breath if you didn't comply. He wanted nothing to do with that good cop bad cop thing.

"Well, maybe I can help you all focus on the reality

under your noses," Daryl said. "Just another perspective from Jordan Maxwell."

"I'm all ears," Nate said, sitting forward on the couch.

"I'm a bit sick of these conspiracies," said Tiff. "Hope it's short."

"It's quite brief," said Daryl.

"I've really got to go," Tiff said.

"Listen," Daryl said. "Word magic is used to trick you into a parasitic game called commerce, which also was an old word for sex. It starts when your mother gives birth to you. When a ship is docked workers unload the cargo."

"What's that got to do with anything?" Nate said. He was eager to get up and move. He stretched his legs out; that helped a bit.

"I wondered that too," Tiff said.

Daryl cleared his throat. "A ship is also a vessel, and when in dock it is a berthed vessel – similar to the word birthed." He sat forward in his chair and coughed. "When a product is unloaded from the dock it goes through a berthing process, the product goes from vessel-stroke-ship onto the dock." He sat up. "This comes under admiralty maritime law, because we are ninety per cent water, the international law of water or cash flow, money and banking; unlike law of the land, which is all about local culture, which involves courts, lawyers who wield the racquets hitting the rhetorical ball back and forth. The judge-stroke-referee sits on a bench-stroke-bank in Latin."

"I feel the punchline's coming," Tiff said. She sat up erect on the couch.

"So it is all literally a fucking game," Nate said.

"Yup," Daryl said, "When a woman's giving birth she's delivering a baby like delivering a product off a ship: the mothership. The product is a baby and the ship the woman's body. So you become a MANUFACTURED product and they make money selling you on the stock market."

"Far out," Nate said. He was really quite blown away by this. What made it seem to ring true was that everybody at some time had heard the state being referred to as *The Ship of State*. It had to have some truth in it. But he reckoned if the average Joe heard this, they'd probably refer to it as just another paranoid conspiracy theory – in other words, bullshit. "I want to hear more," he said.

"Not sure if I do," said Tiff. "We are baptised in water and God gives us living water."

"Well there goes the water motif again." Daryl smirked. "I forgot to say, all churches come under the law of water. By the umbilical cord you were connected to the mother ship, at the naval. You had to travel through her birth canal, which is like a river, a flow of cash, with banks on both sides."

"A real mind blower," Nate said. He stood up, ready to go. It was certainly a different spin on things; words did seem to be a kind of magic and a code. He stroked the tuft on his chin, deep in thought. But this was pretty far out.

"Don't go just yet," Daryl said. "This is key – your mother's waters broke; you were birthed by a dock-tor. He delivers the baby and turns it into a product to be sold at profit; your birth certificate is a certificate of manifest, also a death certificate, you are owned by the government."

Nate yawned and stretched in his seat, but really he was still mesmerised.

Daryl had a full head of steam and couldn't stop. "You are turned into slaves of citizen-stroke-ship." He took a deep breath. "The ship has a captain which is capitalism and the government is a corporation, which has a president and a vice president. Humans are enslaved and become an energy source, both for money and energy like batteries and are charged for the Archons and elite controllers, to feed off. Remember batteries have cells and that's where you will end up if you rock the boat too ferociously."

"Fascinating, but none of it will matter when the Lord comes back. I must go," Tiff said.

"Fucking amazing," Nate said. He wondered if he would ever think about things the same way again, although he'd always had inkling we were somehow controlled. The way he'd thought students had batteries in their backpacks and were controlled by negative and positive reinforcement. He realised now he was being intuitive – something women were supposed to be known for.

"It feeds into the other theories. Another point to remember is the Statue of Liberty's seven spikes are the symbol of seven oceans and continents, some say they mean the sun. But she stands in the harbour not on land. When a sailor pulls into port he is at liberty: free but under the law.

"We are good little guinea pigs, but I have my views," said Tiff.

Daryl chuckled. "Did you know, at no time in the history of the world have the people been free, except for in the American Wild West." His eyes got a bit watery. "I would like to believe somewhere there is a God that will revenge the people."

Nate and Tiff left Daryl to his bizarre thoughts.

They made their way out to the VW. Nate reckoned it was a good time to be driving into town, with most of the school traffic gone and the workers still on the treadmill. A weird feeling filled the air, blending with the longer shadows and autumn chill. Iraq was more than half a world away, but the war impacted subtly in the atmosphere and a certain sadness fell over the traffic, as if they were all going to the same funeral but nobody knew when or where. That's how it seemed to him.

He made a small detour to Wolf and Queenie's villa to pick up a briefcase full of money. He threw it on the back seat and explained to Tiff that Queenie had left it behind and it contained all her work stuff.

Tiff and Nate became so lost in the day's happenings that they were surprised when the Castlemere Public Hospital loomed in front of them. They must have been in the zone.

"Thanks for the ride," Tiff said. She stepped out of the car.

"Not a bad old rattle trap," replied Nate. "It goes." He leaned over to talk to her out the passenger window. "I dare you to go and see Tank."

"I might very well do that," Tiff said, "if I have time."

Nate sniggered to himself as he imagined their impact on one another. He selected first gear and the fifteen hundred air-cooled motor snorted off for its meet with Monsieur Louveteau. The instruction was not to visit Louveteau at his home but to wait for him at the Café Silicon, where Monique and he had enjoyed al fresco drinks once. He carried a plain black briefcase with forty-five stacks of hundred dollar bills wrapped in brown paper bags. Louveteau would tote a matching black briefcase. Inside the case, a hollow book called *Making Profit with Property* contained 500 grams of cocaine in an airtight plastic bag.

It made sense to him – a classic detective story switch. Pretend not to know each other, sit side by side, when the time comes to leave, each pick up the other's briefcase, the deal done. Even under surveillance cameras, nothing much to see.

Louveteau was waiting when he got there. The meet was over in a flash.

After the switch, Nate picked up his cell phone and punched in Wolf's number. "It went without a hitch. Meet me at mine."

By the time Nate arrived home, Wolf was standing chatting to Daryl at the front door. His chopper was parked out of sight from the road between the garage and the house. Daryl smoked a big fat joint.

Nate brought the briefcase over to Wolf.

"I explained to your pal here," Wolf said. "We want a bit of privacy on Pariah Dog business." He indicated the big joint. "That should entertain him for a while."

"Consider me out of town." Daryl inhaled his joint. "I suddenly got a new respect for motorcyclists." He blew smoke.

"I reckon," Nate said, "by the look of your eyeballs. Now go to your room – me and Wolf have got business."

"Whatever." They heard Daryl's door slam shut then the haunting guitar wail of Joe Satriani. Wolf took the briefcase inside and unpacked it on the kitchen table. They shut the door to the passage in case Daryl got nosey.

"Got any kitchen scales?"

Nate rummaged around under the sink and handed them to him.

Wolf weighed the bag. "Well, that appears to be OK,

if the scales are right. They're three grams over." He unzipped the bag and tasted the product. "Well I'll be fucked. The old French prick was straight up, pure, it hasn't been cut." Wolf scrimmaged around in the junk drawer under the bench and found what he was looking for – an old plastic vacuum-sealed bag, which served his purpose. "Hey Nate, have you got any talcum powder?"

"What sort of bum scuttler do you take me for?" Nate went into Tiff's room and came back with a talcum powder shaker from her dresser. He handed it to Wolf, who pulled the cap off and spread the talcum on the stainless steel bench, mixing it with the 250 grams of coke. He put it back into the bag; there were 250 grams of pure coke left.

He gave the small bag to Nate and told him to put it in a safe place. Nate took it into Tiff's room, removed the wooden spark guard with the floral transfer on it, and placed the bag up the chimney on a ledge. Then he replaced the fireguard.

Wolf held the plastic bag up, checked it for leaks and put it back inside the book. He placed the book back in the briefcase and shut it. "That's good enough for the nigger boy with the Trans Am."

"Not a bad profit." Nate smiled smugly.

"Yeah, he won't get any change from a hundred grand. Taxi me over to the Yank and there's an extra grand in it for you."

Nate didn't need to be asked twice.

"Keep the rest of the coke till I want it," said Wolf.

"Sure." Nate said. "Do you wanna hear something funny? Tiff, our Bible-banging flatmate, reckons she might visit Tank."

Wolf chuckled. "Imagine old Tank in her prissy pants. I'd love to be a crab on her frigid twat. It'd be more fun than an ear-biting prize fight or a girly mud wrestle."

Chapter Twenty-one

Tis an old saying, the devil lurks behind the cross.

– Cervantes, *Don Quixote*

FIVE P.M. Wednesday. Tank snoozed with the *Penthouse* centrefold open on his lap. Thankfully for Tiff, the magazine lay face – or more precisely, genitals – down.

She scrutinized the bandaged upper torso of the grotesque, bewhiskered man, removed the magazine from his hand and closed it on the bedside table. She was both repulsed and drawn to him. The world and his genes had certainly not been kind to him. He must have been badly hurt along the way, and all he wanted to do now was take what he could for himself and lash out at everybody else to make them feel his pain. But he'd found a temporary refuge with the Pariah Dogs, who accepted him for who he was. They were probably the nearest thing to family he'd ever had.

Tank stirred, and his eyes gained focus. "Hey! What the fuck … did I ask you to take that? What are ya, a new breed a fuckin' Florence Nightingale, or what?"

She sat down beside the bed and faced Tank with her back to the window. He didn't look good.

He glared at her. "Well? Cat got ya fuckin' clit licker?'

She winced inside. "No, I'm not a nurse and I choose to ignore your depraved terminology." Tiff secured her headscarf. "But I am interested in your welfare – in the eternal sense."

Tank raised his eyebrows. "Speak English, for fuck's sake, woman!"

She hated the expletives. But underneath that rough exterior was a real human being she needed to connect with. "Do you find it absolutely necessary to speak in such obscene language?"

"It's an obscene fuck'en world lady! Some black motherfucker shot me twice, for nothing."

Tiff took a deep breath. "Well, the Good News is there is a way out. The world is this way because people have turned their backs on God and his commandments." She looked out of the window, and down, to the gardens and the river – multitudes of workers were homeward bound after another day at work.

"Ha fucking ha." Tank played with himself. "I've heard all this bullshit before, in the boys' home. No news is fuck'en good news. I already got my own religion – do what ya want but don't get caught."

That attitude would hardly make for a happy healthy human being. It was up to Tiff to try and socialise him to think of others, and stop acting in a selfish and predatory way. She was fully aware it was beyond her, but she would keep trying because he was a soul in distress. The best she could do was be kind to him and pray for him and let him know the truth.

A nurse glided by, slipped them a resentful smile and rattled the curtain round the bed of the patient opposite, who was having terrible trouble holding food down.

"God loves you, Tank, and he wants you to turn from your sins and seek forgiveness."

Tank wriggled in bed and hoisted himself up higher on his pillows. "What are you gonna tell me next? God so loved the world he gave his only begotten son to save them ... unlike my old man and woman, who gave me away to save them fuckin' selves."

"That's awful," said Tiff.

"They abandoned me to the cocksuckers at the orphanage to save them the hassle a' bringing me up. I was so lonely – so ugly. No one wanted to foster me."

"I'm so sorry," said Tiff.

He ignored her. "I didn't even appeal to the perverts." He sighed, resigned, looked around. "I fuckin' hate hospitals. I hate sick people. I hate that antiseptic STD clinic smell. I hate to watch flowers die in vases. And I hate nurses' uniforms."

Tiff tried to console him. "God won't reject you, Tank. God has convicted you right now."

"Fuck me, arsewise and sideways, please – the cops are the only bastards that have done that. The same motherfuckin' enforcers that nailed the so-called Son of God to the cross in the name of the law."

Tiff became insistent, her indignant feelings flushing her cheeks. "It is God's will that we respect our rulers and the law!"

"Fuck you, lady! Ya not getting my candy like I was some innocent fuckin' Sunday school kid. Get outta here and take your doormat dogma with you!"

She calmed a little, oddly placated. "I would like to visit you again."

"Don't bother. Your twat's healed up, sick with religion and I'm more sex offender than priest." He gave Tiff an inane look before she could answer. "I know … often the same thing." I've gotta get outta here and go work my revenge. I'm getting stir crazy."

Tiff squirmed uncomfortably in her chair. He was so hardened in the heart. "You are so rude and crude. Vengeance is mine saith the Lord. I will leave you some tracts. Remember, all have sinned and fall short of the glory of God. That is why it's imperative you invite the Lord Jesus Christ into your life and confess your sins so you can know God our heavenly Father and be saved."

"Hallelujah," Tank said. "Now give me back my girly magazine."

"You're so closed off to kindness," said Tiff. "You must not lust after those brazen hussies in those truly wicked magazines."

"Can't take the competition, eh sister? You wanna feel that." He held his crotch. "That's hard." She came closer, but not to inspect Tank's appendage. He leered at her.

"Have you ever had a real man? I only mind-fuck these glossy paper women 'cause I haven't got a real flesh and blood one. "

"St Paul says it's better to marry than to burn," she quipped.

"He meant burn with lust," fumed Tank.

"That's the devil talking," Tiff said in a smug, matter-of-fact way.

"The devil, yeah – anyone who disagrees with the Bible-study teacher."

From some latent feminine instinct and a fragment of inherent truth, Tiff caught a momentary glimpse of a heroic but frightened little boy lost, the essential Tank, and she melted like an ice block in the sun. She tried to dispatch the Sunday school marm from herself like a big time wrestler but she got caught up in the ropes. "I love you, Tank – as a sister in the Lord."

"Yahoo!" said Tank. "Chuck me your incestuous pants."

"You have a demon." Tiff said.

"Get real," he said.

"You must be born again."

"You got fuckin' shares in God Corp?"

There was silence between them. Tiff looked out the hospital window again. Some people seemed to be without hope.

Then Tank spoke. "You could be hot if it wasn't for the bible bashing – at the moment it's just the forbidden fruit thing. You dredge up more hard core images than a porno magazine. Forget wanting to save my fuckin' soul for brownie points with God. Why not show a little interest in my hornyness. I do have some self-esteem. Otherwise fuck off and let me get some sleep."

"Remember, Tank, God loves you." Tiff went to leave, but he called her back.

"The truth is I prefer them slutty and smelling of cheap perfume, mind-scrambled girls who know the score. The sex is better if their minds roam the universe while their bodies give up to me.

"You're disgraceful!" She held her hands over her ears. But she mustn't give up the challenge.

"Over the years I've learnt mad women fuck the best – next come women over childbearing age, they're so grateful. Ya know, I read in a medical book, in the prison library, a woman's twat is the last thing to shrivel up."

Tiff only heard the last part of the sentence. "You're a sick man."

"Ya know what, Tiff? Women are different but all the same. They don't want equality. They want to be superior. They know what men are like and wield their sex like a weapon to crucify them."

"Look, I'll have to go if you're going to continue with this women hating."

"I might almost be persuaded to believe in a God who created these – depraved, wanton scrubbers for my pleasure." He tried to snatch the magazine back off the table.

"You're too much. I'm sorry, Tank, but I owe it to the Lord not to put myself in the way of such a verbal cesspool. I hope your body and soul will heal soon." With that she walked out.

Tank said nothing, but in his mind he was high on sex. As soon as she left he let rip his fantasies. In his mind he tore her frock like a perforated sheet, to reveal a lacy black bra and flame red knickers, wayward strands of swollen black minge escaped under their elastic pinch. He pulled them transparently over her bulbous thing for maximum definition.

He yanked her bra and pants off. She let go an audible sigh, and he inserted a wedding finger and probed her silky insides. Sensual wanks stirred deep tingles in the pipes of his penis. Face grimaces gave in to the bliss of conjured sperm from spinal lairs.

He was coming. Could he ever get back the buzz of those first times, at the boy's home when he wanked himself silly or bullied another boy into doing it for him? The feelings of horror when he thought he'd used it all up. The first spouts and geysers from the wild cat seams of his balls could not be relived. A fleeting desire to recapture the intensity, when the sticky nectar of his loins orgasmed into sensual nowhere land. The scratch, the primal itch, the fucking pre-orgasmic tingle; the big bang!

He imagined the push of his head, being sucked back inside, a boiled egg in the neck of a matchstick heated milk bottle. He pumped big spurts of sperm, which cooled on his hand and brought him back to the desperate reality of a slimy wizened cock and a hard hospital cot, a prison bed. He wiped himself with his sheets and underclothes knowing he'd be out of there by the time the stains were discovered.

The violent retch, a baritone female voice and an antiseptic smell that stank out ward seven and mingled with the cup, saucer and spoon jiggle of the tea trolley pushed by two Polynesian ladies. It seemed a long time since he had heard such infectious laughter, the swarthy peels of liberty bells.

"Tea or coffee?" the larger one asked.

"Coffee, milk two sugars," Tank said. And it made him feel good.

He should have known it wouldn't last. Inspector Waldron wandered into the ward. "Feeling better Mr Conway?"

"Huh!" said Tank. What a stupid question.

Waldron sat down where Tiff had been. He looked around the room. The ladies offered him a cup of tea, although he wasn't really entitled. He graciously accepted.

"Nice private room," said Waldron. He sipped his tea.

Tank pointed to the patient opposite. "Between vomiting bouts." He could do without this.

Waldron started to probe. "Still can't remember who shot you?"

"Nah! Too dark … those fuckers are so black." He wouldn't have told him if he knew.

Waldron took off his peaked cap and wiped his brow. "If you have a sudden rush of blood to the head …" He stated the obvious: "It's hot in here."

"Hotter than a whore's twat on Father's Day."

"You always did have a unique turn of phrase, Mr Conway."

"Thank the guys on C Block." He was going to make sure he wasn't going back there.

Waldron looked out the window. "Bruce Tomahawk was released today, on bail."

"Axe?"

"I hope we've seen the last of this feuding." He got up to go. "Get better. Bell me if anything comes to mind."

"I will," said Tank. *No fucking way.*

The eight o'clock news crackled on the VW radio as Nate and Wolf turned into Wolverhampton St. They made a sweep in both directions, peered up side streets for suspicious vehicles. All was clear, but Nate felt something wasn't right. Emptiness hung in his stomach – the streets were too quiet.

They parked up behind a flat deck truck covered in slivers of hay in view of the drug house.

Wolf phoned the Yank to warn him. "It doesn't feel

right. I'll pick you up bottle of bourbon."

Nate and Wolf watched the black Trans Am reverse, with lumpy throb, onto the street, and with several carburettor stabs the big block fury settled to an even beat. The Yank straightened up and gunned it towards the first intersection in a belch of black smoke. The radio gave the time: 8.23p.m. They waited.

Nate watched two detectives in a blue Holden reverse out of a house with a big for sale sign on it, on the opposite side of the road, and followed the Yank at a safe distance. He swung into the drive in bottle store.

The cops waited for the Yank to make his purchase, then stopped him and breathalysed him. He tested negative. The other cop checked the tyres, warrant, his license, but everything was correct.

Nate realized the cops had recognised the Yank but may not have a warrant to bust his house – or maybe they were waiting for one big bust to catch the suppliers. One thing was for sure – they'd need to be tricky from now on. With the cops hovering, Wolf dumped the coke under his feet.

They high-tailed it for Sunvale, making sure no cops followed. Nate glimpsed a distinctive yellow and grey Chevy Impala follow them around the roundabout when they turned off towards Sundale. "Fuck! He looked again. "The frigging CA guys."

Wolf swivelled to look out the back window. "CAs alright." He clutched the briefcase between his knees.

The throaty rumble of the big V8 was a hundred metres behind them and closing. Wolf unholstered his cell phone from his belt and dialled Shane. "Fuck, man we're in deep shit," he screamed down the phone. "The CAs are gonna fuck'en steamroller us. They're right up our arse! They're gonna ..." his voice quaked, "make sushi out of us."

The CAs gained on them and tried to ram into the back of the VW. One major hit to the engine would shut it down, and put them at the mercy of the CA who outnumbered them three to one. Nate swerved all over the road. Tyres screeched and there was a smell of burnt rubber. He veered out of the way. "Fucking crazies!" He slowed for the corner. "They're gonna ram us."

The CA slowed, followed the VW into the corner, swung hard left and shunted them around the corner. *Clunk! Eerch! Clunch! Eerch!*

Nate corrected the car and accelerated. "Fucking hell!" he said.

The VW snorted away with some minor rear fender and bumper damage. The dark eyes of the CA gleamed red when the light hit them, like possums stunned in the dark. Nate knew the VW couldn't take many more hits, a tiny bug against a big Chevy tank, and the constant rumble of the big V8 behind them.

"Fuck, they're gaining again," Nate said. He snatched a glimpse in the rear-view mirror.

Wolf looked around. "Floor it!"

The road stretched out for two or three kilometres, water on either side. Nate wound the car up to full throttle but it wasn't enough. The ugly faces of the CA closed in, in full *yahoo! wahoo!* war cry and a flail of baseball bats. The tide was in, and the sewage stench of sea lettuce hung heavy over the inlet.

The CA guys mocked, chanting, "Hedgehogs, Dead Dogs! Here doggie, doggie, doggie. No more pussy for dead doggie!"

The CA accelerated on the straight and drew up alongside. They jeered, waved fists and threw bottles and cans at the car. *Thunk! Oomph! Thwack!* A bottle smashed through Nate's window and gashed his forearm; blood spewed. He swabbed it with his T-shirt. A bottle cracked the back passenger window and more shattered on the road. *Thwack! !* A cocktail of beer, gasoline, and carbon dioxide mingled in the explosive air. Nate tensed up as the big Chevy side-swiped the VW: *Oomph! Thunk! Boomph!* The VW teetered out of control towards the estuary with a smashed-in driver's side. Axe raised his fist from the front passenger seat in a defiant salute. The CA jeered again, bellowing from the interior of the big V8: "We gonna do ya Dog fashion."

Nate and Wolf braced themselves to hit the water, but at the last moment Nate wrenched the wheel and to his relief they swung back onto the road. Now the leather-jacketed cyclops cavalry blazed down the highway, devouring the centreline. Thuds resounded in his head, and the Chev windscreen imploded to the metallic *thwack, crack* and *screech* of motorcycle chains whipping metal and glass – and flesh, if it got in the way. He was scared they were goners.

But then came the *whoop whooping* of the Pariahs, u-turning in hot pursuit of the Chevy like Crete Indians going in for scalps. He cheered as the Chevy hightailed it, hissing and scowling, a wounded jungle cat pursued by the low growl of jackals tearing its metal pelt with sharpened motorcycle chain. He winced as a single gunshot rang out from Finn McCool, the sergeant at arms; it blew out the front left-hand tyre of the Chev. Once courageous, now limping doomed, the Chevy tried to take the loop road that followed the waterline and re-joined the main road a few blocks down.

The last they saw of the Chevy, it was resting upside down in the incoming tide with the headlights shining eerily out into the rippling estuary. One splayed foot was visible. They didn't look for survivors.

This happened the day Baghdad fell to the allies and the war was over, for now – in Iraq.

Nate taxied Wolf to the Mitre to celebrate with the rest of the boys so they could lick their wounds and exaggerate the glorious victory of battle.

"I'll take care of the coke," Wolf said. As they got out of the car, he asked, "Are you gonna stay and party?"

"Nah I gotta go."

Wolf touched him on the shoulder. "You showed

balls today." Light flickered in his eyes and his mouth softened at the edges. "You brought back memories of Dean, my dead son."

It gave Nate a start. He'd never thought of Wolf as a father figure, until now.

Chapter Twenty-two

This life's dim windows of the soul
Distorts the heavens from pole to pole
And leads you to believe a lie
When you see with, not through, the eye.

– William Blake, *The Everlasting Gospel*

THURSDAY, EIGHT forty-four a.m. The music woke Nate from a deep stupor of gruesome dreams of mutilated flesh and blood-splashed cold steel. He couldn't help but hear the dark but benign tones of Pink Floyd's *The Wall* emanating from Daryl's room. He got up to tell him to turn it down, but when he burst through the door he could barely believe his senses. The room smelled of body odour, coagulated smoke and stale farts over heavy floral incense that stuck in his throat. Daryl sat in the middle of his unmade bed applying lipstick, cradling a full ashtray in his loins. His toenails were painted vermilion. He wore pyjama bottoms that gaped at the crotch, and was in a yoga position, going for chemical-induced Samadhi.

"I know everything," said Daryl, talking to himself. "Here is the news, read by P.C. Clare-Voyant: Today the free world choked on a GM Carrot," he raved. "Atomic fission is exact science and science is exactly flawed. Rutherford split the atom, but who can put it back together?"

He babbled on and turned the radio down. "I know everything, because formulas kill and life creates, and live is evil backwards. Dog is God, but the Cabalistic capitalists know that you don't? Spelling is hocus-pocus and hocus-pocus is mumbo jumbo with an agenda."

"What the hell are you on?" Nate said. It must have been a pretty potent cocktail.

Daryl carried on regardless. "The data and symbol system collapsed in nineteen sixty-two to the day and atomic hour. And they have looked to you, citizen, for direction ever since."

"What?" Nate said. He shook him by the shoulder.

"It all comes from the hitherto uncharted regions of my brain, stimulated by a recently updated class A drug washed down with rebel Irish whiskey and an LSD tab for insight."

"You're crazy, man."

"They say what I see and experience are hallucinations – chemical psychosis." He spoke louder. "Da Vinci's last laugh was in the *Mona Lisa*'s smile. I've orbited the inside of my head on a whirling toke of crystalline speed, and plunged into my pounding sheep offal heart, into my hands, my blood flow, the rivulets and deltas, of my scoria sponge lungs, the puff and blow of flying fish from their extinct crater of coral."

Nate tried to shut him up but he was on a roll.

"I've sailed on plumes of every poisonous inhumation of crystalline smoke and succumbed to the vertiginous spin and the galactic buzz in my microcosmic body ... merged with the molecular, atomic and sub atomic bundles of matter arranged from cosmic thought forms and quasars from thousands of years ago, now."

"That must be good shit," Nate said. And he pondered about the art that had been created under the influence of drugs, but even more, the disasters.

"I've navigated neutrinos through the ghostly etheric flux of the universe, which moves through matter and controls the flight of galaxies. I've witnessed gravity break free at creation from the cosmic egg, the Dragon Goddess and the reign of women. I've emerged from the primal cunt wet and bloody."

"I'll go out to the kitchen and get you a bottle of cold water – it might slowly bring you out of it."

When he got back, Daryl was still in full flight.

"The heavy breath of the licentious goat breathed down my neck and droopy hair tits uplifted in the intricate shadow curtain brassiere going down on me." He coughed.

"Here have a drink."

Daryl was just getting warmed up. "Later, I tried to unite a split atom and I melted in devouring waves of heat, which wasted everything in its path. I whiffed coffee while Nero fucked his mother. She bared her blue-veined tits and snorted like an old sow taken by a horny pig farmer in rag week. I felt the sword rip Boadicea's bodice and her heart bleed on English soil for Pakistani Poms and the EU in thoughts of Joan of Arc's virginity."

"Man you should write some of this down. Here, have a drink. You won't believe it in the morning."

Daryl took a long guzzle.

He went on. "Caligula saddled his horse and kissed me goodnight. Jews showered in crematoriums and listened to Brahms and Liszt serenaded by gypsies. Uncle Mengele preserved children's twin eyeballs in the interests of posterity and genetics."

"For real." Nate hoped he'd come down soon, but he wasn't showing any signs of it.

"Yup, and in a mushroom cloud a longhaired dude with nail holes in his feet and hands, wept. On the horizon an oriental army was on the march. An omelette of bald-headed men and women. Children floated in jars like fish on wires – I screamed in silence – hallucinations are real."

What the hell are you talking about?" Nate asked, panic in his voice. "What the fuck have you taken?"

Daryl answered. "I've watched the eternal plight of Purusha and Prakriti learnt at the knee of a dreamtime Brahmin aborigine …" He muttered insensibly, "I am not this body and I've lost my mind. Yah – Bul – On and on and on playing snakes and Jacob's ladder chasing the tail between my legs."

"I hope you're finished."

"Adolf Hitler's picture talks to me and warns me of the two men in suits parked across the road."

"That's nonsense." Nate needed to sober him up.

Daryl blurted: "Politicians and their fucking patsies: a deliberate policy to arse fuck the world with media-fed lies." He came down slow from his drugged state. "I dropped an acid tab Wolf gave …" He didn't get it all out.

"On top of that massive joint?"

"No ordinary joint, man, a special Wolf combo."

"No wonder you're off your face."

"Everything's crystal clear." Daryl chuckled.

Nate turned down the music and shut his door to let him sleep it off. He wandered into the kitchen and clicked the TV on. He caught the end of a news flash: *"Six members of the Culture Assassins ethnic gang last night were rescued from the Sunvale estuary. There were no serious injuries but their car was a write off. Their leader Axe, a.k.a. Bruce Tomahawk, was with them. He had been bailed on fifty thousand dollars on a series of drugs charges the same day. Police believe it was a retaliatory attack by the Pariah Dog Motorcycle Gang, who they recently skirmished with."* There was a brief shot of a reporter wrapped in a scarf while a tow truck winched the upside-down car into the bank.

"Fuck," Nate mouthed. He hoped the cops didn't visit. On a whim he rang Wolf at the pub. "Have you seen the TV?"

"Yes," he said. "Stay cool. See you tomorrow."

Tiff opened the front door and brushed past him while he talked on the phone. She nodded a greeting and strolled into the kitchen with a bag of groceries under her arm. He hung up and the phone immediately rang again. It was Mike.

"I've just seen the TV news, did you …?"

"Nah! Nothing to do with it."

"Anyway, not why I rang."

"What'd you want, then?" Nate said.

"It's Joce's birthday Saturday, and *The Changeling* opens. I've got two complimentary tickets."

"For me? Cool."

"Bring a friend."

"Extra cool." He loved the idea of an opportunity to show Monique off. "I'll have to OK it at work."

"Sure," said Mike. "I'm taking Joce to dinner first."

"Surfing Sunday?"

"I'll let you know on Saturday night."

"Sweet."

"When's the house warming?" Mike said, tongue in cheek. "Catch you later." He hung up.

Nate put the phone down, sauntered into the kitchen and slumped on the sofa.

"Any news?" said Tiff as she made a cup of tea.

"Sorting the weekend."

"I visited Tank, today."

"And you survived."

"He wasn't very receptive to God's word."

"What'd you expect? I'm off to bed."

"He gets out tomorrow."

"You make it sound like jail. Night."

"Good night, God Bless," Tiff said.

At 10.35a.m. the following day, a Friday, the Castlemere Public Hospital car park became a venue for a motorcycle rally. Nate left his car at the new HQ to drive Tank in the Falcon Ute, the Pariah Dog crash truck. Shane and Wolf wheeled Tank down in a chair. He could have walked, but it added to the drama of the situation. Nate watched it all unfold.

The Pariahs revelled in the attention from hospital workers and visitors. Tank was a bedraggled image of a broken down cowpoke, arm in sling and wearing long johns; a Pariah Dog logo on his back.

Wolf and Shane led the way. Their bikes formed the heads of two columns – crash truck behind. The entourage resembled a presidential motorcade, only scruffier. Bikes negotiated the late-morning traffic, and long beards, hair and cut-down denims were in free flow rebellion against the bright morning wind chill and oncoming traffic. Patches and Nazi helmets created a sinister air, and the rumble of big Harlies intimidated pedestrians and motorists alike. Nate could feel sounds in his solar plexus.

By the time he arrived at the HQ facing the road to

St Marie, the Mamas, under Queenie's direction, had arranged the food: barbecue sausages, steak, chicken, ham and bread. The men organized the alcohol and drugs. A mini tanker of draught beer, quarts of bourbon, bullets of marijuana and LSD tabs on tap. Experience showed the guys' temperaments to be bizarre and freaky enough to handle the hallucinogenic drugs well – but heroin, coke and speed weren't on the menu. He knew Wolf didn't supply his guys any hyper-addictive drugs, or anything to cause them to spin out and become psychotic. Any use of the needle or methamphetamines meant expulsion from the club; a user couldn't serve two masters – his brothers and his habit.

Nate recalled a time the press had documented a number of cases involving the pure forms of speed, which had led to senseless and bloody execution-type violence. This didn't influence Wolf in its sale, but why put the club at risk? 'P' got upgraded to a class A drug, a bit of a worry for pushers and manufacturers because penalties were now more severe if caught in possession. But their profit would increase with the extra risks.

He continued to observe a few Pariah dogs erecting a two-metre iron fence, topped by razor wire, around the perimeter; the house, a hundred-year-old villa, stock standard three bedrooms, two living rooms, kitchen and bathroom. It had ornate fireplaces, tin-pressed rose-covered ceilings, a wash house and copper out the back; veranda out the front like in a country song. The quarter acre grounds were a dusty wasteland of rusted out cars His nostrils were stung with a strong smell of barbecued food and dust. The Dogs used the front two living rooms and overflowed onto a low slung deck the guys had constructed. There was plenty of room out front for bikes, which the guys parked in a circle round the activities in the nature of a frontier wagon train.

He watched Tank swagger out of the house in tatty oil-stained denims, a brindled Pariah Dog let off the wowser's chain. His bloodshot bull terrier eyes searched the familiar faces. "OK." His stomach overhung his belt like Boss Hog's inbred second cousin. "Who's gonna get old Tank a beer?"

"Me." Nate snatched a jug and mug off the table on the deck, while the guys packed up to the tanker tighter than the pellets in a scattergun cartridge, jostling for a beer. They smoked, drank and gorged. The women slaved over a hot coal range in the kitchen. He passed Tank a jug and handle of beer. Then he strolled over to where Wolf was tinkering with one of the bikes and asked him for Saturday night off. Wolf's mouth was tight, but then he said, "OK, dude, but in future I wanna know a week ahead."

Nate breathed in relief and followed the action. The double corrugated iron gates opened and a young guy and woman drove into the yard in a *Castlemere News* car, to hostile biker faces. Tank approached the guy in the car. "Well I'll be fucked upside down and sideways, what have we here?"

The guy showed him a card and slid his sunglasses onto his cropped fair head. "Wendel Newton, *Castlemere News*. I'm here to see Wolf Ehrlinger. This here," he said, pointing to the thin girl beside him with a blond bob, "This is Bobby Carr, my photo journalist."

"Hey, over here," Tank shouted at Wolf who was fiddling with the carburettor on Valentino Crass's chopper. He ambled over and the newshounds got out of the car.

"You found us." Wolf seemed impressed by the height of the blond girl. She came up to his chin. She shadowed Wendel, who stood around medium height.

"Gerry, my gaffer, said you would welcome the opportunity to tell your side of the story about the latest clash with the Culture Assassins. Said you'd provide a little background to gang culture."

"Yeah, OK," Wolf said. "Tell your photographer to mingle and feel free to take some candid shots."

They all lazed on the front steps of the house, Nate listening and watching everything as Wolf tackled a barrage of questions from the reporter.

"First, up dude," said Wolf, speaking into Wendel's Dictaphone, "we're not a gang. We're a motorcycle club. A lot of the citizens don't realize this. We're a group of like-minded guys with a fanatical love of motorcycles. We're a fraternal brotherhood who socialize and go on road runs – no more sinister than Masons, the business round table, or the priesthood."

Nate grinned to himself. *Good answer.*

"So you say," said Wendel. "But let me quote what inspector Waldron of the Castlemere Police has said: *Gangs like Pariah Dog and Culture Assassins have become the main suppliers of methamphetamine throughout Pluto's Republic.*"

Wolf sighed, and his eyes turned dark and wild.

This guy was like a junkyard dog. Nate had to wonder how he would answer that.

"He would say that. As a group we're piss easy to scapegoat." Wolf stroked his bushy hair. "You fuck'en tell me, because individual members of a football club have been busted for drugs, is the whole club guilty?" He went on the offensive. "Listen, paper boy, is your scandal rag aware drugs are often supplied through more conservative channels, even government agencies? Not to mention grog."

The crafty old bastard. Nate sat impassively on the steps and stroked the fluff on his chin.

Newton ignored Wolf's question and pursued his line of questioning. "Is Pariah Dog in any way involved in violence or intimidation?"

Nate felt his body clench. How would he get out of that one?

Wolf went silent for a moment. "We do not initiate violence. Be sure we do respond if territorial space is violated, just as a nation state, as in the latest CA incident.

Citizens have nothing to fear."

Yee ha. You should have been a bloody politician. Nate chuckled to himself.

"I'm sure your neighbours will be encouraged to hear that. What about the latest fracas on the causeway with the CA?"

"Self defence."

"And ... accusations that you're involved in prostitution?"

"Well I won't deny that one; it's one of our core businesses."

Yeah well, Nate knew there was no point in denying fact.

"It's reported from some quarters that motorcycle gangs or clubs, like yourselves, participate in gang rapes. It's rumoured the CA attack on Pariah Dog was instigated by one of Felines' prostitutes out of revenge for a brutal gang rape on her." Newton poked the recorder under Wolf's nose.

Nate bit his tongue. This was getting a bit too close to the bone.

"I did wonder about one of our prostitutes, but none of them have the balls for it. It's just the CA playing mind games. I can't speak for other organisations, but wherever we go the gash comes drooling, open-legged," Wolf continued. "There's no need to rape. There's a difference between a rape and a block party – we always have the lady's consent. And anyway, rape is not a good vibe. And on top of that, who wants to risk ten years in the slammer?"

Wendel placed the recorder on the step between them and pulled his sunglasses over his eyes. "Is it true that before a prospect can become a full-patched Pariah Dog, it's necessary to commit a heinous crime or take the rap for another club member to destroy the option of returning to decent society?"

"Once you see through the bullshit, why go back? Eh, Nate?"

"That's right, Boss," Nate said, lying through his teeth.

"These dogs don't return to their vomit," Wolf said.

Nate said nothing.

"I've heard horror stories about women and male prospects being violated by the club mascot – often a dog."

"That's the product of twisted minds," Wolf said.

Nate watched the bikers striking poses for Bobby.

Wendel went on. "What about being required to have oral sex with a woman when she's having her period, or a woman with an STD, or having sex with a dead body and wearing trinkets stolen from the dead. And so it goes."

Nate's lips clenched tight. Even he hadn't heard of this, but who knew?

"No comment other than that we're an outlaw organization and aren't bound by the laws that bind ordinary citizens."

A good political answer. Nate relaxed.

"And can you enlarge on the accusation that you run a string of outcall girls?"

"I have no further comment. You are free to eat and drink and take photos. But there will be no more interview."

The girls saw the tall blond photographer and draped themselves provocatively over the bikes, showing maximum tit and crotch.

Pock Uggles boasted, "I slipped Bobby a leg-opener. I might slip her something else after the drugs have sweet-talked her. She'd have a real scoop when she came back down."

Wendel threw himself into the booze and the raunchy open sexuality with one eye on Bobby.

Nate noticed a tall willowy girl in sprayed-on jeans and cut-down denim jacket toying with him. "Hey, newspaper man. How'd ya like me to show ya some tricks to teach your girlfriend? Or is it a boyfriend in your case?"

Wendel's face turned bright red and the onlookers broke into hysterical laughter.

The crowd simmered and bubbled into one chemical consciousness. Nate's cell phone rang. "Hello, Monique. Pick you up from the Grand – now?"

Louveteau arrived with a thin stranger. Nate could see they'd better get the tall blond out quick to avert a tragedy. The leggy photographer swayed on her feet, reached for her bag on the table and knocked it over, spilling a mixture of filters, film capsules and photos. Wolf and Wendel raced over to help. Wolf picked up a heap of photos. By then Louveteau and friend were peering over his shoulder.

"The slut." Wolf had noticed Monique's distinctive shaggy blond hair, her right arm around Axe and the middle finger on her left hand aloft in one of the photos. Wolf slid it into his inside jacket pocket. "I'll have that."

Uh oh. Nate realised things might be coming to a sort of head. He would have to be bloody careful.

"Sorry to interrupt," said Louveteau. "This is Simon, your landlord."

"Later," Wolf said. "First I gotta chuck out a couple a lowlife scandal mongers."

"I've gotta a taxi job on, I have to go," said Nate.

The member for Harbour East put his Y-fronts back on and leaned back in his chair. Since their last meeting, Monique had determined not to do him, but something inside her reneged. And, like a depraved evangelist, she ministered to this weak and pathetic creature, a man, for want of a better word. Could Chambers read her mind?

"It's everyman's Achilles heel," said the Billy Bunter clone. "I'm talking about sex, of course. Did you know there are certain words verboten to use in the House, words that some might think tailor-made to describe politicians. I recall a few: traitor, liar, hypocrite, cunt and all their picturesque derivatives. Any of the forbidden words were more than explicit enough to define the character of any honourable member in the House of Pluto's Republic."

Monique wasn't surprised. His face was wistful and far away. Anyone who called themselves an honourable member or a worshipful master had to be the scum of the earth.

"I was too busy philandering and taking backhanders to care about screwing my country or my family." His hair was greyer and his skin more flaccid since last time Monique had seen him. His usual flabby face, jaundiced and strained, was a photocopy of Dorian Gray left out in the sun.

He said, "There's a good chance prostitution will be made legal."

She reapplied her lipstick and spat. "The price will plummet."

"Competition is the life blood of the free market," chanted Chambers.

"What if your sweet young daughter sold her peachy self to an overweight politician dribbling at the jowls?"

"That's a difficult one." Chambers blushed red. "Purely hypothetical. I don't envisage that happening. It's a practical matter to ensure sex workers are protected and pay tax."

Monique turned her back on him and whispered:

"You big fat waste of space." She counted to ten.

He checked his watch. "Appointment in fifteen minutes; there's concern around the country over questions of law and order and the emergence of gang sub cultures. The editor of the *Castlemere Press* and local body officials scheduled a meeting this afternoon to discuss how to deal with these issues."

"It's about time," Monique said.

"Yes, I want to initiate a nationwide exposé on local gangs, especially their involvement in the upsurge in methamphetamine use. We'll need to interview anybody with gang connections who could shed light on the secret elements of gang culture – discretion assured."

"Well, good luck with getting people to talk," Monique said.

"I'm sorry," he said to Monique. "I'm going to have to rush you out the door."

If only he knew how desperate she was to get out of there. She picked up her bag and made her way outside. She sat on an antique bench on the riverbank and Nate swung into an empty park nearby. Her hair glowed in the early afternoon sun. He flopped down beside her and soaked in the hot sunrays. She outlined what Chambers said about the gangs.

"Don't you volunteer anything," Nate said.

"I'd like to, for Kath." But she already had.

"Well, don't."

"It'll be alright," she said.

"I've just come from Wolf and a press interview." He looked directly into her pale blue eyes, changing tack. "I've got tickets to the theatre – tomorrow night. Want to come?"

A look of complete surprise came over her face. She held herself as though she wanted to pee, excited as a little girl invited to the circus. "I would absolutely love to." She bent towards him and gave him a short but tender kiss on the lips. "I've never been to that sort of theatre before," she said.

Chapter Twenty-three

*How sweetly she looks! Oh, but there's a wrinkle in
her brow as deep as philosophy.*

– Thomas Middleton and William Rowley, *The
Changeling*

SATURDAY NIGHT. The consensus of overheard opin-ion
showed Middleton and Rowley's classic *The Changeling*
lived up to the pre-show hype and press releases: "*A
whirlpool of depravity, sexual desire, butchery and death.*"

Nate and Monique stood in the foyer, studying the
theatre goers. He had spent the day in the surf and his
skin glowed hot in the unnatural, clammy atmosphere
of the theatre. An attendant placed a *Full House* sign in
the box office window.

"Shouldn't be any criticism about bums on seats,"
Nate said.

They listened in to another conversation.
"Considering our resources, and thanks to you, dear
lady, a very acceptable performance. It can't compete
with the film for atmosphere, without the soundtrack
of Brian Gray and Gary Moore. But … imagine, dearest
Imogen." He touched her overdone lavender hair. "So

charmingly beautiful," added the little man with the New York baseball cap, black sweatshirt and jeans. "Twelve Jimi Hendrix songs were to be used in the original film soundtrack, but at the last moment the Hendrix family wouldn't release the rights."

The matronly lady, the object of his focus, oohed and aahed in all the right places, thoroughly fascinated with him. She was patron to many a struggling artist, so long as they didn't patronize her. Nate smiled to himself.

"Yes," she said, "you should be very proud. As credible a performance as I've seen on Broadway or in the West End."

Monique cuddled into Nate. "Thanks for bringing me." He returned the cuddle and couldn't help thinking that in her little black dress, imitation pearls and fur jacket, she might not have won any animal activist friends, but she could have been a proud daughter of the Establishment.

He nudged Monique. "The man in the baseball cap is Arnold Propp, the theatre director." She huddled closer to him like a schoolgirl on a first date. He wished Goose and Mike would get back with the drinks.

Jocelyn had left the guys at the bar and came over to complain. "I loathe the indignity of queuing for a toilet. I'm going to the ones upstairs. Greta's gone to the one backstage."

Nate's eyes followed the steady flow of foot traffic coming and going to the upstairs toilets. On her descent he noticed the crowd jostled Jocelyn into a corner on the landing and, by sheer pressure, into the arms of Isabelle.

"I reckon the guys must have gone to the upstairs bar for those drinks," Nate said. But really, he was curious about the relationship between Jocelyn and Isabelle.

*****

Isabelle slipped her white, bony hands into Jocelyn's palms. Jocelyn's blue eyes surrendered to the corrosive power of Isabelle's lime-green cat's eyes. The madding crowd wasn't enough to drown out Jocelyn.

"In the touch of this bosom there worketh a spell,
Which is Lord of thy utterance, Christabel …"

Isabelle smiled a perverse smile, and there was a hint of porn star sleaze. "The challenge for me, dear Jocelyn, is to use my charms to seduce a woman so cold, Cartesian and aloof, in control and terrified of her passions, so square holed." She moved in closer to Jocelyn. "When she does finally succumb to surrender, her sexual fire will burn closer and hotter, steamier than rocks in a steam room difficult to extinguish – my word weary tongue will become a passion leech."

And Jocelyn's body language replied: *Have your way with me, Isabelle, darling*.

Meantime, on the stairs, throngs of theatre goers rushed past Isabelle and Jocelyn.

They broke their embrace.

"Are you going to the party at our place?" Isabelle said.

"I don't know … you see it's my birthday today, and–"

"Happy birthday." Isabelle kissed her discreetly on the cheek. "Please do come. Must go, my public awaits." She dropped Jocelyn's hands and lost herself in the downstairs amoebae of bodies.

*****

The crowd thinned to a comfortable foyer full of pretenders who chatted and sipped. Nate sat back down with Monique. "I'd loved to have been a fly on the wall," she said.

He gave Monique a knowing smile. "Well, I guess it's just different strokes for different folks." They both laughed.

Mike, Goose and Greta arrived back, Greta still in her maid's costume. Nate handed the drinks around as they talked shop. Jocelyn came back too. Greta played the virgin stand-in for Beatrice-Joanna on her wedding night. They argued over the casting of Beatrice-Joanna and decided Greta would be more suitable than Isabelle. But Greta said, "The director harbours a gay bias." They soon lost interest in theatre politics in favour of getting lathered.

"The thing is," said Greta, holding the floor, still in costume, "what are we going to do now? We can stay here and pay a premium for our drinks, or go to the after-play party. You're all invited as friends of the cast."

"Suits me." Goose slid his hand over his smooth bald head. "I'm in the mood for a leer up."

"Me too." Mike caught Goose's enthusiasm. "None of us have to get up early in the morning, except the Goose, and he's a big boy."

"At least twenty centimetres," laughed Goose.

Nobody else laughed.

"Monique and I wanna go," Nate said.

"I guess we have a mandate, or a date, then," said Jocelyn. "Do you know where to go?" She told them anyway. "It's a flat in a big mansion, just off Hampton Square, on Wilding St. Look for a silver beamer and a Citreon 2CV. The place will be lit like the Crystal Palace. If you lot go now, Goose and I will come later, after I've changed."

"OK," Mike said. "We'll take Nate and Monique and pick up something at the bottle shop on the way."

"See you there," Greta said. "Come on, Goose, I'll take you backstage."

Nate and Monique found the party house without any trouble, on a street of Victorian houses presiding over a tree-lined square of ancient oaks. Where old houses outlived maintenance costs, they were pulled down, replaced, or renovated into modern apartments, built in architectural sympathy. Nate had seen a TV programme about it.

The house, which was split into several flats, was stark white with coloured leadlight windows and curling flaky paint. Insidious soft gouges of dry rot stood in dilapidated defiance of a bygone age. He wouldn't like to have to paint it.

A magnificent weeping elm filled the front yard, the moon shining through its tormented bare branches, lending the whole place a gothic look. He and Monique shivered. The autumn night air was crisp and clear – there would probably be a frost. The whole place reeked of antique charm and recent rot, romance and grandeur coupled with a contemporary decadence under a bad omened fermenting harvest moon, a lethal mix. The sort of place he imagined experience is heightened unearthed by innocence. A palace of excess leading to God knows what? Blake's nursery and Wilde's retirement home? Or maybe Jim Morrison's ghost? He didn't know.

Lance, Jed and Isabelle welcomed the guests. When Nate and the others arrived at the front door, Isabelle ushered them up the stairs and into a flat to the left at the top of the stairs. The place stank of dusty threadbare carpets and rotten wood. An attempt to cover up with incense created a sickly sweet smell.

The party room enjoyed a view over the square. It filled up fast, enlivened by the animated buzz of the booze-fuelled crowd. The smell of marijuana blended with the incense. Joints were passed hand to mouth and the lights dimmed. Faces strobed in and out of focus along with the tribal beat of the music; to Nate it seemed specially formulated to unleash the instincts.

Nobody spoke. He danced cheek to cheek in a slow dance with Monique, and watched Mike and Goose kick back in the front bay window. They passed a joint back and forth. Greta was engrossed in theatre talk in the kitchen, and Isabelle and Jocelyn slipped out of the room.

Isabelle shut the bedroom door behind Jocelyn the moment she crossed her threshold. She backed Jocelyn against the door and held her arms aloft. Jocelyn's dress clung, exposing the tantalizing orbs of her breasts and classic arc of her crotch. Isabelle's gratification could no longer be delayed. She considered securing Jocelyn's hands to coat hooks with her stockings.

Her hands moved all over Jocelyn with the separate intelligence of raw passion. "Oh! So lovely ... too good for any square ellipsoid." She absorbed Jocelyn's charms by epidermal osmosis, stabbed her with kisses and affectionate nips, burnt her with vampire lusts and amorous rough squeezes through her pants the way they did behind the bike sheds at school – depraved infants terrible sodden between the legs.

"Do what you will, sweet thing," a submissive Jocelyn answered. Foreign words ejaculated from her mouth and she penetrated Isabelle intimately. Isabelle lifted

her gown to allow Jocelyn to slide her fingers inside –
and stir the liquid silk. Isabelle didn't wear knickers.
Her hand stormed Jocelyn's; experienced fingers parted
her bush and burrowed into the receptive vortex of her
vagina. She found the magic spot. Her fingers played
plectrum with her tonsil harp and she whispered dirty
sweet obscenities in her ear, bizarre and unspeakable
things. Thoughts a person could be ostracized or locked
up for, but paroled in their minds and hearts.

Jocelyn's vagina tightened around Isabelle's finger.
Isabelle's sexual repertoire was wide and involved animals,
vegetables, high school girls, depraved headmistresses,
nuns, female prisoners – whatever scenario took her fancy.
She whispered in Jocelyn's ear: "The headmistress said,
"You wicked, wicked girl. You're not wearing regulation
knickers."

"OH!" Jocelyn's shocked whisper came back. "How
dare you utter such sleaze." And then, "Please … sweet
thing … don't stop. OOH! That's nice … ooh!"

And Isabelle whispered, with grit and menace in her
voice: "She inserts her crone fingers into your tight honey
pot, her ancient lumpy tongue … Miss Craven … Oh so
innocent ... Miss Craven burns deep inside … handsome,
sinewy arms … a repressed yin with a closet full of yang."

"Oh! Oh! You witch, I'm orgasming!"

"The headmistress straps on a dildo. You can be first,"
said Isabelle. She held Jocelyn's thighs tight. They rattled
and shook, nipped, sucked and quivered with legs splayed,

wiggled, pushed thighs, vaginas and buttocks under the command of the other's lascivious mute tongues, they tingled from clitoris to nipple tip to sphincter and back again.

Orgasmic corks popped, extracted by winged corkscrews of desire, the reek of sex and marijuana battled with the scent of deodorant, talcum and body odour in Isabelle's nostrils.

"I've been defiled," said Jocelyn. "But I do love you."

"No you don't, it's just infatuation – but now, creature of the deed." Isabelle lit a joint, inhaled and handed it to Jocelyn. "Go ahead, you earned it."

An urgent bang resounded on the door and several male voices shattered their serenity. "What the fuck is going on?"

Isabelle and Jocelyn lay naked and passed the joint back and forth. Jocelyn heard Isabelle's reply as an echo in the recesses of her consciousness.

"Just women's talk," shouted Isabelle. "We'll be out shortly."

Jocelyn started to dress. "We must have been in here three quarters of an hour."

"Maybe," said Isabelle, unconcerned. "The night is young and we must go and circulate."

"Can we meet again?" Jocelyn's face and voice were ambivalent. Her blue eyes rippled pools of joy and sorrow, reflected lime green in Isabelle's corneas.

"Sorry," said Isabelle. "I don't do encores."

They dressed, brushed their hair and fought over the mirror, archetypal females.

Isabelle and Jocelyn re-joined the party crowd. The music reverberated through every cell in their bodies.

"What have you two been up to?" Lance said with a wry smile.

The guys drifted outside for a smoke, to piss and get some fresh air. Nate left Monique with the girls to prepare food.

Lance urinated against the elm tree and turned to Mike. "You're a bigger man than I am, darling." They both looked in the direction of his penis. "I don't mean in that department."

"What, then?" Mike slouched on a rickety old wrought iron bench seat alongside Nate and Goose.

"Some see trust as weakness, darling." Lance shook his penis for excess drops. "She's a friend, but she's an incorrigible whore."

"Who?" Lance lost Mike with his stupid riddles.

"Is-a-fuck-ing-belle, darling."

Goose passed Mike a joint. "I thought you were going to say 'necessary on a bike'?" Nobody laughed.

Mike took a long toke, handed it on to Nate, and said, "I wouldn't mind fucking her."

"Truth is, darlings, guys don't do anything for her. There's a story she did have a boyfriend, once – a real stud, and she sucked him dry."

"Dry?" the others said.

"She's a vegetarian." Lance zipped his fly and stood in front of the guys. "She lives on nuts, seeds and vegetables."

"What the fuck's that got to do with it?" Goose said.

"She sucked him off every night, for years, darlings." Lance tried to disguise his envy. "For her protein fix. He became a physical wreck."

"What're you saying?" Goose said. He wriggled around in his seat, scored another toke and passed it on to Lance who leaned against the tree, facing them.

"I'm saying that's why she's so big and beautiful. Our vital fluid, sperm, is part of her diet. It's full of all the elements and vitamins needed to nourish the body. She has an appetite for women like the worst Casanova or Don Juan." He looked meaningfully at Goose. But Goose ignored him. "So I hope nothing has happened to Jocelyn, darlings?"

"I wouldn't worry," said Mike. "She's a big girl, and besides, as far as I know she hasn't got a penis. She's so linear she'd make a square look bent."

Nate blushed red, knowing this wasn't exactly true.

A short shout from the top of the stairs fractured the cool night air. "Come and get it."

They thumped up the stairs, and Lance regaled them with another story about Isabelle. "The rumour is, darlings, Isabelle is the product of two mothers and a turkey baster."

The food was ready. Nate's stomach rumbled. "Hurry

up guys!" he said, knowing Monique and Jocelyn had prepared most of it – potato chips, crackers, cheeses, dips, slices of wholegrain bread, sausages and saveloys and a salad on the side. Jed was stirred with sexist comments about women being especially talented in the kitchen and the bedroom and then reneged to avoid starvation.

"Women are actually superior to men, in every way, but inferior to the perceived svelteness of some other women's backside." Nate had to laugh at Jed. But he stopped when Francois Louveteau and Jason strolled in. The music died and the revellers milled around the food with paper plates, piling them high. Jason took Jocelyn aside and gave her a gift-wrapped package tied up in blue ribbon, and a card that read: *For a very special lady on your special day*. Nate wondered if Mike could ever be that romantic or look that suave. "I bet you thought I'd forgotten," said Jason.

"Forgotten? I didn't expect anything." She tore the wrapper off in bleary frenzy. "Especially anything as exquisite as this." She held up the Clarice Cliff vase. "Oh, you're so sweet, come closer."

"Have you been eating seafood?" Jason said.

Mike mingled at the other end of the room, and Louveteau was flushed in the face. Louveteau saw Nate and Monique and marched over to them. "Charmed to meet you again, monsieur, mademoiselle." He turned to Monique "I regret I do not have good news, mademoiselle. Monsieur Wolf has discovered that you, my dear, instigated the Culture Assassinations attack and he is out for your blood. He has learned this from a reporter for the *Castlemere News*. It might be expedient, mademoiselle, for you to get out of town."

"What about me?" said Nate?

"He does not know of your involvement, as yet. You have been warned."

That ruined the evening for Monique and Nate. "Thanks for the party, guys." Nate turned to Mike and Goose. "I'll catch you down the beach in the morning, if you're not too hung over." It was a good time to leave, as the supper deteriorated into a venue for sophisticated talk of theatre and sexual politics.

Chapter Twenty-four

Man has his will – but woman has her way.

– Oliver Wendell Holmes, *The Autocrat of the
Breakfast Table*

THE WAVES were about head height. The sun hung low in the sky, reflecting off their glassy lips and warming Nate's back as he, Goose and Mike paddled out. Wisps of benevolent salt spray backhanded them. It seemed to Nate that beyond the breakers, another world undulated, one in which they could meditate and observe the civilized world rise and fall with the primordial pulse of the sea. They might only be a few hundred metres off shore, but they were light years away in serenity. Waves didn't run to bus timetables, and he felt no urgency to catch one. They enjoyed the tranquillity of being without doing.

He broke the silence. "Last night – how many bums did you pinch?"

"Memory's a bit foggy," said Goose. "But it was fun, fun, fun giving the pillow biters a thrill, eh, Mikey?"

Mike didn't say anything.

They pitched and bobbed, unshaven, flat wet hair

against their heads: human flotsam and jetsam. The autumn sea chilled Nate's feet.

"Bloody bum bandits," blurted Goose.

A big set formed way out the back and they paddled, frantic. All three of them caught the same head-height wave and rode it to where it petered out in chest-high water.

Four people appeared on the beach. Nate recognized them – the sand artists from that other time. The surfers spun their boards one eighty and paddled back to sea.

The guys wrung the mickey out of Nate: "You're no longer just a bum surfer, then," Goose said.

"A woman, a job, a mortgage," added Mike. "The whole catastrophe."

"I'm really only interested in the surf," Nate said.

Cold water was literally poured on their conversation – they duck dived under a wave that broke over them, and paddled in silence until they straddled their boards out the back.

"OK guys, fess up time." Nate nervously tugged his tuft. "Monique betrayed the Pariah Dog to the Culture Assassins."

"You fucking idiot!" Goose spun round to face Nate.

Mike seemed to understand. "What! They don't know …?"

"They'll find out," Nate said. "They always do."

"Well, I tried," Goose said. "And so did Mike."

"I know." Nate hitched a ride on the next wave in.

He looked on as the artists doodled in the sand. This time they were sculpting an ornery horned bull and a warrior woman holding a double-edged axe, standing together under a crescent moon. No male artists were present. They showed more artistry than they had with the pyramids, but the Sphinx had impressed him. But why put so much effort into these works of art only to have them demolished by the next full tide? He didn't bother talking to them this time. He wasn't in the mood. He sat down on the rocks, dried himself off and watched Mike and Goose slice through the transparent waves. Conditions were near perfect. Heaps of surfers seemed drawn to the other end of the beach.

"I'm surprised you're not out there," came a familiar voice from behind him. "Mind if I sit down?" Nate turned to put a face to the voice. It belonged to an old beachcomber he often saw but didn't speak to. His back was stooped, and his skin was wrinkled and sallow. His eyes were dark, almost black, and the ragged grey beard lent him a Middle Eastern appearance.

Nate didn't answer, but the old guy sat anyway and watched the two surfers.

"Your friends," he said.

"Yep."

"I used to surf when I was about your age."

Nate found the image of the old man and young surfer hard to put together. But he humoured him.

"When you're young you don't think you'll ever

grow old and arthritic," said the old man, showing Nate his bent and gnarled hands.

"You just wanna have a good time and be free," said Nate.

"Exactly. I wanted to lie in the sun all day, surf and run after young women."

"And did you?"

"For a time, while I lived at home. But I knew the time would soon come when I had to make my own way in life."

"I know what you mean," Nate said.

"I became a professor of history – an exponent of academic freedom and the open society. I learnt early, that the victors wrote history." His gaze was far out to sea and his stance was like a bowed tree in a prevailing wind. "I discovered my colleagues, for the most part, to be moral cowards, servile to the dominant discourse, contemptuous of students and the wider community." They watched Mike and Goose commandeer the same wave and ride it a long way up the beach. The old guy sighed a sigh tinged with bitter emotion.

"Sorry to hear that," Nate said.

"They kept their mouths shut when required by statute to be society's guardians. Yes." He gazed skyward. "I soon learnt how partisan objectivity can be when it's in its own interest." He cleared his throat. "We need a new society where political rule depends on knowledge, in the head and the heart, and not on money and power." Then he apologized. "I'm sorry; you got me going my boy."

"I've started to realise too there's a fix in the system – it kind of undermines the innocent enjoyment of life." He was tempted to tell him Daryl's ideas, but it might be better to wait until he knew him better before discussing that sort of thing. "You … you're Abe Solomon."

"Yes! We meet at last, young Nathaniel. And might I say, I really enjoyed my conversations with your mother on her cleaning rounds at the university. She was a breath of fresh air. Such a gentle woman, endowed with a fine natural intelligence. You should be proud, my boy."

"I am," Nate said. "And thanks, for all you've done for me. You'll have to come up home, sometime."

"I'd like that, my boy. But I haven't quite finished regaling you. Your mother was a very wise woman. She opened my mind to the notion of the sacred masculine which identifies with industry science, technology, explorers, colonists and aggressors in history." He eyeballed Nate. "And the sacred feminine, the intuitive, creative, feeling, indigenous peoples who place heart above the brain and mysticism over rationalism."

"I had always thought a bit along those lines, that there was no classic male or female type – we're all along a spectrum between the two. And I found it hard to believe people are totally gay. I never talked to anyone about it."

Abe took a deep breath. "You have ideas like your mum. Currently these qualities are unbalanced, and goals like owning the most property and making exorbitant amounts of money have become the aim of many people. This has led to greed and war." He sighed.

"Well, thanks for the lecture. It's made me think. But first the world has to get over being pussy struck."

Abe tittered. "That's an age thing. World resources are used without regard for the future. Both men and women try to increase their power and insecurities by embracing the false masculinity. As you have realised, within us we all have both aspects of the sacred masculine and sacred feminine, to different degrees. When we return to a balance of these qualities we become as solid as a tree deeply rooted in the earth."

"Interesting," Nate said. "Mum never talked to me about that stuff; mind you she was always busy working." Abe seemed to put the fix down more to individual greed than elite or dark manipulation.

Abe disappeared down the beach when he saw the guys drubbing out of the water. They stopped for a moment at the sand doodles, then trudged over to where Nate sunned himself on a comfortable rock, and dried off.

"Fancy a beer?" Goose read their silence as affirmation. "I'll go and get us one from the car." He came back with a slab and peeled off a can each. He ripped the tab off his and swallowed hard. He placed the rest on the rocks with a wet towel over them, and turned to Mike. "You're the educated one. What do you make of those works in the sand?"

Nate lit a smoke and sat on a rock beside Goose. Mike squatted on the towel, facing them with his back to the sea.

"I'm no expert."

"Come on," Goose said. "No time for false modesty."

"One idea is …"

"Yeah? Go on," said Goose.

"About three thousand years ago, before the male takeover of society, the world was ruled by women under the worship of the Goddess."

"Sounds a bit suss to me." Goose folded a towel under himself to soften his seat.

"In this society, women were the rulers and men the servants."

"Well that hasn't changed – women still rule from the bedroom."

"Woman worshipped the phallus and men were their sex toys."

Goose chuckled. "I don't believe that. They're more attracted to overweight men in business suits."

"Men carried this phallus worship over into patriarchal society, later."

"Sounds a bit cockeyed," Goose said. "So how did we make the transition to vagina worship?"

Mike's brow furrowed in thought. "A part natural and part political over correction in purusha and prakriti, the co-eternal female and male energy, after millennia of suppression. Did you know women introduced agriculture and industrialization, arts and the sciences?"

"Who's shitting who?" Goose said.

Nate stroked his beard and interjected. "So they are the fuckers who invented wage slavery?"

"I wouldn't like to commit to that one. I think it was Adam Smith that kicked off capitalism." Mike laughed and folded his legs into a yogi flying position. "Men raped and bullied women into submission, wrote them out of history and brought in a male God."

Goose guffawed. "And kept generations of fucking theologians in work over whether he had a cock or not."

Mike's mouth quivered in amusement. "Women were seen as the evil descendants of Eve, who made the wrong choice in a lose-lose situation. They didn't have a soul, but they did have a vagina."

Goose laughed, and almost toppled off his rock. "Which they used as start-up capital for the oldest profession."

They all laughed.

Goose went on, tongue in cheek. "This led to vaginal-inspired capitalism, beginning with the production of consumers before spreading to global conglomerates and multinationals."

"I take it this isn't a criticism of your precious free market," said Mike, smiling as though he'd won a philosophical victory.

"The free market is not sexist," Goose said. "It rewards

performance and abhors a vacuum. A hole opened up in the market so it got stuffed with tampons, panty liners, lubricants, birth control pills, vibrators, sexy lingerie, perfumes, fashions, chocolates, flowers, books, films, TV – obstetrics, gynaecology and plastic surgery. The list is not exhaustive." Goose jumped off his rock.

Nate made an association with what Abe Solomon had said: the winners write the losers out of history.

Mike got to his feet, his legs shaky as a new-born foal's. "I hope you didn't find my explanation convoluted."

"I did," Goose said. "But it helped me clarify my views on the efficacy of the free market." They all sat back on the rocks. A low-flying seagull left white-splattered deposits on Goose's bald head. Mike and Nate rolled around in the sand with laughter.

Mike got to his feet, stifling a laugh. "Supposed to be good luck."

"Very fucking funny." Goose wiped his head clean with a towel. "You haven't finished telling us what these are." Goose pointed to the drawings in the sand.

"OK." Mike stretched his arms out sideways. "The bull, the warrior woman, the axe, the crescent moon are symbols of the re-emergence of woman as rulers."

"Thank you, Professor Willis," Goose said. "But I think you'll find the experts have discredited all this women having ruled shit. I saw it on the History Channel. Matriarchy is just a figment in the imagination of shit-scared white men seeing their traditional power erode."

Mike ignored him. "The bottom line is …" he got to his feet and shook his aching legs, "that all the ills of the world are caused by men, and they will go away when we return to an empathetic, less competitive, fair society."

"I am a capitalist, but I'm not stupid," Goose said. "I don't know how you make it fair – it's an exploitative system and I can't for the life of me understand why women have struggled for a hundred-odd years just to become wage slaves equal to their brothers, with their strings pulled by the lure of the almighty dollar." Goose grabbed his cell phone out of a pile of clothes on the rocks.

Goose dialled Greta's number. "Hi, Garbs, party sounds as though it's well underway."

Greta said, "Yeah, don't be late."

He heard Lance shout. "Hurry home, Daddy, darling."

Goose said, "I don't know when I'll be home – I've got to go in to work."

Greta, Isabelle, Lance and Jed were drinking mulled wine, snacking on crackers and cheese, talking idly.

Greta had an inkling she knew where this would end up, and it wasn't in hugs and kisses.

"That smile's positively pornographic, darling," Lance said to Isabelle. "Did you check out each other's shutter speed, the other night?"

Isabelle retaliated with a wry smile. "A lady never

kisses and tells," she said. She sipped her wine with the self-satisfied grin of one who has scored sexually. "Fortunately I'm no lady."

Greta was impatient with their innuendoes. "Don't you two ever think of anything else?"

"Occasionally I think of falling in love, darlings, but the best ones are either married or straight. I dream of giving birth."

"Yuck!" Isabelle said. "So demeaning. Love is so shallow, and babies ruin the sex urge and the body – not to mention the social life."

Jed stirred the cauldron. "Keep them barefoot and pregnant, I say."

"That's like so last century," Lance said.

"I would be happy with the pregnant bit," Greta said.

"You ignoble savage," Isabelle said.

"Keep your crotchless knickers on."

"I don't wear knickers," Isabelle said. "But watch out – my growler's got wisdom teeth!"

"The party's getting rough, take me away from this, Greta, darling," Lance said. "Tell your husband I asked after him."

"Sure." There was no way she would do that, the way he thought about gays.

"We do really have to go," Isabelle said. "We haven't cleaned up from the party yet."

"I'd better lend a hand." Jed followed them towards the door.

"Wait just a minute." Greta grabbed him by the belt.

"I'll catch you up shortly," Jed said to the others. They shouted their goodbyes to Greta.

The moment the door closed, Greta stroked Jed's hair, and whispered in his ear. "I find you very attractive." She lowered his hand to her crotch, more encouragement than he needed. "Goose won't be home for hours."

He followed her lead. "Why can't every woman be so straightforward about lying back?" he said.

Greta realized now was the optimum time to get her egg fertilized. She dropped to the carpeted floor and lifted her frock over her head while Jed removed her sensible cotton pants. Jed didn't waste time on foreplay.

The time was right, and she wasn't getting any younger. She laughed to herself. He plunged into her and she clasped him. She rocked him, and herself, to orgasm between her dimpled thighs and flaccid freckled buttocks. "Don't worry … I'm on the pill," she gasped. "Fill me up, gorgeous, fill me up." She could have been an advertisement for ink cartridges. Her hands clawed his buttocks, which puckered and flexed like a squeezed douche bag, and filled her with all the ejaculate his testes could muster.

Chapter Twenty-five

Nothing worth knowing can be taught.

– Oscar Wilde

MONDAY MORNING arrived fast. Daryl got up at seven thirty, but he needn't have, because he didn't have a job. He stole a newspaper from next door's letterbox, the alternative free market. He knew they'd get a special delivery after they rung up to say they'd been short delivered. He skulked back inside the house and read the headlines: *ARCHITECT OF THREE-YEAR PLANS, POLITICIANS AND PRESIDENT TO VISIT WITH CASTLEMERE BUSINESS LEADERS*. He pushed open the kitchen door. "That Lewis Chambers and his quisling compadres have innocent blood on their hands." Daryl shook the newspaper and sat down at the table opposite Nate.

Nate chewed on a piece of toast. "Monique visits him at the Grand."

"Why would she … visit him?" Daryl said.

"She does his haircuts and manicures."

"The bastard! The Grand, you say?"

"The whole of suite 553."

"Interesting."

"Politics give me a slack." Nate buttered himself another piece of toast. "I try not to listen to the news."

"I'll manicure him up the arse with a chainsaw file."

"Now now, Daryl. That's foul hate coming out of your mouth," Tiff said. She handed him two pieces of toast and a cup of tea. "Learn to respect your leaders. They are appointed by God; when you disobey them you sin against God."

"Give me a break. That man and his fucking cronies virtually killed my father – they shut down the railway workshops. That was his life, rolling stock and rock music."

"I'm going for a surf." Nate gulped down his lukewarm tea and made for the front door.

Tiff shouted behind him. "If you see Tank, tell him I'm asking after him."

"I don't expect to." The front door slammed.

Nate grabbed his surfboard and mountain bike from outside the front door. He tucked the board under his left arm, walked the bike to the road, threw his right leg over and freewheeled down the hill to the cove.

A flock of seagulls picked over rubbish in the car park as he freewheeled in. He locked his bike up against a fence rail and clambered through the sand hills with his board. He watched small, waist-high waves tumbling in.

He leaned his board on the marram grass, sunk his back into a sand dune and soaked in the sun. He tried to comprehend everything that had happened. For the first time in ages he thought about his mother, and what old Abe said: a gentle woman, a woman of fine natural intelligence. "I suppose she was," he said, out loud. He'd never noticed it when he lived at home. All her advice had gone pretty much over his head. And unconsciously, he followed his father. Always going for the quick fix and the main chance, and losing out long term.

He still couldn't understand why his mother thought honesty was the best policy and an honest person has no superiors. And he thought of another thing she used to say: "A prophet is no good in his own country." The separation of death seemed to give her voice extra authority. Another one he liked, "A smooth sea doesn't make a good mariner." He supposed he could alter that to surfer, and it gave him new heart. "Thanks, Mum," he mouthed. The quality of freedom depended on a person's response to life. And person was almost an anagram of response – spooky – or did he have too much time on his hands?

He reckoned freedom didn't mean selling out, it meant finding a creative outlet that made you happy and provided a living

His cell phone rang. "Okay, Wolf, I'll be there in half an hour. What do ya mean; you can't tell me on the phone? Surprise me, then." Nate clicked off, wrapped his phone in his towel, and ran out into the surf with dreams of being a pro surfer. He had to wonder, what did Wolf have in mind? Did they know about him and Monique?

Nate arrived at Felines at seven p.m., according to the clock over reception. Wolf and Queenie were waiting for him in the staff room, and he searched their faces for any clue that they suspected him. Wolf threw him a set of car keys with a Ford logo. He jumped in shock.

"Your new wheels, dude. Only for work, otherwise it stays in the garage out back." Wolf took Nate aside. "Monique fucked up big time, slung her slutty little arse over the line – betrayed us to the CA guys. I'm relying on you to help us bring her in."

Nate bit his bottom lip with bitter resolve and worried about their fate – both dog tucker. Wolf took him into the lounge. The TV blared without an audience.

"By the way." Wolf placed a fatherly hand on his shoulder. "I hope that coke's still safe and secure."

"Sure is." Nate's eyes stuck on a revealing camera shot of steamy sex on the TV.

"Just call it a bonus." Wolf slipped him a brown envelope. "For babysitting." Nate flicked through the wad of notes – ten one-hundred-dollar bills.

He trembled. "No problem."

"Things look pretty fine." The action on the TV distracted Wolf. "Fuck, that dude's got a big one … I finally offloaded that five hundred grams of shit on the Yank for a hundred grand. You may be a bit standoffish when it comes to the crunch, but you're a good omen for the Dog."

"I'm glad." Nate shivered.

Queenie came over and said facetiously, "Aren't you working tonight?"

"Sure," Nate said. "Just getting my riding instructions."

Queenie said, "I want you to take Tara and Ginger into the city. Some loving wife has organized a threesome for her darling husband's fortieth." She slipped Nate the address.

Tara and Ginger waited at the reception in whorish poses, Tara in fishnets and short leather mini; Ginger in a short black singlet dress.

"Come on, ladies." Nate sauntered over to the desk in shaky bravado. "Let's try out the new wheels." They click-clacked behind him in high heels.

He unlocked the car and they all climbed in. The car had that distinctive new car smell, battling for dominance with Tara's and Ginger's pungent powdery aroma. The steering was tight and responsive. He let the women out at an inner city brick and tile gentleman's residence and collected the parlour fee. Then he drove to Monique's.

He pulled up outside her Victorian flat and bounded up the stairs two at a time. He banged on the door and she let him in after checking him out in the peephole. He flopped onto the couch and she offered him a hot drink.

He didn't want one.

"We've got to get out."

She sat down beside him. "They don't know about us, do they?"

"No, but it won't be long."

"What can we do?"

"Mike's good in these situations." He pulled out his cell phone and dialled. Mike answered. "Wolf knows about Monique. We need to scarper fast."

"You won't get any resistance from me." Nate put his phone on speaker so Monique could hear. "Where to, you reckon?"

"Up north, at my father's farm stay … contact Goose for a car. Good luck! Get a pen and I'll give you instructions."

Monique tossed him one and he sketched a rough map, folded it in half and shoved it in his jacket pocket.

"Remember, buddy," Mike said. "I'm only a phone call away. I'll tell the old man to expect you."

Nate ended the call and looked at Monique. "Did you get that?"

"Mike's father can hide us?"

"Right."

Monique got up and paced the floor, staring vacantly through the living room window onto the street. "You've got a new car?"

"Yeah, the firm's."

"I'll have to ring Mum."

"Don't tell her where you're going. Make sure you're packed and ready to go by the time I finish my shift tonight."

"I'll be ready," she said, and opened her arms for a hug, her expression wistful.

He held her and they kissed deep and long. His cell phone rang. "OK, Mel, got it – pick you up at Felines and drop you at Sunvale."

Once in the car, Melanie bubbled with shoptalk. "I don't know about the game being legalized. It could be another scam by the government aimed at the protection of sex workers on one hand and gathering revenue with the other. They'll bugger it for the unskilled. I'm not going to pick up this sort of money in an office or a call centre."

"I know," Nate said, trying to empathize. "What address is it again?"

"The next block. He's a regular, likes me to change his nappies. I only hope they're not full of number twos. How sick is that?"

"He's a customer." He let her out, collected the fee from a guy like the man next door and drove home. Tiff and Daryl needed to know he'd be out of town for a while.

They were in the kitchen when he arrived home; he could hear them.

He shoved his head through the open door. "I've

been called away on business. I don't know how long for. See you when I get back."

Daryl smirked. "Got yourself a clandestine shag, eh?"

Tiff glared at Daryl. "Take care."

He shut the kitchen door and raced into Tiff's room to get the cocaine. He grabbed it from its place up the chimney; there was an avalanche of soot. He stuffed clothes from the tall boy in his room into an overnight bag, along with the cocaine, and carried the bag out to the car.

In the car, he dialled Goose. Greta answered and handed it over.

"Listen, Goose, the shit's hit the fan. Monique and I need to get out of town yesterday or we're friggin' dead meat. We need a vehicle."

"I've got a Camry – hasn't been detailed yet. Meet me down at the yard now and I'll give you the keys. I'm going out on a limb – so don't prang it!"

He waited about twenty minutes for Goose to come across town, but it worked out because it gave him time to pick Melanie up from Sunvale. He didn't know what vehicle to look for, because Goose usually just drove anything off the lot. This time he drove a Land Cruiser. Nate got out of his car and they strode into the yard together. Goose plucked the car keys off a board in his office, then they ambled into the workshop and Goose opened the double doors.

"I appreciate what you're doing for us," Nate said.

Goose threw him the keys. "If it helps you get away from that scum. Besides, it's good to escape from Greta's constant talk about babies. Don't let that woman of yours talk you into kids, they're not goldfish – you can't flush them down the toilet when you're sick of them."

"I'll bear that in mind," Nate said.

"After a couple of years, the fucking bitches can claim half of your assets."

"I get the point," Nate said.

"Be careful."

Nate backed the car out and drove around to the forecourt. Goose came through the building and met him out front. "Park it out on the street and lock it up. Get a taxi over tonight."

Nate did as he said and came back to see Goose. "Thanks. You might have saved our necks."

"I hope so."

He got in the firm's Falcon and went to meet Melanie. She was leaning against a lamppost outside, puffing on a cigarette when he swung into the curb.

She flicked the remains of her cigarette into the gutter and climbed into the car. "Well, I'm glad that's over."

"Where to now?" Nate said.

"Drop me off at home," she said. "I'm not doing any more punters tonight."

All the way to her place she talked about Monique's plans for a parlour of their own. "We intend to give the girls the respect they deserve, and employ graduates and more sophisticated types."

"That sounds cool." But he wasn't convinced.

"Yeah, we'll solicit a corporate type of client that might like to take the girls out for dinner and a show before shagging them. Sometimes presentable educated men don't want to be bothered with the whole courtship thing, but are happy to pay for a woman to take to a business dinner or just for company when the time or inclination presents itself. These guys are our target market."

He let this flow over him, while he plotted the getaway.

When they arrived at Melanie's he was barely aware of her getting out of the car.

He got a call. "OK, Maya, the Monte Royal Hotel, a German couple for a ménage à trois." Nate had trouble getting his tongue around it. Maya was more Singapore Airlines stewardess than hooker – she exuded Asian charm from her tallish frame. She'd told him once that threesomes were often the husband's idea, and the wife was sometimes persuaded against her better judgement. Sensitivity on the hooker's part was necessary.

He accompanied her to pick up the fee, and a chubby butch blond fraulein with cropped hair and studded dog collar opened the door. He knew that rich Europeans were prepared to travel the world for the novelty of a bit of dark or yellow snatch. When she saw Maya she drooled at the mouth like a hungry pug dog.

He asked to come in to meet the husband, to ensure no one else skulked. The husband, a fat man in his forties, proposed to get his jollies watching his wife and Maya get it on.

Nate left with the parlour fee and all sorts of cultural exchanges in his head, which in reality probably amounted to five finger exercises in surgical gloves.

The rest of the night proved to be routine; the usual lonely men in suburban bungalows seeking female companionship and sexual relief. They wanted the presence of a woman for an hour or so after the kids were tucked up in bed, and pretended to their sad selves they didn't have to pay for it.

But he was aware that even in the so-called stable relationships, men and women paid for it one way or another, and ransomed their independence for love and sexual release.

He returned to Felines, locked the Falcon in the garage and cashed up with Queenie. He didn't want to give her a reason to think this might be his last shift at Felines.

"See you tomorrow," she said.

"Yeah. Catch you later." Nate strode off into the night to keep his rendezvous with Monique.

Chapter Twenty-six

'Tis all a Chequer-board of Nights and Days
Where Destiny with Men for Pieces plays

– Omar Kayyam

NATE'S WATCH said one thirty-five a.m. The motor's hypnotic hum provided the backing track for the headlights of the Toyota that cut through the night into the wee hours of Tuesday morning. The terrain was different now; a river wound its way through beech-clad hills, black trunks and branches reached stark against leaves. They crossed the river and climbed higher, to a summit which in daylight had vistas of a beautiful rugged coast. At night it revealed itself on the ozone breeze.

He'd visited that coast, on school holidays with his mother and father. His father had liked to take his boat out there, but his mother had never enjoyed it. She worried the repossession people would take it away because he failed to make the payments. It never deterred Nate from a good time. They saw lots of whales up close; caught crayfish, and sometimes his father let him steer the boat.

The Toyota descended and followed the road up the

coast, past seals hidden in the dark, through the narrow, solid rock road tunnels he'd enjoyed as a kid.

The road arched around the coast and further north to the brow of a hill that crested above the small settlement of Crayden. Tourist shops, pubs and motels faced a basin of sea edged by Norfolk pines with spectacular backdrops to the Colossus Mountains, which seemed to rise out of the sea. He pulled over into a layby. Monique snoozed against a pillow held up to the cold passenger window. She woke with a start and shivered in the warm car. "Are we there?"

"Not quite." He turned the overhead light on and slid a hand into his jacket pocket for the map. "Fuck, the friggin' map's not there." And there was no one to ask for directions, gone three thirty in the morning; no all-night service stations. "Fuck it!"

But he knew it was roughly an hour north and half an hour inland to the foot of the Colossus Mountains, if they didn't miss the turn off. He remembered where that was from the map – by an old red railway hut over the Torrance River Bridge – then he'd need to find the right farm, not easy in the dark.

Monique fell asleep again, snoring to the hum of the engine, and they continued north following the familiar rugged coast. There was still no hint of daylight, and the Toyota's lights bounced off the black rocks and splash of ocean foam. The road veered inland to the Torrance. The river was low and the car lights reflected off giant boulders and the remains of bleached beech trees strewn like pick-up sticks flung by a giant.

The railway hut loomed, and so did a new blue and white B&B sign.

He turned off onto a gravel road. About fifteen minutes later it branched right, but he didn't turn off because he remembered the map said go to the end of the road and turn left. The instructions came back to him now. He needn't have worried – when they approached the fork in the road, a sign read *Eldorado Farm Stay*. An arrow pointed left and another road went up over the hill to the right. Mike was obviously not up with the latest developments at home. Following the arrow, they drove around a bluff through a long avenue of poplars to a large area of river flats backed onto foothills of the Colossus Mountains.

"We're here." He looked over at Monique, but she still dozed.

He turned his attention to the homestead complex, which was on an elevated site set to the coast. A plantation of pines shadowed the foothills around them, and the Torrance River ran through the south side of the valley below. A large area in front of the house presumably enabled tour buses to turn around, and there were five rustic chalets set into the hillside at the side of the house, with views to the river.

The first signs of daylight flared at the horizon as he pulled the Toyota into the car park. The air chilled the moment he switched the engine off, and he shivered. The time on Monique's watch said five a.m. He cuddled up with her and slept, until he was awakened at seven thirty by Mike's father tapping on the window, now covered in frost.

Mike's father was a thicker-set version of Mike, with a distinctive deep voice and thin grey hair. "Welcome to Eldorado Farm Stay, folks." He beamed. "Mike filled me in, breakfast waits."

Nate swallowed the wafts of a full farm breakfast – bacon, eggs, and sausages – coming from the house. His stomach did a quickstep in hungry anticipation. "Thanks." He stepped out of the car. "We'll take our stuff in first."

"Of course." Ted showed them to the first chalet, which had magnificent views of the river and over the whole valley.

"This is paradise," said Monique, as she helped Nate stack their gear on the balcony, looking down the valley towards the coast.

"We like it," Ted said. "I'll leave you to unpack."

Monique checked out the modern kitchen and bathroom and threw herself on the queen-sized bed, bouncing on it in a wanton way. "Hey come and check this out."

He lay down beside her and pulled out his cell phone. "I'll give them a quick ring at home."

"Do you have to?" Monique's bottom lip drooped in

a sulky way.

He selected the numbers with his thumb.

"You just caught me," Tiff said, "I was about to leave for work."

"Everything OK?"

"You've only been gone overnight."

"How's Daryl?"

"Asleep."

"I'll keep in touch." He ended the call.

But Daryl wasn't asleep. He lay on his bed and brooded on the headlines about the gathering of the architect of the three-year plans and his cronies. He grew surly at the injustice of it all. How did the three-year plans benefit the little man?

The story of the real creators of wealth was never told. The little man – the disgruntled pimple on the licentious butt of history: imperialistic exploitation of the masses didn't make good press. TINA which meant: there was no alternative to the by-line of political spiel that came from the mouth of Dodger Blackwatch, a curious blend of Adolph Hitler and Charlie Chaplin and the principal architect of the three-year plans. But he didn't get the trains to run on time and he wasn't a natural comedian. He found it necessary to sell the family silver for a pittance to keep the wolf from the treasury door. Blackwatch didn't phrase it that way, even though his politics were clichéd. Adam Smith's fiscal snake oil sold to the dupes to transform a poverty-stricken nation into a super-efficient cash cow.

"No pain, no gain," became the monetary mantra of the neoliberal yogis, and the iodine salve of the unemployed and destitute, while Blackwatch and Co slashed and burned their way through the economy. They hung a carrot of deceit under the donkey noses of the great unwashed, with platitudes of how everything would be wonderful six months out. Meanwhile, they changed the legislation without mandate, and so quickly that conditions worsened and critics suffered stymied whiplash.

The political architects went to extremes to imbed policies so deep into the economic, political and legal infrastructure that future regimes would find it difficult, if not impossible to undo. Their agenda was to get the economy right for the big shakers and movers, and the benefits would trickle down. "Yeah, yeah, like a fuck'en golden shower!" Daryl snarled to himself. The people were substantially poorer – health, education, employment and mental health had all been hit. The overseas debt had quadrupled.

Part of the insidiousness of political art was that there existed a certain demographic that would happily pay to be urinated on – the rationale behind asset sales, indirect tax and consumer exploitation. "Fuck it!" Daryl shouted. He threw a lascivious eye over a voluptuous, airbrushed Penthouse pet hanging on the wall opposite "Another day of wretched poverty," he blurted. He asked himself, is it better to have all the time in the world and no money, or vice versa?

Daryl didn't kid himself. He'd been born into servitude, sweated labour in a service station owned by an oil company that paid their casuals eight dollars an hour to watch consumers pump gas. His lifetime of misery had been sparked by his parents during five minutes of ecstasy in the back of his father's souped-up Chevy.

His only consolation was the bored housewives who might let him dip his stick, while hubby worked to earn the aphrodisiac. But it was getting increasingly difficult for a poor man to get an arbitrary fuck.

And he reckoned that soon, an unemployed one would have to resort to sheep molesting. But he knew that was taking poetic license too far.

He reached for his drug stash. The sun wasn't even over his armpit, but reality was just too hostile. He took out a joint and lit it, sucked a long toke. It took the edge off. His head spun with banker conspiracies from Paul Warburg to Paul White. He lifted his sheath knife down from the wall – the one he used when he went on pig hunts with his father. Taking it from its trusty scabbard, he studied it – its curved blade, its serrated back. He would hunt with it again, for the more profligate two-legged degenerate hybrid, snout-ensconced-in-the-trough politician.

He felt the dope slur his phrases, which became less lucid, bitter and grandiose. He spat at random. "Revolt. The law stinks of ravishment. Take what's yours and give me mine." And he fostered visions. He led a great insurrection. They stormed the press gallery and biffed flour and eggs, moved in with imaginary bayonets fixed, cold steel barbecued on hot flesh sure to enliven the rhetoric. He savoured the fear in their eyes and the lumps in their chests, the flutter of feral moths in their stomachs.

The sky, earth and the sea wept for the betrayal of generations of taxpayers and nation-builders to ghettos of hopelessness, while rewards went to those who worshipped at the altar of a flawed ideal. He held the power of life and death in his hand, the Grim Reaper with a sheath knife, on speed. He needed Dutch courage, so he took a puff of crystal meth, one of the few products still made locally. He felt a violent rush and he didn't know if it was from the drug or from his violation at the hands of the Republic. He sucked in a huge lungful and exhaled with a huge smile on his face. He finished off the smoke, got dressed and rang for a taxi.

The taxi was prompt for a change, and dropped him outside the Grand Hotel.

The day was bright and hot, without much wind. He wore jeans and a white T-shirt, under a grey light-knit woollen sweater. His dark brown hair gleamed in the sun and his doggy eyes were keen yet furtive. His stomach bulged to one side where his knife was tucked into his jeans covered by his sweater.

When he arrived a busload of suckered Japanese tourists had just disembarked, and the hotel staff were fully extended checking them in. The doorman didn't notice him wriggling his way through the crowd into the pink marbled foyer and the lifts. The conference room, Suite 553, was on the tenth floor. He held the lift door open on floor ten and looked around for security guards. The corridors were clear. The place had a stifled, closeted, air-conditioned atmosphere. He sauntered down to suite 553, the third door down. And much to his surprise the door was open wide enough to see certain political faces he recognized, grazing on caviar washed down with Moet. A sign read *Leave your cell phone in the box provided.*

He shuffled in and grabbed the President of the Republic, Rosa Dark, who was lost in meaningful baritone banter with a stunning red-headed female reporter dressed in a Harris Tweed suit. She held a microphone up to Rosa's mouth in a suggestive manner.

Rosa's expression changed from rapt attention to overt terror when she felt the cold steel of the sheath knife against her throbbing jugular. "It's strange," she said. "The song 'Mack the Knife' has come into my head. Contemporary society owes a lot to the celebration of the knife, especially the switchblade, for among other things, cost cutting and nips and tucks."

"Not to mention 'The Threepenny Opera'," shouted Daryl. He kept the knife pressure on her jugular and said in a tough guy voice: "Don't anybody move or she gets it."

That somehow got everybody's attention. The reporter escaped.

"I take it you have some sort of submission to present?" Rosa said. "What is it this time? You want to ban battery hens and legislate free-range pigs?"

"No," Daryl said. He smirked. "That's already happening. Strange as it might seem, I simply want you to represent the people and tell me which international bank we owe the megabucks to."

"Be a good chap, run along. That would breach our privacy laws and national security." She turned to face the members of the party and spoke boldly, without the aid of a microphone. "Let me assure you there's no conspiracy. It's just as everybody knows – money rules."

"You could just print the money to pay the debt," he said.

"Nonsense. That would only lead to inflation. I have a dream–"

"Leading to nocturnal emissions," shouted Dick Stone, an opposition party member. He was followed by noisy applause.

Daryl still had a death grip on her.

"I have a dream," she went on, "leading to fiscal deficits, that I know is shared by many honourable members on the other side of the house." She took a breath. "I have a dream where ..." She managed to free one hand to place on her vagina in a pledge. "I have a dream where girls and women will smash the glass ceilings and kick in the doors leading to institutionalised patriarchy."

She was going for the female vote as well as the supportive and disillusioned males, but it was really about self-promotion. Daryl could see through that.

She stood erect. "I have a dream, that our lady gardens, the symbol of a fairer and kinder society, are reverenced by all. I have a dream, where poverty is ended in all its forms and where we have a world that respects human rights, human dignity, and the rule of law, justice and non-discrimination, not to mention an answer to climate change."

The whole conference room cheered.

"Rubbish!" shouted Daryl. He increased the pressure on her jugular. "Your dream is a rort. You have to be asleep to believe it. Females are lauded, and at the same time sold into wage slavery alongside their captive brothers. You can stop with the campaign speech. We are all manipulated by overseas debt and austerity measures and the free market."

Boos and heckles came from the crowd; shouts of "socialist," "conspiracy theorist."

There were more heckles, boos and a few high-pitched hysterical laughs. He shouted over them. "The strings are pulled by bloodsucking, flesh-pedalling elites and Archons."

A shout from the crowd: "Somebody ring the mental hot line."

He held Rosa firm. "Society has to wake up to political and economic agendas of previous and future governments that have been in the interests of wealth for a few: a New World Order."

More boos and heckles. Rosa tried to wriggle loose, but he had her in too tight a grip. "In the long term the power brokers will decree, through law, that dissenters or haters be euthanized along with the poor, the sick, the weak, and the redundant, not to mention the fat and ugly, and it will all be managed sensitively. And pensions, benefits, wages will be cut for non-cooperation."

"You are so offensive and politically incorrect," Rosa said. She almost squirmed loose.

Daryl held her tighter and shouted, "Families and reproduction will be controlled by the state: to get the world population down to an efficient one billion."

The crowd went wild. Shouts of: "Low-life hater!" echoed through the conference room.

"Fuck the government," Daryl said. This was useless. "In fact, fuck the government with a policeman's truncheon." Even if he did form a political party called something like the Rabid Underdogs Party, he doubted he'd reach the threshold to get members into power. Society had been duped – people were too busy watching

TV and getting stoned. It was business as usual. The oppressed were allowed once every few years to decide which particular representatives of the oppressing class would represent and repress them.

He shouted, "The real power brokers still worship the phallus in secret and view women as something to be exploited while pretending to go along as sensitive lovers."

Rosa said, "I'm all in favour of sexual congress. After all, I am President of the Republic and as such have an honorary penis. Of course, that's off the record."

"It will take more than an honorary penis to smash the glass ceiling, as a minimum you'll need a real one," said Daryl. "Are you gay?"

"Read my labia," Rosa said. "I am not gay."

Daryl's mouth dropped open. "I thought the President of the Republic would be at least as good as me. Isn't that what gay stands for: as good as you?"

"He's obviously some form of mutant Social Creditor," said Dick Stone, professional party hopper, model citizen and railways saboteur. Daryl couldn't take his eyes off him. Stone's hair was the colour of a silver fox but he had the suave demeanour of an American pit bull. He, like the architects of the three-year plans, gauged their power by the extent of pain they inflicted on the powerless. They modelled themselves on Gestapo, and little boys who pulled the wings off butterflies. They orgasmed on other people's pain and trained by smashing unemployed workers' jobs against otherwise redundant railway wagons, just like a typical Archon.

Dark was captive to these politics, later adopted by the conservatives which voters forgot her party had begun in the first place. The hairs bristled on the nape of Daryl's neck.

Blackwatch's palm was munificently greased for efficient sale of his country into hopeless debt and wage slavery. He got an open cheque from an obscure branch of Metro Bank made out to Benjamin Arnold Enterprises. He experimented with pig farming using every free market and Kama Sutra strategy, but failed miserably.

But Daryl knew all along: a silk purse can't be fashioned from a sow's ear – or a prosperous nation from an economic basket case using trickle-down economic theories.

The free market required some sort of catheter, some conduit to fit the new right urethra to avoid pissing on them. The bag could then be more efficiently dumped in the laps of the plebes, where it belonged. Not if he could help it. None of them cared about the lives they destroyed in the process. The speed of implementing change and deconstructing a nation was euphoric – a bigger high than snorting cocaine. To quote Lewis Chambers: "All rather exhilarating and really just jolly good fun, what?"

"You killed my father and murdered Paul White," screamed Daryl. He increased the pressure on Rosa's jugular.

"Let him have his say." It was the modulated voice of Blackwatch. "It's the democratic principle in action, like the vote. It will make him feel better but it won't do him any good." Chambers moved along the table and picked at the chips with the elegance of a penguin pigging out on sprats. "Democracy is the precursor of tyranny," Chambers said.

"Oh do shut up," Blackwatch said. His moustache twitched like a poodle preening. "You'll give the show away. We must keep up appearances."

Rosa interjected. "And our Swiss bank accounts."

"Hear hear!" shouted Blackwatch. "I'll drink to that. Charge your glass, Chambers. Rosa?" He felt his crotch with his other hand. "I have an odd sensation in my loins. No matter how much we hurt them they come back for more like they were anaesthetized."

Chambers raised his glass and spoke: "Long live the ignorance of the great unwashed and the efficiency of the free market and the plutocratic manipulated economy." They snorted in collective triumph. Blackwatch added a rejoinder: "To efficiency, the blood of innocents and the great fascist dictators of all time!"

"You fucking psychopaths – you have to be stopped! Traitors and murderers!" Daryl screamed. He tightened his grip on Rosa; his head spun, this was Huxley's Brave New World, a technological authoritarian world where humans were genetically bred, brainwashed and drugged to accept the status quo, and Orwell's Nineteen

Eighty-Four, where self-expression was outlawed and people were under constant surveillance. Then he saw the camera on the wall.

Dick Stone bristled, in his element. He pushed his chest out and said, "I've been called worse than that, in the house, by female members."

"In fact, many do have balls and members," Chambers said. He smirked at his own joke. "That they strap on for the opening of parliament."

"That'll be enough of that." Rosa wrestled with the knife and stroked her Tubal-Cain badge. "People will wonder what sort of place parliament is."

"Best kept in the Dark," Blackwatch said.

"Like all dark deeds," Rosa said.

The blood ran to Daryl's face. His head was a gyrocopter fuelled by methamphetamines. He'd thought it would be easy to come in here and vent his spleen. But they were beyond ordinary decency or understanding. They felt no remorse whatsoever for the pain they inflicted on others – it was a game, wealth creation for the boys, by the girls if necessary, and they made up the rules as they went along. And his sense of outrage was just another absurdity in their otherwise Pythonesque lives.

He knew the drill – kissing babies with one breath while dispatching middle-aged dinosaurs like his father to slow suicide or fast alcoholism and insanity.

Daryl released Rosa who fell into the arms of the

reporter. He moved over to the balcony.

"It's hopeless," he said. "I feel as though I'm the only one inside or outside this room, apart from the indigenous people, who feel this country has been betrayed – led into captivity by the new one world Pharaohs."

"It's healthy to be angry and outraged," said the Flintstonesque Sunday cricketer who'd just walked in. "But there's not much we can do until a lot more people feel that way. He flushed red with self-conscious humility. "Keep me on the parliamentary gravy train and I might buy all the assets back."

Daryl knew, meantime, he would live in surreptitious splendour, wearing the red flag on his sleeve and fostering the delusions of benevolent dictatorship in his chest.

"What about an enquiry into the suspicious death of Paul White?" demanded Daryl. The Flintstone-type character went red in the face in apoplectic sympathy with the establishment. In his best Past Masters' voice he said: "There is no defence against deceit." And that was all.

A shot rang out. Daryl hadn't seen the armed offenders squad entering the glass tower opposite. But the camera on the wall had recorded everything. The last thing he heard was the pop of a gun. He took the fast way down, slumping off the balcony with the grace of a wingless fledgling DOA. His splattered blood made an interesting Rorschach test on the pavement; a red, jagged full stop.

Rosa walked to the edge of the balcony and looked down. "Poor fellow. His life was in vain. It signified nothing. He should have created an underdogs party, but who would have voted for him?"

"It's not as if he was a lost vote," quipped Dick Stone. "It's a bonus the unemployment and mental health statistics have just gone down." His words were followed by guffaws, grunts, snorts and stapled belly laughs.

Rosa frowned. "I guess that's a consolation. Put it down to the joys of citizenship."

A dapper man in a shiny Singapore suit put his head around the corner of suite 553, symbolic of throwing his cap into a circus ring.

"One law, one people, one land, one title," he said. "To each according to his need." His hand was up the skirt of a ventriloquist doll of a middle-aged good time girl. The doll kept on repeating: "Con is very nice man. Con is intelligent, very nice man. Con is not racist. Con is not wolf. Con is wolf in sheep's clothing."

"To each according to ability," Con said. A whisper rose from the crowd.

"He's quoting Karl Marx," shouted a lone voice from the Youth in Asia Necrophilia Party."

Chapter Twenty-seven

If the radiance of a thousand suns
Were to burst at once into the sky
That would be like the splendour of the mighty one –
I am become death, the shatterer of worlds.

– Bhagavad Gita

TIFFANY PUSHED through the front door and dropped her work things in the hall. She urgently needed to pee. She'd just got comfortable when somebody knocked at the front door. She prized herself off the toilet seat and opened the door to a uniformed constable.

"This is the only address I have for Daryl Jones, and you're his flat mate I take it? I regret to tell you Daryl passed away this afternoon after being shot and falling several storeys. His family up north have been informed."

Tiffany didn't say a word, but fell to the floor in shock and tears. The constable lifted her to her feet. When she recovered enough she showed him to Daryl's room. They were both surprised to find a note pinned to his bed head. She glanced at it quickly. It wasn't exactly a suicide note, but what was it?

MDCCLXXVI

Assassins of Franz Ferdinand, the Tsar, and JFK
Bury us alive under Mosaic property, religion and law.
Triple hexagon eagle flies, in the one world temple's
fibre optic eye;

Gay brides French kiss Moloch's arse behind hoodwinks
And eat kosher chicken and scoff abominable seafood,
Off the body of a naked women bent over backwards

On an altar of hewn stone; sycophantic pawns of
geometric laws
Sacrifice their first born to propitiate a one-eyed God,
Conquer the world while worshipful brothers throw

Themselves on thrice-crowing cocks to make donuts;
Neutered slaves breed embryos from eugenic spores
Flung against shit-splattered walls of no conscience;

Sister of the Nile whores sing: "All for one and one for
all,"
While banks use multiplication and long division
To foreclose on you and Paul White's haunted ghost
And Rattle GE seed money calling it business as usual?

PS. There can be some things worse than death,
And what are those?
You could never know, no never comprehend.

The unknown cannot be trounced from the known:
Any more than Gold sinks to the bottom of the pan,
And Scum rises up. We are them they are us!

"He was obviously in a disturbed state when he wrote that," said the young Teutonic officer, his official voice croaky. "If he wasn't dead he'd be under very serious charges of abduction and threatening to kill the President."

Tiff's tears overwhelmed her. "Excuse me," she sobbed. "I'll be in my room if you want me."

"I understand," he said. He went off to search Daryl's room.

Tiff lay on her bed stroking her floral sun dress. Her body and soul ached. Melancholy bubbled from the artesian depths of her being. For the first time in her life she felt her belief inadequate and she inwardly accused her Lord. Why, together, hadn't they been able to save Daryl's tortured soul? Daryl asked her to understand him, but she considered her God held the trump cards – life was a smug one-way street, which didn't permit rogue traffic. She knew now of his weird spirituality based on fair play, a fatal attraction to the underdog and, until now, a fidelity to the bittersweet mystery and reality of life.

Tears welled in her eyes. She'd wanted to know and understand Daryl better, but now that chance was gone. What if Daryl was right? What if belief in God was a pack of lies to hold the gullible in slavery to those who invented Christianity? Were the feminists correct? Three thousand years of misogynist society under a despotic male god? She'd never questioned her beliefs before. She'd always accepted implicitly every word in the Bible to be the indisputable word of God. And accordingly, she'd respected the powers that be, because God willed we respect them – or was it St Paul?

She felt used and cheated, even humiliated, in the worst sense.

The constable knocked on her open door and rustled the poem. "I've found what I need," he said. "I'll pass it on to his mother. She can pick up the rest of his things at her convenience – does that suit you?"

"Yes." Tiff got up from her bed. "That will be fine. I'd like a copy of Daryl's poem, though."

"Perhaps you can talk to his mother about that." The cop strode to the front door.

Daryl's mother was his only close relative, and she lived in a halfway house for psychiatric patients.

The constable left, and a few minutes later there was another bang on the front door. Tiff opened it. Tank stood beside Wolf, and Shane behind. Their faces said they weren't in the mood to exchange pleasantries – but Wolf introduced them all anyway. This was the first time she had met Shane and Wolf.

Shane brooded behind them, tall, dark and tattooed – a diabolical shadow of the others, it seemed to her. Wolf's tall frame, matted flecked beard and hair, tattered originals, flushed complexion and the grimace on his face intimidated her. Tank slouched, unkempt, paunchy and squat, his bald spot covered with lank strands of greasy hair. All smelt of leather and motorcycle oil. She expected to see bikes out the front but saw a XR6 Falcon.

"Where is he?" Wolf demanded. "And what was the filth doing here?"

"Have they taken him in?" Tank said.

"One thing at a time," said Tiff. "We've had a terrible tragedy here today."

Wolf's eyes were wide.

"He's had an accident?" Tank said.

"No," she said. She rubbed her eye. "It's Daryl. He was off his face on drugs, and held Rosa Dark at knife point. He was shot by the police."

"Silly boy. Another of my customers gone west. Now, where's Nate? He didn't show at work, and he's got something of mine. Do you mind if we come in?" He slammed her out of the way.

She tried to stop them but they tore into everything. They started in Daryl's room, uprooted his bed, pulled books off shelves, clothes out of the wardrobe, drawers out of his tallboy, soot out of the chimney.

She physically blocked her doorway – no way would she let them in there. So for the moment she was forced to watch while they pillaged Nate's room, dismantling it piece by piece. When he emerged, Wolf was fuming, purple with rage. He'd found a recent photo of Nate and

Monique in an embrace. "The two-timing tip rat." Wolf smashed the picture on the floor and ground his boot into it.

They came back down the hall and she barred her doorway.

"Take her into the kitchen," Wolf ordered Shane. "Me and Tank will search her room."

Shane frog-marched her into the kitchen. "Who can help you now, sweetie? I like the sun dress, nice easy access."

She prayed Shane wouldn't do anything, but he did. It happened fast. "I always wanted to do it to a nun," he said. "You're the nearest thing." He held her arms and opened her legs with his right knee. She screamed and then spat in his face. He slapped her. She fell to the floor. "Please, please. I've dedicated my life to the Lord and I'm saving myself for my future husband."

"Shut up. You belong to me now. Playing hard to get makes me hotter."

"Ah! You monster," she said.

He whipped her knickers off, entered her and thrust with demonic stabs. The blood on the couch testified to her broken virginity. For her, the abomination wrenched off the veil of innocence into carnality. And she knew she could never return to her original state. The act of rape both horrified and awakened her dormant sexuality, against her will. Shane had his fill and pulled up his jeans from his ankles. She put her knickers back on and straightened her dress.

"Thanks, bitch. Was it good for you?"

Tank and Wolf barged into the room. "Are you sure you don't know where that fucking traitorous piece of vermin is?" Wolf held up the remains of the battered photo.

"I can't help you," Tiff said. She sniffed, wiping away tears and mucus with her hand.

"Don't worry your frigid little snatch." Wolf glared at her.

She shivered.

"We'll find them, and when we do …" He moved his finger across his throat. "But for now …" He squeezed her left boob and leered at her body. "I'll send Shane an' the guys around when they get horny, to finish the job."

Shane smiled the way a Doberman does, lifting his upper lip to show bad teeth. He mocked. "I'll bring a marriage certificate, you bring the dowry."

"I'll be in." Tanks bleary eyes raked her body. "Now, thanks to Shane, she's public property."

She vomited. They took that as a cue to go. She didn't hear the car start straight away. They talked quietly; the passenger window was down and she could just make out what they were saying. She prayed they would go.

"What's this?" She saw Wolf smoothing out a piece of crumpled paper.

"Fucked if I know," said the other two. Wolf turned on the overhead light.

"It's a map, up north, near the Colossus Mountains. That's Nate's writing. So that's where the weasel fuckers are."

Tiff heard the car start and accelerate away at speed into the night. The Pariahs left her lying in a pool of blood, her hymen split asunder. She quivered. She couldn't go to the police if she wanted to stay alive. She felt dirty, unclean, physically and spiritually.

She took a quick shower, not thinking about the DNA evidence destroyed.

She cleaned the blood off the settee and pretended nothing had happened. But Shane's nicotine breath still hung in the air and passively asphyxiated the remains of her violated being.

After the double tragedy, the house languished in an aura of silence and sadness. Daryl's death was a catalyst for all the doubts and unanswered questions she'd had over the years. She questioned her God and her beliefs more and more. *Why did this happen to me —your faithful servant? Why did you allow six million Jews to be killed? It's all lies. Filthy manipulated hateful lies. Don't tell me of hatred in the name of love anymore! How many women burnt at the stake, in the name of a God of love?*

She screamed: "Because you must not suffer a witch to live!"

How many raped and abused in self-interested whispers of male adoration and love? How many ravished in hatred? No more! Lies, all lies! Does any man know what love is? Don't even ask a woman!

"If everything you created was good," she screamed, "who created evil?" And she heard a voice in her head reply: free will did. But it only made her madder.

Daryl would have said Jesuit priests and business leaders turned the devil into a religion, but it was really Christianity that had done that. She experienced herself in free fall, further and further into a dark and deep blasphemous abyss.

It was eight o'clock the next morning, Wednesday, before the Pariahs were heading towards the Colossus Mountains in hot pursuit of Nate and Monique.

They dropped the Falcon at Felines and decided Wolf and Tank would travel in the crash truck, with Shane and Finn McCool leading the way on their Hogs, in an official sort of way.

It was the first month of winter and the day began clear and fresh. The deciduous trees were already bare. It was a pleasant day to be on a bike, and Finn McCool and Shane motored ahead of the ute. They were enjoying the hills, throwing and leaning their bikes low and hard into the corners. The traffic was light, apart from logging and sheep trucks and camper vans.

Wolf and Tank had a good view of traffic around the bend in the road ahead, because they were further back and could see beyond the bluff. A truck and trailer unit rattled and banged on the other side of the bend where the road flattened out. Shane should've been able to see it because he was riding on the shoulder of the road.

He white-lined it ready for maximum lean into the corner. Tank had a horrible foreboding. He looked on as the bike tilted to the right over the white line and then left. Shane accelerated hard. By the time he saw the truck it was too late. Time stopped, followed by a terrible hollow thud. It was so fast. Tank froze as Shane's body was flung in the air about fifty feet, hammer-thrown across the road, coming to rest on the lush green verge.

Tank wanted to be sick. The motorcycle was jammed under the front wheel of the truck, a hideous scene. Everything was quiet, except for the haunted bleats from the sheep truck, on the death road.

Tank got out of the ute and rushed over. It hit him hard, the smell of hot metal and spilt fuel mixed with freshly mown grass on the verge. Finn McCool was a long way up the road before he realized Shane wasn't there, and turned around to investigate. The driver of the truck on the other side of the road hung over a five-wire fence, ghostly white, and vomited. Wolf hovered by Shane and dialled an ambulance.

Tank cradled Shane in his arms and reassured him, but Shane's face was smashed beyond recognition and his dark eyes were glazed, fixated on something Tank couldn't see.

"You'll be right, old mate. Hang on; don't die on the old Tank, now." Tears formed in his eyes. He got no verbal response from Shane, just a guttural rattle, as if he might want to have said something but it wasn't possible.

Tank had never felt so helpless. He thought of all the good times they'd shared. Shane was the brother he'd never had. He winced at Shane's bloodied raw face. "Please God," he begged, desperately. "Save him."

Who the fuck am I kidding, if there is such a being, he isn't going to help the likes of us.

He didn't know whether to curse or to pray. In despair he called on the name of Jesus Christ. A wave of guilt towards Tiff stung in his chest. "If you aren't bullshit," he said, "save my best friend Shane." He burbled on … "Save us miserable sinners, forgive us? Please …" He'd never said please or thank you, in his life.

It was instant. Tank's heart orgasmed with the strangest, warmest internal caress – a shot of real love fortified with a deep-down spiritual vibe. The surrounds filtered with the bluest of blue hues, and Tank floated, but his feet were anchored to the ground. He held his buddy in his arms and the most beautiful butterfly, coloured yellow, purple and red, alighted on Shane's head.

It communicated with Tank in a subtle but significant way. *Perfect trust*. The antennae swayed. *Be like the butterfly*. The voice spoke from within and beyond the butterfly. The message seeped into his consciousness. *The butterfly has perfect trust*, the voice in his head seemed to say. With that, Shane's breath stopped, and his eyes stared in wonderment at what they saw, and they stayed like that even though now he was dead. Tank wondered if the guttural noises were Shane's attempt at repentance.

The ambulance arrived quickly, but too late. Shane's injuries were too serious. Tank held Shane in his arms when the meat wagon came for his body. Finn McCool and Wolf leaned against the ute and smoked.

"It's always sad to lose a brother," Wolf said, "but do I have to remind you guys we have to catch those two little skanks? We'll do it for Shane."

Tank's heart sank as a breakdown truck hauled the remains of the bike away and police interviewed the truck driver. They scribbled down the Pariahs' statements, then they were free to go. Tank mounted his bike and Finn McCool led the way, but rode more sedately.

The rest of the journey for Tank was a steady but uneventful run to the farm stay. They parked by the bluff, and he rested his elbows on the roof of the ute and surveyed the homestead through binoculars. He watched a pale green Toyota sedan, a tractor and trailer with hay bales on the back, a small flat deck truck and a late model Toyota Land Cruiser. Two men came out of the house and roared off towards the river flats on the tractor; the younger one fed out hay from the trailer.

He handed the binoculars to Wolf. "I reckon now would be a good time to make our move."

Wolf surveyed the chalets.

Tank could see, even with his naked eye, that only one

chalet showed signs of life and movement. He assumed this was the one they were in.

Wolf got them to move the vehicles off the road to avoid attention. He yelled at Tank. "Get the sawn-off from behind the seat – bring some ammo."

They crept stealthily along the line of poplars towards the complex. They stalked the chalet, and overheard Monique and Nate talking, oblivious to what waited for them outside. Wolf whispered: "On the count of three: one … two … three." They burst in, and Tank levelled the sawn-off pump-action shotgun at them.

"Surprise surprise!" Wolf said. "Thought we were home safe, did we? Sorry to disturb the little house-playing fantasy." He smiled. "But it's the end of the fucking line – meter's expired, dudes."

"You should'a known betta than betway a Pawiah Dog," Finn said.

"Rip one of those tea towels up and use it to tie their hands behind their backs," Wolf said. "We'll drag them along the metal road and finish them off with the shotty."

Nate and Monique stood deathly pale in the one room chalet as Finn ripped the towels into useable strips and Tank tied their hands behind their backs."

They shuddered.

Wolf grabbed Nate by the scruff of the neck. "Where's my fuckin' coke? You little sewer rat."

"It's at home," Nate bluffed. "If anything happens to us you'll never find it."

"I don't think it will be a problem." Wolf smirked at the others. "I think you'll fess up when you see what a metal road can do to the moisturized skin of your slut girlfriend. By the way, did she tell you, she's partial to a bit through the back door?"

Finn shredded the towels and used the pieces to tie Nate's and Monique's hands behind them.

Nate envisioned dying a horrible death. But he nurtured a thin hope, while he knew where the coke was and Wolf didn't. Maybe he could hold them off long enough for help to arrive in one form or another. Mike's father and brother would be back from feeding out soon.

They shuffled down the path from the chalet. He and Monique were in front, their hands behind their backs. The ripped towels didn't make for good ropes, and already he'd loosened them by wiggling his hands vigorously. They were all but loose. He would wait for a chance to make a run for it in the direction of Mike's father. Fat chance at the moment, with Tank holding the sawn-off at their backs.

Finn and Wolf followed. They got to the pale green Toyota Camry.

Suddenly Tank spun around on Finn and Wolf. "On the ground." He aimed the gun from one to the other.

They wrestled Tank for the gun.

Nate had unloosed himself and jumped in to help. There was a bang. In the fracas, Tank snatched the gun back and Nate dropped lifeless to the ground, a gunshot wound to the head.

Wolf stepped forward and Tank fired off a round at his feet. Gravel and pellets ricocheted at Wolf's shins and thighs.

Wolf glowered. "You crazy fucking bastard. What's got into you?"

"The Lord." Tank grinned. "Now stay back. You've just killed Nate."

"So what," Wolf scoffed. "At least I'm not pussy struck by a Bible-banging slut that begrudges you a whiff of her knickers. Shane beat you to it."

"Shut up." Tank pointed the barrel under Wolf's nose. "Shut your filthy mouth or I'll blow your fucking head off. Pick up Nate and put him in the car."

Monique was sobbing.

Tank kept the sawn-off on Finn and Wolf, and snatched Wolf's cell phone from his jacket pocket.

Wolf and Finn took a step back.

Tank untied Monique, and she got into the car. Monique drove while Tank kept the shot gun levelled at Wolf and Finn from the passenger seat window. He jumped into the car and they roared off, leaving Finn and Wolf stranded. They stopped where the ute and Finn's bike were parked. Three shotgun blasts sounded as Tank blasted out the back tyres of the ute and the motorcycle.

"Let them follow if they will," Tank said.

Chapter Twenty-eight

There is none more enslaved than those who think they are free.

– Goethe

THREE UNLIKELY characters motored south towards Castlemere on a sunny Wednesday afternoon in early winter. Monique was in the driver's seat while Nate lay lifeless in the back; Tank a desperado-riding shotgun. The novelty of freedom numbed them to silence. Monique checked the rear-vision mirror furtively, as though she had a paranoid nervous tic. She began to think of the possibilities, run scenarios through her head. There had been two other vehicles in the yard, and they may have had keys in them. And, if they'd managed to hot-wire one of them, they might be not too far behind.

It was good Tank had taken Wolf's cell phone, but Wolf might have forced entry to the house to ring for back up, while Mike's father and brother were down the paddocks. Or, Wolf might have spun a hard luck story to Mike's father when they came back up the paddock. She worried that a posse of Pariahs might come to meet them from the South, but she didn't tell Tank her thoughts, while he gave her a commentary on his encounter with the Lord. Just then there was a groan from the back seat. She pulled the car to the side of the road. It was some sort of miracle. She and Tank opened the passenger door and Nate sat up.

"What happened?" he said.

"Remember, Wolf and Finn."

"Of fucking course."

"We thought you were a goner," said Tank.

"The wound looks black and bloody," Monique said, "but it must have pretty much been a graze. I can see a few pellets stuck in your forehead." She used her handkerchief and a bottle of water to wipe it down.

"We'll get you to the emergency department in town," Tank said, "but in the meantime I'm gonna call the cops."

"I never thought I'd see the day old die-hard outlaw Tank would call the cops." Nate sat up."

"I'm a different man." Tank placed Wolf's phone to his ear. "Hello, Castlemere Central Police? I have a tip off for ya. Pariah Dog motorcycle gang have a large quantity of cocaine stashed under the front passenger seat of their blue Ford sedan, which is parked up in the garage at Felines Massage Parlour." There was silence. "Waddya mean, you fucking know? You can't divulge sources, who am I? Never mind." He clicked off. "They've already had a tip off," he said to the others.

*****

If not for the circumstances, the return trip would have been enjoyable. Nate sat in the back seat and Monique drove. He let go a long languid yawn. The sun shone brightly on the ocean and seals frolicked with be whiskered noses in the air like old-fashioned garden ornaments minus the ball. His grandmother had had one that held a birdbath. And she'd had a giant butterfly stuck on a wall of the house. Inside, on a kitchen wall, there had been three ceramic ducks in flight. And a giant goose pecked at the exposed cheek of a little boy's bum by the piano in the lounge. Funny what sparked your memory.

Tank rankled like a cracked seventy-eight or gramophone tube from Grandma's house. But Nate couldn't dispute that whatever had happened to him must have been a profound, life-changing experience. The truth was, Tank had probably done most of his serious sinning so he wasn't going to miss much. So far so good.

But then, suddenly, Wolf and Finn McCool were right behind them and they were trying to ram their car. Tank handed him the shotty. He blasted the back window out of the Camry, reloaded and unloaded a couple of rounds into the SUV's two front tyres. The vehicle swerved into the grass verge. They heard the sirens of a police car behind them. Lucky for them it stopped at the SUV. And out the back window his eyes were riveted on the two officers who had Wolf and Finn McCool spread-eagled against the SUV on the grass verge.

Near the outskirts they heard another siren behind them. The police car got in behind the Camry and signalled them to pull over. A tall wiry officer got out. "What's the hurry, lady?" He leaned in the window, looking at Monique. He saw the gun beside Nate and noticed Tank's gang patch.

They explained what had happened, and the officer took the gun.

"I should arrest you for discharging a firearm in a public place, but the priority is to get this young man to the emergency department."

Further along the road were several parked-up police cars, their blue and red lights flashing. Pariah Dogs Valentino Crass, Puck Uggles and Pedro Purplehaze were being shoved into a police van by officers. They drove past and nobody gave them a second look.

The cop put his siren on and waved to Tiff and the others to follow to the emergency department.

Nate was treated, and then went downtown with the others to the police station. He was surprised – it didn't take long. Their statements were taken but no charges were laid. Tank was let off the hook because he'd helped them escape. But they said he may have to go to court if he was implicated with the drugs they had found.

"I'll stay in the car," Tank said when they arrived. Tank remained in the passenger's seat. "Until you catch up."

Monique and Nate clambered out of the car and went inside.

Tiff was reading the paper at the kitchen table and got up, overwhelmed to see them as they came in. She rushed up and gave Nate a hug, not wanting to let him go, then broke down and burst into tears.

"I wish I could have contacted you," Nate said.

Tiffs eyes flooded with tears. "It's been terrible. Daryl died horribly." She wiped her tears away with her sleeve. "I was viciously raped by that Dog – Shane." She turned to Nate. "What did you have that belonged to Wolf? They tipped the whole place upside down looking for it, whatever it was."

"I'm so sorry. I should never have got involved with them in the first place. Poor, poor, hopeless Daryl. And I'm so sorry about you too. It's my fault."

Tiff's face reddened. "Your friends supplied the drugs."

"If I could undo things," he croaked, "I would."

"That devil Shane put me through hell." She quivered. "I still quake in fear when I think of him, and that repulsive Tank. I've even begun to question God's existence."

Monique put a comforting arm round her.

"You're normal, after all," Nate said.

"Nate!" Monique scowled.

"Well, as my mother used to say, "it's an ill wind that doesn't blow somebody some good.""

"That's insensitive and out of context." She glared at him.

"Perhaps God does exist," he said. "Shane is dead: a head-on with a sheep truck. And Tank has been born again."

A light came back into Tiff's eyes and her whole face shone Praise God." She raised her eyes heavenward. "Please forgive me and give me the strength to love my enemy."

To Nate, loving your enemy sounded like a recipe for being beaten up. He doubted he could ever submit to that. But for him, at least, life slowly returned to normal after Daryl's funeral. Several Pariah Dog members were remanded on drug charges, Tank did go to court as an accessory, and the judge took the change of heart into account, a seemingly genuine conversion.

It was lucky for him and Monique that they weren't charged. But they were forbidden to be in contact with gang members, apart from Tank.

Tank got two hundred hours of community work, and moved into Daryl's old room. Tiff found it in her heart to forgive him.

Nate learnt the police had rounded up and raided the Dog's premises on a tip off from the Culture Assassins. Wolf got eight years for possession of a class A drug and wounding with intent. Nate breathed a sigh of relief, because without Wolf's leadership, Pariah Dogs would disintegrate into a disorganized rabble of maverick bikers unlikely to retaliate. It was a case of kill the head and the body dies.

The Press finished its exposé on the gangs, and this coincided with Wolf's trial. Felines closed and prostitution was legalised. Monique and Melanie employed some of the classier girls from Felines for M&M Escorts, which did a brisk trade in a more executive sort of market for visiting businessmen. Nate was their manager.

He often joked with the working girls about how profitable "the wages of sin" were, on the occasions he bumped into them.

Things were going well, so he decided it was time for a long overdue housewarming party. He put the word out to the girls and his friends to bring others if they wished. Guests should bring their own food, and he'd supply the booze.

The afternoon of the barbecue came with brilliant winter sunshine. It was the shortest day and the longest night of the year. The air was thin, and a sharp frozen blast from the Alps made Nate shiver. But they were on the other side of the hill, huddled beneath the brow, which was warm in the sun. He didn't usually feel comfortable in the role of host, but his business experience boosted his confidence. People arrived and wandered through the house, explored the yard and admired the view. People he didn't know. He warmed to the diversity of people he found around him.

"Magnificent," said a woman with an upper-class English accent. "Exquisite views."

"A surfer owns this?" said a young male German tourist with spiky hair, leaning his mountain bike against the house.

A lanky blond guy with an LA accent said, "The plot alone's gotta be, like, two hundred grand."

Nate turned sausages on the barbecue. He wore an apron, which sported huge breasts and dark curly vagina.

"Thanks, pal. I'll have onions and sauce on mine," said a big Canadian guy.

"Farting tucker," said a young curly headed guy with an Australian accent.

"More cans inside," Nate said.

Two young Chinese guys searched for a drink, and another Asian couple shuffled in, a man and women – difficult to tell, but he thought they were Japanese. Some of these guys were partners of the girls from work.

Mike, Goose and the girls, plus some of the theatre crowd arrived. Nate welcomed them and they mingled in little cliques, waiting for their food to cook.

"Hey, you guys," Nate said, passing tongs and a fish slice to Mike and Goose. "You've gotta earn your keep around here." They turned the steaks and sausages. The women played at being men, standing back and drinking beer.

"I can't help but admire your apron." Isabelle towered

over Jocelyn and Greta, who tittered.

"How long do we have to wait for a sausage around here?" said Greta, poking her tongue out in a licentious way.

Jocelyn pushed her breasts out, sucked in and stroked her stomach.

Lance and Jed ambled in. "As long as it takes to drop my pants."

"Show off." Lance flirted with Jed. "Ooh, ooh, darling, do you have sauce on yours?"

Nate brought over a bucket of mussels he'd picked off the rocks down at the cove. He spread some on the hot plate, and was amazed how they sprang open. He chuckled to himself. Faster than a politician's mouth. He passed them around on paper plates. "Thought I'd get in before the indigenous people or the government took the bolt cutters to the old Queen's chain."

"They're so disgusting," said Greta. She plucked a mussel out of its shell.

"They look just like a little … with a big …" said Goose.

"Don't you dare!" Greta fluffed her auburn hair.

"He was only telling the truth," Nate said.

Isabelle picked one up, scrutinized it, and said, before sliding it seductively into her mouth, "A little vagina with a big clitoris."

Nate said, "Grab it by the clit bit, the penis-like bit, and scoff the rest. Spit the hairy bit out." He laughed and was amazed the politically correct among them hadn't pounced on their smutty foolery.

Isabelle tucked in.

He couldn't stop laughing. The other women feigned disgust in front of the men at Isabelle eating replica vaginas.

"I thought you were a vegetarian." Greta narrowed her hazel eyes at Isabelle.

"I eat seafood and I'm very partial to ..." Isabelle swallowed in glee "... salad and vinaigrette lashed with crude innuendo." That shut them all up.

The sausages and steak were ready. Nate put them on a plate and left them on the table for others. They were smoked and charcoaled medium rare. The aromas caused a sensation like ravening piranhas around a living carcass frothing in his stomach; time for a scoff at last. He put his utensils down and joined in the fracas. The crowd assembled and helped themselves to meat, salad and tomato sauce on the table.

Greta caught Jed's eye and said, "I have an announcement to make. Goose and I are having a baby." She raised both arms into the air and conducted a spontaneous cheer. Jason walked in. And Lance said, "You know when to arrive, darling."

Nate suspected trouble. He was a bit worried about Jason, who moved through the gathering with the ease of a stiletto-heeled tightrope walker. The partygoers filled their plates and searched for something to plonk their buttocks on that wasn't hard or penetrating. In a perverse way they managed to gravitate towards people they wanted to distance themselves from. He sat down next to Lance and Goose and surveyed the scene.

"I hate to bring up shop talk," Lance said to Goose, "but I think that car of mine has been wound back, darling. And I know of others who bought cars from Superior Imports with the same complaint."

"That's nonsense," Goose said. "All our odometers are certified correct."

"I've consulted Louveteau, who believes a case against Superior Imports for odometer fraud could be brought."

Goose turned red in the face.

It needn't come to that, darling," said Lance.

Nate couldn't believe his ears, but as far as he was concerned, it would go no further. He remembered talking to Goose about odometers being doctored. He'd admitted it, saying it was simply down to market forces. And, he'd said "Why don't people understand basic economics? Haven't the media persuaded the critics that odometer fraud doesn't happen anymore?" He'd said a firm denial was all that was needed, politicians used it all the time. It didn't matter what sleaze existed below – the surface of the water must never be rippled. Proof could always be given cement boots and buried at sea, later.

Nate was distracted by Jocelyn and Isabelle, who

were just drunk enough not to worry about what they were saying.

"Please," said Isabelle. She stroked Jocelyn's hair. "You look pretty, just like her." She stroked her cheek. "I know what I said. But please, please be my mummy," she urged with baby tears in her green eyes. "I promise to be a good girl." She pouted.

Jocelyn blushed and looked around to see if anyone was listening. Nate deliberately looked away. There was only a group of tree ferns between them. Jocelyn tried to compose herself. They spoke in whispers, but he could still hear them. Jocelyn said, "I find that strangely erotic. How could I reject you?"

Jason tossed Jocelyn a glance but she averted her eyes.

Jocelyn pushed Isabelle away. "Not here. People are staring, besides … I'm only five years older than you."

Nate's attention was caught by Tiff, Tank and Monique, who brought some extra salad and buttered bread from the kitchen. Tank didn't look threatening in jeans and a pale blue polo shirt. He could pass for an overweight barman.

Nate knew Tiff was still fragile, but had come to terms with Tank and her violation with support from her God and Monique.

Mike drifted over to replenish his plate. Isabelle devoured more bean salad and had recovered her composure. She approached the table with Jocelyn for some bread and salad.

"Well, it's finally happened," he said. "They've decriminalized prostitution, the last bastion of Victorian morality." He slid into his best demagoguery. "The great jewel in the free market tiara. A universe where every action of every being is a market transaction, conducted in competition with every other human being."

Tiff coloured up and her mouth set in a line. "Always has been and always will be a mortal sin." She'd been hiding in the background until now. "But we must render unto Caesar. They used to have temple prostitutes, you know."

Mike picked up the gauntlet. "The greatest and most meaningful form of expression known to humanity reduced to a dirty, filthy cash transaction in the stroke of a vote." He glanced in Isabelle's direction.

Nate chuckled to himself. *He's really milking it.*

"Traditional marriage is prostitution," said Isabelle. "A paternalistic, homophobic and claustrophobic institution that's used to rubber stamp the worst kind of female exploitation and rape, angled as a cornerstone of the patriarchy to keep women enslaved to one man and one male god."

"It's healthy to have strong opinions," said Mike, his voice rising.

"It's a bit more than that," Isabelle said. "It's the fucking white male plan."

Nate laughed inside. He expected Isabelle to have her claws out by now.

She continued, her face glowing red. "Today, through corporate feminism, patriarchy celebrates its domination as female and by deception champions the rights of women while exploiting them at the same time."

"Pretty tricky," Nate said. He lifted his can in a mock toast. There was no doubt about it, they seemed to be pushing this women thing, especially to get women as CEOs and directors of companies, but it was pretty much the *girls can do anything* message overall, and ordinary men were useless unless film stars or football players. Otherwise men were yesterday's heroes and surplus to requirements. As long as they had sperm banks and other technology, women didn't even need them to reproduce.

It was as if Monique read his mind. "They also foment war between the sexes. I see a lot of angry men in my work because of this."

"Exactly," Mike said. "As long as men and women fight each other, they are not fighting 'the politicians and elite's' them."

Goose came over to get a sausage wrapped in bread. He wore his baseball cap back to front. "It's what people want. Prostitution – the democratic reality of the times. What's wrong with a quick fuck, without complications or drama, for a fast buck?" He lifted the bread of his sausage and smeared it with tomato sauce. "Without the *I've got a headache, my period. I'm too tired. Have you put the cat and rubbish out and taken your socks off?*"

Tank joined in and was blunt. "Prostitution is the evil of all roots, a form of contractual sex, like fucking honest work that is done out of the necessity to live."

"A sign of the times," said Tiff. "Blatant as a scarlet sunset or climate change – it's the love of money that's wrong. Tank's right, nobody should have to make a living under any form of exploitation. Sale of the mind and body is slow murder of the heart and soul."

"That's not very neoliberal," Nate said. There was a bit of a chuckle from others.

"No matter." Mike smirked. "They're not marketable commodities."

"Unlike your mouth and arsehole," Monique said.

They all laughed.

"Mike couldn't resist. "Our political masters aren't interested in providing meaningful, well-paid work and dignity and leisure for the plebes. Ours is to pay taxes, finance the plutocrats and die before we collect a pension."

"Right on!" Nate punched a fist into the air, and couldn't work out why the masses hadn't woken up to this.

"You're preaching to the converted," Monique said. Do you have to have a PhD in cynicism to work it out for yourself?" She followed Nate out into the garden.

Abe said: "Your mother and I enjoyed ourselves here."

Nate looked at him as if to say, what was she doing here? From where they stood they had a wonderful view over the cove and bay below.

"She used to visit sometimes," Abe said.

Monique approached and Nate introduced her.

"Charmed indeed." Abe shook Monique's hand. "Such a beautiful young woman, you're a very lucky young man, Nathaniel."

Monique blushed red.

"Abe's an old friend of the family," Nate said."

They stared in silence down across the bay, and Nate saw movement out the corner of his eye. He lifted the binoculars around his neck. "The *Osprey*, owned by Francois Louveteau."

"Fine man by all accounts," Abe said. "Outstanding barrister. Must say, never cared much for him, myself. Don't know why."

"I could give you a few reasons," Nate said. "Some other time, perhaps."

They watched in serenity, as the yacht, under diesel power, sliced through the late-afternoon haze. Nate ushered Monique aside, reminding her of her appointment to do Chambers at four o'clock. "I'll ring the taxi," he said. "You don't want to be late."

And with those words, something exploded in his heart and head, and he realised he'd striven for nothing. The very people he hated and despised, he had become – all in the name of the free market plutocratic republic.

A faint rainbow arched off the faraway headland, one leg on the land and one in the sea. Purple clouds fermented from the South. The air was still and quiet.

Isabelle spoke, her voice carrying eerily in the burgeoning mist. "In the beginning was Tiamat, the Mother of the Gods, Creator of All."

About the Author

Leon Paulin grew up in Auckland and Dunedin, New Zealand. After leaving high school, he moved to Christchurch and hung out with a group of surfers around North New Brighton. He was soon riding the waves and soaking up the beach culture.

He worked in many manual jobs, but later moved on to university. Eventually, he opened a string of used-book stores and took up the pen.

His articles and short stories have appeared in newspapers, magazines and online.

This is his first novel, but is published second. *Republic* was penned in June 2002, completed in 2004, and remained in a drawer, virtually forgotten, for the following fifteen years.